THE RABBIT'S FOOT

All rabbit shifter Alpin Dawkins wanted was some peace and quiet. Being kidnapped and trundled off to a lab to undergo six years of sadistic experiments wasn't what he had in mind. And now all he wants is to go home.

Although Malachi Kurian spent years training to be a First, the leader of his wolf pack, he had no desire to be at anyone's beck and call, so he ran. Life as a lone wolf worked out great - until the night he heard the screams.

He might have escaped, but Alp is certain this time he's going to die. When a wolf kills his pursuers, Alp fears he's about to be on the menu.

He never expects the wolf will save him, or come to love him.

Now all they have to do is rescue the others still held in the labs....

THE RABBIT'S FOOT

THE WALD PACK: BOOK ONE

PARKER WILLIAMS

Edited by
TRICIA KRISTUFEK

The Rabbit's Foot

Edited by Tricia Kristufek

Cover Art by Cate Ashwood

To everyone who realizes that opposites attract.

Special thanks to Tricia Kristufek for her marvelous editing skills and Cate Ashwood for the stellar cover!

CHAPTER 1

MALACHI KURIAN SQUEEZED the icy-cold Miller bottle in front of him. All he'd wanted was to come into the bar, have a couple drinks, find someone for a few hours of companionship, and then go out, shift, and run. Was that too fucking much to ask?

The night had started fine. He'd awoken hungry, thirsty, and more than a little horny. He decided he needed something he hadn't had in far too long: sex. The best place to get that, especially in this buttcrack of a town, would be at a bar, so he hopped on his motorcycle and headed for the unincorporated Swenson, Oregon. The population was only 175, but the last time Mal had come through a few years ago, there'd been some real lookers. Men, women—Mal didn't much care, as long as he relieved the ache in his balls.

He'd taken a seat at the long wood and chrome bar in the Brushback Tavern, the only one around for thirty miles, and ordered a steak, some whipped potatoes, and two bottles of beer. Once he satisfied those urges, then he'd work on taking care of his other issue. Though there weren't more than a dozen people in the place, Mal saw three that would suit him just fine: a young man standing by the jukebox, swaying his slender hips; a woman with a generous amount of boobage and legs that Mal knew would squeeze him hard as she rode him; and someone who smelled of a man, but had hair dyed the color of the setting sun and was dressed in the sheerest clothes Mal had ever seen, including a gauzy midriff top and teeny tiny shorts that showed off a supple ass. Mal smiled at the fact that he'd have to peel the person out of those clothes, and that thought excited him to no end.

Everything had been going to plan. Until it went to shit.

"Are you flirting with my husband?" a woman shrieked.

The one Mal had decided to set his sights on stepped back, his eyes wide. "What? Ew, no! Why the hell would I want your gnarly, wrinkled old man?" His gaze scanned the room, landing on Mal. He gave a triumphant smirk. "I'd rather have him fuck me than let your prune get within three inches of me." He held up his hand, fingers parted slightly. "Because, you know, that's about all he's got in his pants. Probably explains why you're so bitter."

And that set the woman off big-time. She threw herself at the object of Mal's lust, and the two of them fell to the floor, tussling. Mal huffed out a sigh. *Well, it won't be him tonight.* Oh, well. Still two other viable—

Then every goddamn person in the bar took sides, and the fists started flying, letting Mal know the night was going to be a bust. Goddamn humans and their petty squabbles. The least they could have done was waited until he'd gotten off.

The thud of heavy boots coming up from behind had Mal shaking his head. "Trust me, you don't want to be missing anything important when the night is over. Go back to your table, sit down, and shut up," he growled, his voice low. The feet retreated quickly. Mal turned on the stool and glared at the people. "All of you, sit the fuck down!"

It got so quiet, you could have heard a pin drop. Everyone scurried to their seats or headed for the exit as fast as they could.

"Thanks, man," the bartender said, his voice quaking. He slid another beer to Mal. "On the house."

"Appreciated," Mal replied, twisting the top off the beer and chugging it down.

Mal hadn't done it for him. He didn't know the man, and the guy wasn't on the list of the pickings for the night, so Mal lost interest in the conversation quickly. Since there wasn't going to be any fun in the sack, Mal decided he'd head back to his temporary den. In the morning he'd head out once more. Maybe this time he'd go to Washington state. Plenty of forests to run there. He needed to get out before local law enforcement started asking questions, which they always seemed to do after an altercation.

He stood, dropping ten on the bar. "Thanks for the meal. It was excellent."

"You could stay, if you wanted," the bartender said, his gaze raking over Mal's body.

Any other time, maybe Mal would have taken him up on it. True, he hadn't been one of the three, but a warm body to plunder was always a good thing.

"Nah, I have to hit the road in the morning." He moved toward the door. "Ya have a good night, though, okay?" He winked, and the pheromones leaking from the man ramped up. Sadly, though potent, they didn't stir Mal's already-crushed libido.

He slammed through the door and headed for his bike. The 1951 Vincent Black Shadow was a fucking work of art. Mal had taken it from some lowlife losers who thought they could roust him for money. He'd taught them the error of their ways and hadn't even shifted to do it. Truth was, Mal was a First wolf. Big in both forms, and to screw with him was taking your life in your hands.

Once he'd... liberated the bike, Mal had spent a few thousand restoring the black paint, gold pinstriping, and brushed aluminum pieces the motorcycle was known for. It had taken several months, considering the only money he used was from his transient jobs and hustling pool. At least now the bike gleamed and drew envious gazes wherever Mal went. Hell, it was probably the bike that had gotten him laid the most in the last ten years. Whenever someone felt it thrum between their legs, their grip on Mal tightened and the pheromones went through the roof.

He shook his head. He really wished he'd gotten laid tonight. Having a warm set of lips around his cock was a lot better than his callused hand any day. Maybe he should go back and see if the bartender would.... no, he'd already walked away from that. And anyway, in the distance, Mal could hear a siren approaching. Best for him to be elsewhere as soon as possible.

He kicked the bike to life, the purr of the engine soothing his nerves, twisted the gas, and roared down the road, the wind whipping his hair into a frenzy. He should ride with a helmet, he knew that, but the open road was too intoxicating, and if he did have an accident, it would take a lot to do more than hurt a First.

He snorted. A First. Could he even call himself that? Technically, he was, but Mal had no pack, had no desire for one. When he'd been with the Forest Walker pack in Maryland, he'd been bored out of his mind. It was the largest, and one of the richest packs around, and Mal hated being there. He didn't want to deal with the bullshit his First, Damon Walker, did. All the politics and the whiny wolves who thought the First should settle any disputes, even stupid arguments over what one couple was going to have for breakfast.

No way. Mal knew his First was grooming him to take over after he stepped down, but Mal wanted no part of that. So one night, nearly fifteen years ago, he snuck out and left, never once looking back. Better to be a lone wolf, responsible for no one but himself. He could eat when he wanted, sleep when he felt like it, and fuck whenever the urge hit him. The structured life wasn't for him at all.

Mal was about ten miles from the bar when he heard the loud crack as it echoed off the trees. It sounded like a gunshot, followed by shouts of "Don't let it get away!" and "Hyde will have our heads if we come back without it." Every instinct told Mal to keep going. This wasn't his problem, and he didn't want it to become one.

He'd almost convinced himself of it, at least until a plaintive whine reached his ears. Fuck it all to hell! Mal slammed on the brakes and skidded across the blacktop and onto the gravel shoulder. He lifted his head and sniffed. Some kind of shifter, though being so far away, Mal didn't recognize the species yet, and he was being chased by four humans. The acrid scent of the gun oil, the residue from the recent shots, and the terror of the shifter all slammed into Mal's brain at the same time.

"Fuck," he snarled. He stripped off his leathers and shifted to his tawny wolf. The scent of the other shifter was stronger now, but so was the smell of the rot and decay. Something was wrong with the animal, and it spurred Mal on, desperate to reach the creature before the hunters got to him.

He dashed through the trees, dove under the low-hanging branches, barreled through the bramble bushes, and burst out into a clearing. There he could see the tiny fluff ball with strips of fur missing, his body listing to one side and—it was a fucking bunny.

Then Mal noticed what was causing the smell of rotted meat. The rabbit's foot was missing, and infection had obviously set in. It snapped at the men, who laughed in return. The men smelled of chemicals and death. Mal knew they'd killed recently, and anger surged through him. Though he was no one's leader, Mal was still not going to let these men hurt the tiny shifter.

"Don't worry, kid. Hyde will take good care of you. He still has a lot more things he wants to try out," one of them said in a coaxing voice. "Be a good boy and come along with us. We don't want to hurt you."

"Much," called out another, which set off a round of laughter that had Mal seeing red.

The rabbit turned and did his best to run, stumbling several times. The men, their laughter ugly and dark, stalked it. Mal could see it had no energy left. When the rabbit went down one last time, it lay on its side, heaving for breath. Then the men were on it. They pummeled and kicked the animal, sending it skittering across the hard-packed soil. When it came to rest, its soft whimpers and terror inflamed Mal. He rushed forward and smashed into the group, knocking them to the ground. He was up before they could react.

"Fuck!" one of them screamed. "Kill it!"

Mal flicked a quick glance at the rabbit, who lay bleeding. He could see the missing foot clearly now, including the bones protruding from beneath the dirty fur. Obviously these fuckers knew what the rabbit was, but they never thought something more vicious would be out in the woods tonight.

The one man who'd kicked the rabbit raised a gun, likely the one Mal had heard the shots from. His hand shook as he tried to aim, but Mal didn't give him a chance. He lunged for the man, leaping up and locking his jaws around the exposed throat, then yanking to the side, ripping out his larynx and leaving him to drown in his own blood. And what nasty blood it was. Laden with chemicals, it probably would have killed the man eventually, so Mal was doing him a service.

The second man got up and tried to run, but Mal leapt on his shoulders, sank his fangs into the back of the man's neck, and crunched through his spinal cord. In the unlikely event he survived, he'd be paralyzed and pissing through a tube for the remainder of his days.

He didn't last but a few moments.

The third and fourth men shouted and ran for the woods.

One thing Mal had had to relearn when he became a lone wolf was hunting. No longer having a pack to take down larger prey, he'd adapted and honed his technique. Now, instead of the pack taking the animal down as a unit, Mal would have to keep it from running. To slow the first man down, Mal tore out his Achilles tendon, sending him crashing to the ground. Then he went after the last guy. One jump into the air, and a mess of claws and teeth, ripped open the man's jacket. The coppery scent of blood let Mal know he wouldn't be getting up again. After that man breathed his last, Mal went back to where the other was dragging himself across the ground, pleading for his life.

I'm sure the rabbit would have done the same. I'll show you the same mercy you gave him.

Mal tilted his head up and howled long and loud, the sound echoing everywhere. The man covered his head and screamed, which sent a shiver of delight through Mal. He loved it when his prey was terrified. And these men definitely should have been. When Mal lunged and raked claws across the guy's throat, there was a satisfying cry before he fell over, dead.

After a quick trip to ensure there were no survivors, Mal hurried over to where the rabbit lay. At first he thought the tiny thing was dead. He nudged it gently, and was surprised when its eyes popped open. It saw him, and Mal could hear the heartbeat race. It tried to stand, but flopped over. Mal quickly shifted to his human form and lay beside the rabbit.

"Hey, I'm not going to hurt you." His gaze went to the other men. Had they said the same thing? The rabbit would have no reason to trust him. "I know what they did to you." He swallowed hard. "I want to help you, but I need you to trust me. Can you do that?"

The rabbit's eyes fluttered, then closed. Mal took that as a yes. He slid his hands under the small body and had to stop from jerking back when the little thing tensed and screamed.

"It hurts, I know. I wish I could take that away from you, but I can't. Can you be strong for a little longer?"

It would be a mercy to kill the shifter here and now. The damage it had taken would require weeks to heal, if it could be done at all. Abraded skin showed, even beneath the fur. Scores raked across its body, some fresh, others very old. How long had they kept this poor thing like this? More importantly, who would do such a disgusting thing?

The rabbit slumped into Mal's hands.

"Thank you for trusting me," he whispered, holding the rabbit to his naked chest, hoping to provide some heat. "I'm going to get you out of here."

The rabbit turned its head and stared at the bodies.

"Hey, no," Mal said, putting a hand over the bluest eyes he'd ever seen on any animal. "Don't look. My howl alerted the predators in the area. Most will avoid them, but enough will take chunks out to make it look like the men were killed by the animals around here."

The rabbit snorted, then closed his eyes and seemed to fall unconscious. Mal was grateful for that, because they had some rough terrain to get through, and without being able to use his wolf, it would be a difficult trip. But he'd promised to help, and he would.

It took nearly an hour to get back to where he'd parked the bike. He opened the saddlebag, stuffed his jacket inside, then placed the rabbit on top of it before closing it again. Then he dressed, jumped on the cycle, and a moment later, they were zipping toward Mal's den.

"What the hell am I doing?" Mal berated himself. "Don't get involved. Ever. That's why I left the Walker pack. I didn't want any part of that life."

Yet here he was, rushing into the dark night, with precious cargo that he'd vowed to save.

He was such an idiot.

ALPIN DAWKINS OPENED his eyes and found he was once again in complete darkness. Fear slammed into him, thinking he'd been caught and brought back to the lab and was still being experimented on. Still listening to the screams of the others as the fuckers shot acids and chemicals into their bodies, poked out eyes, lopped off ears, or in his case, part of his bunny's front leg. In human form, he was missing his left hand.

And now he was back in the room and—wait. His nose wiggled and he sagged in relief. He wasn't in the lab. He was nestled in something soft that didn't smell of harsh chemicals, but instead held a musky aroma. It was then Alp remembered the wolf. When he opened his eyes and saw it standing over him, he was so certain it was about to eat him. To think he'd escaped the horrors of the lab, only to end up in a wolf's stomach. Then again, why not? It was the way his luck ran. Apparently rabbit's feet weren't nearly as lucky as the legends claimed.

Then the wolf had shifted and Alp wasn't certain if he was saved or if a worse fate was about to befall him. When the wolf touched him, Alp worried he was going to die. Of course, every moment of the last six years had left him with that fear coursing through his body.

Since the day he'd been dragged into the lab by Hyde, Alp hadn't known a moment of peace. Why hadn't he just given up? Let death claim him, as it had so many others?

That answer was as easy as it was obvious. He wanted to fucking live! He was twenty-two, for the Maker's sake. He had plans for his life. He'd wanted to get a goddamn job. He'd wanted a chance to live on his own, without his thirteen annoying brothers and sisters always being underfoot. He'd wanted... Maker, he'd wanted a fucking life.

That wasn't what he got, though. They'd taken him at a gas station. The day after he'd turned sixteen, Alpin had *borrowed* the family car, intent on seeing at least part of the world before he was dragged home again. He never made it beyond the Tucson city limits before he was grabbed and injected with something. He fought as hard as he could, but rabbits weren't known for their strength—they were more about speed and escape. As his mind clouded and his vision dimmed, Alp hoped that his parents wouldn't be too angry with him about the car.

That had been six years ago. Six years of torn flesh, searing pain, terror, and waking up each night certain it was going to be his last. Alp wasn't sure what the wolf was going to do to him, but better the devil you know. Especially when he killed the ones who'd hurt Alp so badly.

Well, some of them. Hyde was still out there. Still experimenting on and killing others.

And one way or another, Alp would stop him, even if he died in the process.

For the moment, though, Alpin was safe. He snuggled into the soft leather and closed his eyes. Years of not being able to sleep through the night were catching up to him, and despite the pain searing through his body, he needed rest in the worst way.

Tomorrow was another day, and Alpin couldn't wait to see his first sunrise in forever. Because as far as Alpin was concerned, it would be one day closer to the last for Hyde.

CHAPTER 2

MAL SLID the bag off his bike, doing his best not to jostle the rabbit. He'd known when the little thing had fallen asleep, because the hammering heartbeat had slowed, and the damn thing snored like a chainsaw. He smiled to himself. At least he'd been able to keep it safe.

He carried it into the cave he'd been living in for the past few weeks. It wasn't tidy, but it was—oh, shit. He'd forgotten dinner from the other night was still laying against the wall where he'd pushed it. It wouldn't do for the rabbit to wake up and see... well, one of its distant relatives. Mal picked the body up from the floor and rushed it outside, then buried it in a hole he'd dug.

Returning to the cave, he opened his bag. The rabbit was still buzzing away. Mal stripped off his shirt and put it on the floor of the cave, then lifted the bunny out of the bag and placed him on the garment. The scent from his missing leg was overpowering. Chemicals, blood, decay. Mal needed to get it as clean as possible. Unfortunately, there wasn't water around that Mal would deem clean enough to apply to a wound. He'd have to go to town again and find what he could at the drugstore. He hoped the pharmacist would know the best way to treat a rabbit.

Taking his jacket out of the bag, Mal thought about putting it on, but then placed it over the rabbit, wanting him to be warm. He tucked the corners around the small body, knowing that because of his scent, predators wouldn't come near. After, he retrieved his other clean shirt from the worn, leather-bound satchel. He made a mental checklist of what he'd need while in town, beyond the first aid stuff. Something for the rabbit to eat. Some clothes. Some... shit, he had no idea about sizes. Shifters bodies were usually a percentage of the human. Small shifter meant a small human. Big shifter, like Mal, would mean a much larger body. The bunny was tiny by any standard. Clearly it hadn't been fed in far too long.

Heading back out to his bike, he cast a last glance at the cave, then rolled the motorcycle a fair distance away before he kicked it on. As he opened the throttle and headed off toward town, Mal hoped he was far enough away not to disturb his guest.

Swenson was abuzz about the bar fight when Mal entered the city limits. The bartender had told the police that a stranger had been eating when it broke out and that he'd calmed the crowd with a few words before he left. Now the police wanted to have a conversation with the man.

Fucking great. Last thing Mal needed was to draw attention to himself.

He was shocked that Swenson only had the one store, but it claimed to have everything, so Mal headed there. Once he entered, he grabbed a cart that he proceeded to add bandages, peroxide, and iodine to—all the things his mother had kept on her shelves when Mal was a kid. Adults healed quicker than humans, but kids? Their enhanced metabolism wouldn't kick in until puberty, so scraped knees were treated seriously in his household. He wondered what his mother would say about a foot that had been lopped off.

He also went for some clothes, but uncertain what the human would look like, Mal couldn't judge sizes. He decided to grab some socks, but balked at shoes, not knowing what to do about the rabbit's foot yet. Anything else could wait until the bunny was able to shift. When that happened, he could wear Mal's clothes until they were able to get him some.

He shuddered, thinking about what would happen when the

shifter returned to form and found he'd been hobbled. Mal knew little about rabbits, but one of the things he did remember was they went into shock easily. He hoped it wouldn't be fatal. After all, he was spending a lot of money to get him healthy.

He stopped in the freezer section and pulled out a few bottles of orange juice from the floor cooler, then hurried through the remaining aisles, grabbing loaves of bread, some peanut butter, grape jelly, bottles of water, a few bags of carrot sticks, apples, a couple of small hay bales from their pet department, a water dish, and then another sleeping bag for his guest.

When the cashier told him it would be nearly $200, Mal groaned. Not because of the money. He had plenty of that. More because if he ran low, he'd need to hustle again, and he wasn't keen on doing that too often.

Then, even though he didn't want to think about money, an idea came to Mal. "Is there a vet in town? I've got a sick... rabbit."

The cashier gave a big, genuine smile. "We have Dr. Hamilton. She runs the small animal clinic out on the highway. There's also Dr. Marrin, but he's kind of"—she leaned in and whispered conspiratorially—"a dick."

Mal grinned. "Okay, then. I guess I'll be stopping to see Dr. Hamilton. Could you tell me where to find her?"

The woman deftly took Mal's money and made change while giving him detailed instructions at the same time. She was hyperefficient.

"Thank you. I appreciate the help."

She grinned. "When you see Mom, tell her I said hi, and I'll call her later this week. Oh, and remind her about my finder's fee."

Mal couldn't help but grin. She'd totally played him.

"But seriously, Mom is the best," she promised. "If anyone can help your rabbit, it'll be her."

"Thank you again," Mal said as he picked up the bags and carried them out the doors to his... aw, shit.

"How the hell am I going to get all this stuff on the bike?" he growled, staring at the bike that wasn't meant for being a pack mule.

It took Mal nearly an hour to get everything situated enough where it wouldn't fall, and by then he was in a foul mood. It got worse when the sky darkened and the first drops of the coming deluge struck his face. Big, wet glops of water ran in rivulets down his cheeks.

"Nothing can ever be fucking easy," he bitched. He got on the bike, then headed back to the cave. Crawling along on a machine that he'd easily pushed over 125? Talk about making it feel like a minivan.

By the time he got back to the cave, Mal was soaked, as was his cargo. He carried the bags inside, making two trips to keep them from ripping, and found his friend was still asleep. That was good, because rest would help.

Help fix a missing foot? Don't be stupid.

Mal bit back a growl. He was in unfamiliar territory here. If a wolf became infirm, they were generally rejected by the pack. And for stupid reasons. They weren't animals; they weren't humans. They were the best of both worlds, but too many packs figured that only the strong survived and the weak needed to be cast out. Not all were like that, but many. The Forest Walker pack had been one of them.

The rabbit twitched, then lifted its head. Mal put everything down and approached slowly, his hand outstretched.

"Hey, hi. Remember me? My name is Mal, and you're in...well, a cave with me. Don't worry, I'm not planning on eating you or anything." He winced, remembering the rabbit he'd buried earlier. He needed to figure out a few things before they moved forward. "Can you hear me?"

The bunny tilted his head, then nodded.

"And no problems understanding me?"

If a bunny could scowl, this one was. It put its face nearer to the floor, and a strange rumbling came from it while the beast shook its head.

"Good. I only know wolves, so I'm not really sure how things work for rabbits." Mal pointed toward the bags. "Are you hungry? I figure if we can get some food into you, maybe you'll be able to shift and help heal...." He looked down at the same time the rabbit did. "I'm sorry," he whispered.

The bunny's nose fluttered, and Mal couldn't help but smile.

"Hungry? Good. I... don't know what kind of food you eat. I went with fruit and hay, but after you shift, you can tell me what you like, and I'll go back to town to get it for you." A loud peal of thunder rattled the cave. "Maybe after the storm passes."

He went to the first bag, pleased the hay bales were wrapped in plastic so at least they'd be dry. He undid the clasp and pulled out one of them, then went over and placed it beside the rabbit. He sniffed it a few times, then leaned in and nibbled.

"Good. I've got some fruit to go with that. Water too. We need to hydrate you."

He set about getting everything ready while listening to the bunny chomping on the timothy hay.

"I have to ask, and I'm sorry for being blunt. We wolves aren't really good with subtlety. You know about your foot, right?"

The bunny sighed and nodded.

"Okay. Was it from an accident?"

This time the rabbit's lips curled back to show its teeth. It shook its head violently.

"Right. Someone did that to you." Mal's blood heated again. Fuckers would have to die. He went back to the bags, grateful for something to occupy his hands. "Let me get you some water."

He pulled out one of the plastic bottles and unscrewed the top, then filled the dish with it. He placed it in front of the rabbit, who sniffed it.

"I swear, it's not poison. Here." He swallowed down the remainder of the water, taking relief to his parched throat. When he finished, he wiped off his mouth. "See? It's... well, I wouldn't exactly say good, but it's clean so it's better than nothing."

The rabbit dipped his head into the bowl and lapped at the water, a curious purring emanating from him.

Mal wasn't sure where this was going to lead. Should it lead anywhere? He could leave, since the rabbit was awake now. But....

Fuck. He couldn't leave the rabbit alone. He hadn't saved it from those men to walk away now. No, he would see this through. Then, once it was all settled, he could leave with a clear conscience.

Probably.

ALP BIT BACK a moan as the water sluiced down his parched throat. Maker, how long had it been since he had an unlimited supply of water and not just enough to keep him docile? How many times had they taken it away from him when he wouldn't obey, then left him without for days on end until he practically begged them for some?

When the wolf—Mal—moved, Alp shuffled around the water, guarding it greedily.

"Drink all you want," he murmured from behind Alp. "I have five more bottles."

Maker, this was surely heaven after having been in hell for years. He drained what was in his dish, and before he could plead for more, Mal was there, refilling the bowl.

Between the hay and the water, Alp's stomach, which had been empty far too long, was filling. He drew back, fearful that if he gorged himself, he'd be sick, and since rabbits couldn't throw up and he wasn't able to shift, it wasn't a bright idea. He would wait until he had his strength back, and *then* he'd eat his fill. Maker, his stomach rumbled at the thought of his mom's pasta primavera. She always loaded it with red onion, carrot, broccoli, bell pepper, yellow squash, zucchini, tomatoes, and garlic, and a thick sauce, poured over shell pasta so every bite was laden with taste.

At the thought of his mother, Alp sagged. He missed her so bad, it hurt.

"Hey, you okay?" When Alp turned, Mal's eyes widened. "Shh, it's all right. We'll get you to shift, I promise."

Needing closeness, Alp stood. He nearly keeled over as weakness swamped him, but he steadied his wobbly legs and semihopped toward Mal, who reached out and stroked a hand over his ears, bending them until they were flat on his head. It was an affectionate thing everyone in his family did. They all loved being touched and held. At night, they'd shift into rabbit form and huddle in the living room to sleep.

Alp's eyes burned. Why had he wanted to get away from that? He'd give anything to be sprawled in the living room, mashed between his siblings Sylvia and Andrew, even if Andrew did have a tendency to fart on occasion. It was always the sly giggle afterward, like no one knew who did it, that made Alp laugh.

Maker, he couldn't believe he missed Andrew's farts.

Strong arms lifted Alp from the cold cave floor and pulled him in, clutching him against Mal's powerful body.

"I wish you could tell me what was wrong," he said. "I'd help if I knew."

And the way he was holding Alp, cradling him, he believed Mal—with his gruff voice, his enormous body, and his rough hands—would help him. He closed his eyes again, willing himself to become human, but there wasn't anything there for him to grab. The necessary energy stayed agonizingly out of reach.

"I have to clean your leg," Mal said, reaching over and pulling a bag closer. "This might burn, and I'm sorry, but…. You know."

Yeah, Alp knew. But he doubted anything Mal would do could be worse than what Hyde had. He lay quietly as Mal worked. There was discomfort, but also warmth as Mal held Alp to his chest. When he hit something painful, Alp jolted and tried to push away.

"Shh, I'm sorry. I'm trying to be as gentle as I can. You gotta remember, I'm a wolf, so we're a little ham-handed. I'll try to do better."

Then Mal tightened his grip a little and started humming. He had a good voice. Strong, certain, like Mal knew his place in the world.

"I sing for the bunny, I know it sounds funny, but the bunny can't sing for himself."

"I'm holding a bunny, because the weather is… um… runny, and I'm sure he feels all alone."

He hummed a little more, then continued the impromptu song.

"Holding the rabbit, it could become habit, because he's all soft and fuzzy and warm."

"But I need him to tell me, if... uh... what happened to him, so I can make it right again."

Now Alp couldn't keep from whimpering. It had been far too long since anyone cared about what happened to him, and here it was a wolf, an animal that should have gobbled him up as soon as they met, but instead was comforting him. He snuggled deeper into the embrace, while Mal continued humming and cleaning.

Mal held Alp up, staring him in the face. "Sorry, I ran out of rhymes."

It didn't matter to Alp. The words were what was important. After years of screaming, now he could simply be quiet.

"We should both get some sleep," Mal said, standing and taking Alp back to where he'd put him in the first place. "I bought you a sleeping bag. Let me go and—"

Alp didn't want that. He needed the closeness to remind himself he was alive. He grabbed Mal's hand gently in his teeth.

"Hey, what are you—oh. You don't want me to leave again? Don't worry, even I'm not dumb enough to ride a motorcycle in this weather. I'm not going anywhere."

But that wasn't all Alp wanted. He'd give anything if Mal would continue to hold him. He wanted—needed—closeness. Fuck, it had been far too long since he'd been able to let go of his fear, and he worried that if Mal put him down again, it would all come right back to him.

"No, that's not what's worrying you." He squeezed gently. "You want me to stay nearby."

Yes, Maker please! Don't go.

"How about this? I'll unpack the sleeping bag, and if it's not too wet, we can stretch it out and I'll lay next to you."

That would be great. Only.... Again, need surged through Alp. It wasn't logical, but he needed touch, comfort. A reminder that he'd beaten Hyde and survived, and that he was tethered to the world where so many others had gone to the Maker. And while it was unkind, Alp had many times thought they were the lucky ones, because they were free of the constant pain, the terror, and the soul-crushing uncertainty.

Alp knew what he wanted. The wolf was his protector, and he needed that now. True, the wolf and the man were the same, but the wolf had stood over him, had killed for him, had saved him from being dragged back to the lab where this time Alp was sure he would have died.

"That's not what you want either, is it?" Mal slid a finger over Alp's ears, and Alp shivered. "How about this then? I'm going to try something, and if it scares you or feels wrong, nudge me and I'll move, okay?"

He lay Alp atop the little nest Mal had made for him, then stood and stripped off his clothes. Any other time, Alp might have enjoyed the sights of a well-muscled man sliding out of wet clothes, but right now, a desperate need filled him. As soon as Mal had the shirt off and dropped it on top of his other sopping items, he closed his eyes, took a quick breath, and then a second later, a cream and tan wolf stood where moments ago there'd been a man.

Mal strode with purpose toward Alp. Then he lay down beside him, leaned closer, and locked his teeth gently onto Alp's scruff to pull him in. Alp breathed in the wolf's musky aroma, letting it settle him. Then he curled up against Mal, who wound around him and lay with his head over Alp's back.

And for the first time in far too long, Alp was able to sleep without worrying that every little sound in the darkness was something coming for him. He knew that he was safe, because the wolf would stand between Alp and the world.

And win.

CHAPTER 3

MAL LAY PERFECTLY STILL, watching as the rabbit's tiny chest rose and fell. He leaned in and sniffed the foot again, wrinkling his nose at the odor. His cleaning hadn't done nearly enough. Tomorrow he'd have to take the rabbit to the vet—there was no way around it. If he didn't, Mal feared the bunny would lose more than a foot. He licked at the leg, wincing at the taste of chemicals and sickness, but that didn't stop him from doing it again. Mal wasn't sure why, but he had to do something to soothe his charge. It was then that he noticed how warm the rabbit was. It seemed too hot, especially for such a little thing, but what was a rabbit's temperature normally? Maybe they were naturally this warm.

He nudged the bunny, wanting to wake it, but it lay still. Far too still, as far as Mal was concerned. Panic gripped him. He hadn't saved the thing's life for it to die in a dark, filthy cave with him. He freed himself from the rabbit, then stood and shifted. He grabbed dry clothes from his bag and dressed quickly, never taking his gaze from the rabbit. He lifted the tiny thing in one hand, then snagged the shirt he'd had used for his bed earlier. He put that into his saddlebag before laying the rabbit on top of it, finally pulling the edges around, doing his best to make the rabbit comfortable.

The sun was scarcely more than a corona of color that had begun to make itself known, so it was only around five, give or take. Far too early for the vet to be in, but Mal's heart thundered at the likelihood that his charge would die, and he couldn't think of anything else to do. He jumped on the bike and sped off down the highway, remembering the instructions the young woman at the store had given him. It took nearly thirty minutes to find the clinic, and Mal's shoulders sagged when there weren't any lights on that he could see.

Anger surged through him. This wasn't right. The rabbit was doing better. He was! Mal stomped to the door, raised a hand, and pounded on it. The area was so quiet, the sound echoed all around. And then dogs started barking. Mal waited a minute, then did it again. He'd pound on that door as long as he had to.

The click to his right was far louder than Mal's insistent banging.

"I don't know who you are, but if I blow your head off, the sheriff will thank me for saving him the paperwork."

Mal turned and found himself face to face with an older woman, with a dark complexion, eyes that reminded him of honey, and a voice that sounded as though she smoked heavily, though Mal couldn't smell it on her.

"Please, you have to help me," he said, injecting as much desperation into his voice as he could. He needed her to hear him.

"Help you with what?" the woman asked, her eyes narrowed but gun not wavering in the least.

Mal glanced toward the bike and sadness swamped him. "The bunny.... He.... Please, don't let it die."

That caught her attention. She lowered the gun. "Where is he? Bring him in through the back."

Mal raced to the motorcycle, undid the straps of the bag, and carried it through the back door. The barking was loud, so Mal did a little trick his own First had taught him. He sent out a subvocal command, telling the mutts to shut the fuck up, and a moment later, everything went deathly still.

"Bring him to the exam room," she told Mal. He followed close behind, clutching the bag to his chest. When they got in the room, she took the bag from him and set it down on an exam table. "Okay, let me do my job." She opened the bag and gasped, then turned and pointed to another door. "You go sit out in the waiting room."

"But—"

"Now!" she growled. "I can't work with you hovering." She glanced up and her eyes softened. "I'll do my best—you have my word. But even if he survives, this isn't going to be cheap."

"Whatever it takes. I don't care about the money."

And he didn't. He'd made more than enough hustling pool to last him twenty years or more. Drunk humans were so stupid when they thought that because they plied Mal with liquor, he was an easy mark. A werewolf metabolized the alcohol quickly, which made it hard for Mal to get drunk. He played that part up, losing a game or two, and then the inevitable statement would slide out: "We should make this interesting, ya know?" Then Mal got serious and took them for all the money he could, before he vanished into the night and was off to the next town.

"There's coffee at the desk. Help yourself. This will take a while. If you can, feel free to stretch out on the couch and get some sleep. We don't open until nine, so no one will bother you until Shelly comes in at eight. If I know anything before then, I'll come get you."

Mal turned and went through the door the doctor had indicated. The waiting room was a jumble of scents; from disinfectant to dog and cat treats, and sick and injured pets. The whole thing made Mal nauseous. He could smell the pair who were going to die due to cancer, despite the vet's best intentions, and from the low whimpers coming from what Mal figured was the kennel area, the dogs were ready to go.

Humans were such an odd mix. Most, it seemed, had no problems killing animals for food, but then they lavished toys and expensive beds on the ones that lived in their houses. Mal couldn't see the difference between the doe his pack took down and the dog whose owner let run the streets at night. What made one a pet and the other food? It never made sense to him.

Yet, here he was, sitting at the vet with the bunny. Sure, it was a shifter, but still an animal. Why should Mal care if it lived or died?

Circle of life, kumbaya, and all that other crap, right? He looked down and found himself twisting his hands together. It did matter if the rabbit died. It had to live so it could know the men who'd hurt it were dead now. So it had a chance to move on.

"Please don't die," he whispered.

A few moments later, the lack of sleep from the last two days caught up with him, and Mal drifted off.

"Sir?"

A hand landed on Mal's arm, and he instinctively jerked away with a snarl. When he saw the pixie-faced woman beside him, he swiped a hand over his eyes.

"I'm sorry. Haven't been sleeping—the bunny!" Mal worried she'd come to give him bad news, and he wasn't sure he was ready to handle that. Hell, he wasn't sure what was wrong with him since the rabbit came into his life. Any other time, he wouldn't have cared and would have just gone. Now? He was invested in the rabbit's life.

"The doctor would like to see you. She's in the exam room."

Mal's heart thumped hard. "Is... is it okay?"

She gave him a smile. "He's in the pen, on an IV to replenish his fluids. He's all right, but the doctor wants to talk with you. She's finishing the paperwork and will be out in a few minutes."

Mal stood. "Thank you. Again, sorry about being snappy."

She grinned. "Most of our clients are snappy, and their dogs and cats aren't a whole lot better."

She laughed at her joke, then turned and went back to the counter. How exhausted must Mal be to not have sensed her approach? He sat down again and closed his eyes. The rabbit would be okay, and that knowledge lifted a huge weight from Mal's shoulders.

"So your rabbit...," said a voice from above.

The voice startled Mal, and he realized he'd again drifted off. He cursed to himself, because a wolf that was unaware of his surroundings was also known as a dead wolf. He jerked up.

"Sorry, I didn't mean to wake you," the vet said, as she stared at the paperwork in her hand.

But Mal didn't care. He might be tired, but the vet was dead on her feet. Anyone could see that. Her brown hair, which had been in a haphazard bun earlier, was now sticking out like bits of straw poking out of a bale. Her honey-colored eyes were cupped by dark circles. And even more telling, the pinch of her face said she was in pain.

"It's okay." He glanced down at her feet and noticed she was favoring the heels. "I'm sorry about all this."

"Sorry?" she asked, looking at him, obviously incredulous. "Why?"

"I woke you up and—"

"I wasn't asleep. I'm usually doing my paperwork then, because it's the quietest time around here, barking dogs and needy cats notwithstanding."

"But you should have been asleep, and now you'll be awake all day."

She gave him a wan smile. "Do you know where you are?"

Mal blinked. "Geographically? Swenson."

"Yup. At one time it was a bustling town. The military kept us all jumping as they came through. Then that dried up. Now? We have 175 people who live here, and about a hundred pets. Do you know how many of those are spayed or neutered? Lemme tell you. Probably not even a third. No time, no money, pets are replaceable for a lot less than the cost of a surgery. When someone goes to the trouble of bringing a rabbit in, that says something to me about their character."

Mal wanted to tell her he wasn't just a rabbit, but the less humans knew about shifters, the better.

"I have to ask, how did the rabbit get so hurt?"

"I don't know," Mal said. "I found it like that, and I couldn't leave it."

"Well," the vet said, an edge to her tone. "I want to know who would dump such a precious thing. It's emaciated, dehydrated, and don't even get me started on that foot. It looked like someone went after it with a cleaver or something. There were shards of bone protruding from the leg and...." She dipped her chin. "I'm sorry, you don't need to know all that. Let me just say that rabbit was lucky you found him, because without your help, he'd be dead right now. I've never seen an infection like the one he had. My strongest antibiotics barely helped. I was going to suggest putting him to sleep, to keep him from suffering. Then he seemed to rebound. If the thing didn't have such a strong will to live, he'd be dead right now. As it is, he'll sleep the rest of the day, and probably a good chunk of tomorrow."

Mal sagged at the good news. "Thank you, doctor. Your daughter was right. You're amazing."

Her cheeks pinked. "My daughter said that?" She snorted. "I wonder what she's going to be asking me for this time."

"It's obvious she cares for you. Though she did mention something about a finder's fee."

The vet laughed. "She must be low on stuff to make dinner. She wants me to invite her." She let out a sigh. "I love her too. She's my little black sheep of the family. My mama had a fit when Dinah came out. First she was a vegan. Then she was a vegan atheist. Now she's a vegan, atheist, queer woman." The vet chuckled. "Mama practically blew a blood vessel at each step. But as much as she hated it, she loved Dinah with her whole heart, and told her she needed to do what makes her happy." She snapped her head up, her face red. "I'm sorry. I don't even know why I'm telling you this."

Because Firsts, no matter the species, foster goodwill. They are the ones you can unload your burdens on.

"So anyway, the rabbit." She sighed as her gaze darted over the paperwork. "I've never seen any animal with a will to live like he's got. If I didn't know better, I would say his body was trying to heal itself."

She was way too close to the truth. "Of course that's ridiculous."

"Right. Ridiculous."

Mal could hear the suspicion in her voice, so he veered off into a safer topic. "How much do I owe you?"

The doctor consulted her notes, then turned a sad gaze at Mal. "Right now, the bill is $2800, and that includes—"

Mal took out his wallet. "Doesn't matter." He pulled out three thousand. "Here."

The vet's eyes widened, but that didn't stop her from reaching for the money. "I thought we'd have to haggle. Most people around here would never be able to afford a bill like this, let alone spend it for a rabbit. Let me get your change."

"Nah, keep it. The rabbit might need something else, or you can use it to buy something for your daughter. She was really great, and I appreciate her getting me to you."

"You're... not leaving him, are you?" There was hurt in her voice. "I mean, I thought you'd—"

Nope. Mal had made him a promise, and he would never go back on his word. "No, I'm sticking around. At least for a while."

Which was a bad idea, especially seeing as how the same sheriff the vet had threatened him with was actively looking for Mal.

"Where are you staying? We can contact you if there's any change."

And another fly in the ointment. "I'm not... I mean...." Shit. "I'm on my way through town. I only stopped to help the rabbit, but I need to be sure he's okay before I go. I don't have a phone, so can't be reached that way."

"Oh, I understand." She pursed her lips. "Look, I have a friend who owns the motel in town. Why don't I see if you can stay there? The rates are cheap, the rooms are clean, and if you're going to be sticking around for a while, at least you'll have a roof over your head."

The idea did sound good. If the bunny got better, Mal didn't want him sleeping in a dank cave. But there was that whole sheriff thing.

"I'm gonna be honest with you. When I was in the bar eating, there was a fight, and the bartender—"

"His name is Tad. He's the owner's son."

"Okay. Tad. He told the cops that I was part of it, even though all I did was tell the people to sit down and shut the fuck—" He winced. "Sorry."

"Please. Compared to Dinah, you're practically a saint. Girl has a mouth on her that would make a sailor blush. As for the sheriff, don't worry about him. He's not a bad guy. You just tell him what happened. I'm sure he'll listen. And from what I hear, the only reason he wants to talk to you is because you stopped the fight, and there's a rumor that one of the boys that was in the bar is interested in finding out more about you."

She winked, and all that tension that had been knotting in the base of Mal's spine seeped out.

"I know we're a small town, but I can promise you we're not hicks. We have LGBTQ people, we have a throuple that owns the bed and breakfast, but they're out at a convention right now, and we even have our own Pride parade. There's usually six or seven of us marching, but more turn out for support. I admit, it's a little strange, but we respect our people."

The honesty in her words, raw and powerful, soaked into Mal. He'd kept his distance from humans unless it was for sex or for getting money from them. Dr. Hamilton wore her heart on her sleeve, and the fact that she was so open shamed Mal in a way he'd never experienced before.

"You should know, I'm not really a good guy. I've—"

"Rescued a bunny that most others would have walked by. You paid to have him taken care of. Tell me what part of *good* doesn't fit you." She crossed her arms. "Go on. I'll wait."

Mal chuckled. "I hustle pool to make money so my bike has gas and I have food, and I can—"

She scowled. "You hustle pool?"

He nodded, and her sneer turned into a wide grin.

"Oh, you and I are *so* gonna play. Bring your wallet, because Mama needs a new pair of forceps."

The conversation was too much for Mal. Too open. He was used to hiding, and Dr. Hamilton was dragging him into the light.

"Maybe it's best if I come back later. I don't want to—"

She tilted her head and glared at him. "Are you arguing with me? I'm the mother of a teenage girl. Don't even think you'll win. Now, do as you're told and everything will be fine." She smirked. "Seriously, the whole thing with the bunny clinched it for me. It makes me trust the kind of man you are."

Not a man. At least not *just* a man. "You don't know me."

"Again, saved a bunny. Am I putting a lot of faith in you? Yeah, I am, and I admit it. But animals are my life, and they have no guile. Well, cats do, because they're assholes, but they're honest assholes." She stood. "Come with me." She turned and strode off toward another room.

Mal's head was done in by this woman. He was surprised to find himself trailing behind her. She entered the kennel room that Mal had noted earlier, with Mal hot on her heels. He wasn't sure about this. Animals were generally afraid of werewolves, because they saw animals as fluffy snacks. When they stepped into the enclosure room, every dog sat and stared up at Mal. They didn't bark, didn't whine. Just... stared.

"Seems to me they trust you. Dogs don't give trust easily."

That was so not true. They trusted everyone. Mal lifted his eyebrows. "Really?"

She laughed. "Okay, they're stupid friendly, but when they're in stressful situations, they look for comfort. That's what they're doing now."

Again, Mal had that whole First vibe, and the animals were reacting to it.

"Now," Dr. Hamilton said, her voice filled with pride. "Let's talk about you sticking around a while."

CHAPTER 4

ALP WOKE, his throat hoarse and parched. He needed water in the worst way. He opened his eyes, and panic set in as he realized he was once again in a cage. Once again a prisoner. Where was the wolf? He'd promised to—

"You're awake" came that voice that vibrated through Alp. A moment later, a face appeared in front of the bars, and Alp blew out a breath. "I know you're hurting. I can smell it. They did a lot of work to save you. Seems you were a sick little bunny."

Mal smiled and reached a finger inside the cage. Alp wanted to bite the smarmy bastard, but instead tilted his head closer. Mal stroked the digit over Alp's ears, just the way Alp liked it.

"You were so sick, and you weren't waking up. I wasn't sure what to do, so I brought you here. The doctor? She worked all night to get you healthier again. You're going to be weak, and it's best if you sleep, but I didn't want you to wake up in a scary place without a familiar face."

Alp noted that the room was dark. He pushed his head against Mal's hand, pleased when he took the hint and rubbed harder.

"The doctor let me stay, because I insisted you shouldn't be alone. It's about two in the morning. She was dead on her feet, so she went home."

Mal pulled a chair from the corner of the room and set it in front of the cage. He opened the door, reached in, and gently lifted Alp from the bed and cuddled him to his leather-clad chest.

"Y'know, I'm glad you're okay. I was... nervous. Think you can shift for me?"

Alp again reached for the energy that would allow it, but there was nothing there.

"Yeah, I didn't figure you'd be able, but decided it wouldn't hurt to ask." He continued to rub Alp's neck, and it soothed him. "You know when you shift back, you're going to be missing a hand, right?"

Oh, Alp knew. When he was in the lab, he was constantly being forced to shift from human to rabbit and back again. They wanted to know how much damage he could heal and how quickly. Then, a few days after his eighteenth birthday, they decided that the best test of his healing ability would be if they removed a hand. Alp screamed at them and told them he couldn't lose a limb and have it grow back, but they were certain he wasn't being honest.

They'd locked manacles around his wrists, pinning them to the chair, and then brought out their tool kit.

"What are you doing?" Alp had cried.

"It won't hurt," they told him, as though he was stupid. "The area has been numbed."

Fuck that! He struggled, but the clamp was too tight. He tried screaming, pleading with them not to do this, but it was as though they were deaf. When the saw touched his wrist, Alp lost it. He kicked one guy in the knee, dropping him to the floor. He thrashed so much, they added further restraints.

"You're making this harder than it needs to be," Hyde had said.

"Fuck you!" Alp spat. Then anger turned to desperation. "I can't lose a fucking hand! I need them."

"We'll see. I still believe you can regrow it."

"I said I couldn't," Alp whimpered, clenching his hands tight.

"And you've lied about so many other things. In fact, of everyone here, you're the most intransigent." The doctor put the blade to Alp's wrist. "We need to learn more about your kind, and that takes research. And research takes great risks to achieve the best rewards," he said, right before he pressed the saw into Alp's flesh and Alp started screaming.

"Hey, what's wrong?"

Mal's voice. Deep and soothing. Alp burrowed further into his embrace, hoping to blot out the memories that threatened to overwhelm him yet again.

"You're shaking."

No shit, asshole. What would you do if you couldn't get the images of them taking your hand out of your nightmares? And worse? The sounds as they hit bone, then continued. It was unlike anything Alp had ever heard in his life.

When they were done, they threw the fucking hand into a jar of some sort and took it off to study, then did some cursory shit to stop the bleeding. And there had been so much blood. Then they shocked him with prods to force him to shift again before they stuffed him in the tiny cage they kept him locked away in. He lay on the stinky towels, licking his paw... well, where his paw should have been, until the sedative wore off and Alp passed out from the pain.

"Do you need my wolf?" Mal asked.

Though he was ashamed to admit it, Alp did. The wolf might not be his First, but he was a First. He nuzzled Mal's hand.

"I'll take that as a yes."

Mal stood and stripped off his clothes, folding them and laying them on the chair he'd been sitting on. Alp was amazed at how fluid the change from man to wolf was. When he finished, Mal picked Alp up by the scruff and pulled him down to the floor, then curled into a ball, with Alp in the center, surrounded by warmth and fur and musk. It was several long minutes before Alp's heart stopped thudding and resumed a rhythm. It was also then that he noticed Mal's subvocalization. For humans, it was the words in your head when you read something, but for shifters, it was something more. A thrum that settled inside their bodies, sorting out the chaos and bringing peace, as well as comfort. Alp shoved his face into the fur and let the warmth seep into his body.

When the warm tongue slid over Alp's face, he knew Mal had heard his snuffles and was trying to comfort him. Why did this have to happen to him? Alp had wondered that so many times in the last few years. Sure, he wasn't what anyone would call settled in his skin. He didn't know any other rabbits that wanted to live outside their community, but Alp had wanted that with a desperation.

Now? He'd give his other hand to be at home with his parents, sitting down to dinner with everyone gathered around the table, arguing over whose turn it was to do dishes. Every nightmare he'd had while in the lab had centered around him being taken from his family. How the men who held him were cold and cruel. How the guy in the lab coat—Hyde—acted like none of them were human, that they had no feelings and were things to be experimented on. Alp had seen old men die during these heinous experiments. He'd also witnessed babies cut from their mothers, then discarded after they'd served whatever purpose Hyde and the others in the lab had used them for. And they did it with such... glee.

Mal's tongue was more insistent now. Apparently he'd realized it wasn't calming Alp at all. That didn't stop him from trying, though. And that was the closest Alp had come to kindness since they'd taken him. He closed his eyes and lay there, breathing in Mal's scent. The one that promised safety. That calmed him enough to let him doze.

When he jerked awake, Alp could smell coffee brewing and the sounds of someone in the outer office talking to themselves. He and Mal were still shifted. For him it was fine, but what would the vet do if she found a wolf in her clinic? Worse, what would happen when she found him with a rabbit? Alp leaned over and gently bit Mal's ear. He opened one sleepy eye, sighed, and then his eye drifted closed again. In a panic, Alp smacked his head against Mal's. The solid thud was enough to make Alp dizzy, but it got the desired effect when Mal blinked, which was followed by a yawn, and then his eyes went wide. If Alp thought he'd jump up and dislodge Alp, he was wrong. Mal took his scruff in those powerful jaws before he stood and placed Alp gently on the chair. He shifted quickly, then grabbed his clothes.

"Fuck, I can't believe I fell asleep," he groused. Once he was dressed, he cupped Alp in his hands, then put him back in the cage before closing and locking it. A few moments after that, the door opened and a woman stepped into the room. Her eyes widened when she saw Mal.

"Oh, I wasn't expecting to see you here," the vet said, but as far as Alp could tell, there was no suspicion in her voice.

"I'm sorry," Mal said, casting a gaze in Alp's direction. "I was sitting here last night and talking with the rabbit, and I must have fallen asleep.

She smiled, and it seemed genuine. "I've owned this clinic for fifteen years, and only once in all that time has anyone been worried enough about their animal friend to want to stay. So tell me again how you're not a good man."

Alp knew teasing when he heard it. Mal must have said something to her, and she wasn't buying it. Neither would Alp. Mal had saved him—ripped four men apart for him—and no matter the fact that he was a wolf, Alp trusted him with his life.

"I have donuts in the break room, if you're hungry."

"I should really get back to—"

"I called Rebecca, my friend with the motel, last night. She has a room all ready for you. It's twenty-five a night, which is about a third of what it normally costs."

"Dr. Hamilton, I—"

"Lydia," she said, peering into the first cage. "To call me doctor feels pretentious. It's a small town—I grew up with these people. Went to school with them. Around here no one calls me anything other than Lydia." She grinned. "Well, there are a few names that aren't as nice, but you get the point."

"Lydia," Mal started again, "I shouldn't—"

"And I called the sheriff. He told me to tell you he's grateful you were at the bar, because he hates having to do any kind of paperwork, and according to everyone he spoke with, you stopped what could have been a big fight." She arched her eyebrows. "Next excuse I can shoot down for you?"

Mal sighed and his shoulders slumped. It was kind of funny

seeing a First being browbeat by a human. All his life, Alp had been told to stay away from both predators and humans. His parents insisted he should stick with his own kind, that humans were dangerous and that any predator would snatch you off the lawn and make a meal of you before anyone could blink.

Alp had never believed it. He'd known to his soul that humans weren't as wicked as his parents made them out to be. Boy, Hyde had taught Alp that it was a lesson he should have listened to. But this vet? She seemed so kind and open. And she took care of him, brought him back from an infection that by all rights probably should have killed him. Alp grabbed the bars of the cage with his teeth and rattled them. The doctor smiled.

"Someone is feeling better," she said cheerfully. "And I'm willing to bet he wants you to stay too."

It defied rationality, but Alp didn't want Mal to leave. He wanted him to stick around until Alp could shift, then to head back to the burrow with him in tow to show his family that not all wolves were bad. No, that wasn't right. He wanted to introduce Mal as the wolf who'd saved him. He wanted all of them to sit down to dinner together, to watch as Mal tasted his first mouthful of Mom's cooking. To eat until he was so stuffed, he could scarcely move. Then he'd head into the living room with Alp's father and listen as the two of them bickered about football and who had the better team this year.

He wanted this with a ferocity. He was free of the lab, and he could chart his own life now.

But wasn't that desire what had gotten him into trouble in the first place? His refusal to listen to anyone had brought him to the lab, where he'd lost six years of his life. No, deep down, Alp knew what he wanted. To go home. To sleep with his siblings, who by now had their own families. Alp wanted to cuddle up with them, to tell them stories, and to listen as they spoke to him about all manner of silly and inconsequential things. He wanted the life that Hyde had stripped away from him.

The thing was, he still wanted his protector there with him for all that.

The vet opened the pen door and ran a hand over Alp's flank. "Hey there, sweetie. I have to look at you and see how things are going. I'd rather not put you back under, so if you promise not to hurt me while I examine you, I think we can both be happier."

Alp didn't want to sleep again. He wanted to go back with Mal to the cave, or to the motel room the vet mentioned. He wanted to stay with Mal until he was better, because Mal was the only one he trusted. So he lay limply as the vet checked his leg.

"It's awful, but it looks a lot better than what it did. I cleaned away the necrotic tissue and trimmed the bone on the residual limb back so it wasn't as jagged." She nuzzled Alp, and he appreciated the comfort. "I wish I could do more. I'd give anything for bunny-sized prosthetics."

She didn't need to worry about that. Alp had—mostly—come to terms with the loss years ago. He'd seen the arm after they'd cut it off, and he knew what it looked like. True, he still had dreams, but he also knew that he couldn't dwell on it. The hand was gone, and nothing could change that. At least he had the satisfaction of screwing up Hyde's work. Then he realized that there were still people in the lab. Shifters, like him, who Hyde had experimented on, killed, all in the name of some perverted science.

And many of those who had been left the night Alp bolted had been children who were ripped from their parents and then experimented on while their folks were left to die.

He jerked, and the vet gasped.

"I think I should put him back," she said.

"How about if you let me hold him?" Mal asked. "Maybe I can keep him calm."

This time she looked dubious, but handed Alp over. "If he gets too rambunctious, put him back in his pen."

"He'll be fine," Mal assured her, stroking that big hand from head to tail. "Won't you?"

Alp snuggled in again, happy to have Mal's scent filling his lungs. True, it wasn't as pungent as the wolf, but it was still Mal.

"Huh." The vet shook her head. "You've got a talent with animals, it seems."

Mal continued his ministrations, and Alp felt himself relax further. "Well, some of my best friends are animals."

If only the vet understood how true those words were, but honestly? At the moment, Alp couldn't care. The twinges of pain that had always accompanied him lessened when Mal touched him. The fear that he'd be captured and taken back? Nearly gone. Alp wasn't sure why, but he knew that Mal was the cause. He knew, without a shadow of a doubt, his parents were going to fall in love with the big wolf.

As long as they didn't run screaming when they saw him.

CHAPTER 5

THE ROOM WAS PRETTY austere even as motels went. It was definitely no-frills. A small bathroom with a sink, toilet, and shower done up in the hideous avocado gold that had been popular in the 70s. The bed was a queen, but the comforter smelled new. There was a small television, a tiny sofa, a clock that stood on the nightstand, and an empty wet bar that Mal had filled with bottles of water for the rabbit.

When he mentioned taking the bunny with him, the vet—Lydia—hedged. She said that he'd need constant care, but Mal assured her if she told him what to do, he could handle it. So she set about teaching him the proper care of the wound, the feeding of the rabbit so he'd get enough nutrients—which required another trip to the store—and a promise that if *anything* seemed off, he'd call her immediately.

As soon as they walked into the room, Mal carried the rabbit to the bed and nestled him on one of the pillows, fluffing the covers around him to make a nest. He swore he heard the rabbit sigh.

"This has to be better than the cave, right? Or being out on your own?"

Bright eyes flicked up to him, and the little butt wiggled deeper into the makeshift warren, the rabbit going so far as to grab the edge of the blanket and dragging it over himself. He seemed content, but

Mal was still worried. He had so many questions. Who were the men who chased one small rabbit? Why? Sure, they'd obviously known he was a shifter, but was it a hate crime? Were they curious if shifter rabbit tasted the same as a regular bunny? Mal didn't think that was the reason. They'd smelled too much of chemicals, and their blood had been so disgusting.

"I wish we could talk," he said. "I need answers, and you're the only one who has them."

The eyes that had been so happy a few moments ago closed, and Mal felt like an ass. The trauma the rabbit had been through obviously was horrifying, and instead of letting him rest and gather his strength, Mal was bringing it up again.

"I'm sorry," he said quietly. "I didn't mean to do that. It's just... I said I'd be responsible for you, and it's rough not knowing what I'm protecting you from, ya know?"

A small nod came before Mal felt the swirling energy that precipitated a shift. The rabbit was trying again, but as had happened before, Mal knew he wasn't going to be able to do it. He needed rest, food, and to get back strength before he tried to shift to his human form.

"Hey, stop," Mal insisted, and the rabbit went limp. "It'll come in time. What you need to do now is sleep. How about a banana chip?"

The ears perked up, and the rabbit turned a hungry gaze in Mal's direction.

He chuckled. "Okay, you like those." He went to his bag and pulled out the box of freeze-dried chips Lydia had given him and shook it. "Gee, I don't know. There doesn't seem to be many here. Maybe we should ration them. What do you think?"

The tiny ball of fluff bared his teeth, and Mal couldn't help but laugh.

"Okay, no rationing the treats. Understood." He pulled open the bag of freeze-dried berries and fruit chips, then reached in for the dried yellow treat. The moment he held it out, the rabbit snapped it away from Mal, then sat back and munched away. "Yeah, no way you like those, huh?" Mal sat on the edge of the bad and reached for the rabbit, who snarled at him. Mal arched his brows. "You did not just do that," he said, his voice deep and growly. Fuck, he was pulling the First tone out.

The rabbit dropped the treat and shrank away. Mal picked up the half that was left and held it back out.

"I'm sorry!" he insisted. "I didn't mean to do that, I swear. I have no idea what you've gone through, and I shouldn't be so hasty and so much an asshole."

The rabbit didn't move, his gaze tracking Mal. He could sense the fear, and he hated knowing that he was the cause. He set the chip on the bed, then picked the rabbit up and snuggled him to his chest.

"Life is hard," he said. "I left home because I didn't want all the rules and shit that came with being a First. I ran away like a coward in the night, swearing I would never be a First. That I would never have a pack." He nuzzled between the rabbit's ears. "Then I met this bunny. Cute little thing. And I sensed his terror, and... I don't know, it called to my wolf to protect it. For the first time since I left my pack, my wolf decided it wanted to be a First again, and it decided you were our pack." He snorted. "I know how it sounds, but I swear it's the truth. So, please, forgive me? I'll do my best to just be Mal, and not let my wolf dictate what's going to happen, if you'll be patient with me."

He retrieved the fruit and held it back out to the bunny, who eyed him for a moment, then gingerly took it from his fingers and went back to munching. Mal set him down on the pillow again, then drew the covers over him once more.

"After you eat, you'll take a nap." He winced at the order in his voice. What the hell was going on? "Sorry!"

The rabbit made a weird sound, but Mal knew what it was.

"You're laughing at me?"

And though it should have annoyed him, Mal found it... endearing.

◦~

ALP WAS STUFFED. Mal had given him a small alfalfa bale, some fresh water, and put out a box of straw for him to use to.... well, poop and pee. Back in the warren, such things were common, but for some weird reason, Alp didn't want Mal seeing the droppings. He'd have to figure that out later.

When Mal told him about not wanting to be a First, Alp's heart had quivered. He *needed* that. The direction, the feeling of safety. His own father, though a lovely man, was a rabbit through and through. They had no First, and it showed. Sure, the kids eventually came around, but, like Alp, they could be little shits until they matured. And parents accepted that from them. Alp needed Mal to not do that. He wanted him to be the First, to set the rules, because Alp's awful choices had gotten him into this mess.

Mal snorted and rolled to his side, his arm thrown above Alp's head. Though he knew he should stay where he was, Alp slowly rose, then gingerly made his way to where Mal slept. It had bad idea written all over it, but Alp needed his First. And wasn't that a kick in the pants?

"You're not sleeping," Mal said. "Bad dreams?"

A big hand scooped Alp up and cradled him as Mal lay on his back and put Alp atop his chest.

"I want to make you a deal," Mal said softly. "My wolf wants us to care for you. To make you our pack. Can we do that? At least until you're healed up enough to go out on your own?"

Hell, yes! Alp moved up and put his head on Mal's chin. When Mal again reached up and rubbed Alp's ears, Alp was certain he died in the labs and now was in heaven.

Somewhere during the massage, Alp fell asleep.

It couldn't have been long, but the rapping on the door jolted Alp. He sat up, his nose wiggling. Why was *she* here? Not that Alp wasn't grateful for everything the vet had done, but why was she coming to Mal's room?

Mal got up and put Alp in his cage. "Sorry," he said, a frown marring his features. "Not sure why she's here, but I'll get rid of her."

Well, that made Alp a little happier. He watched as Mal made his way across the room and pulled open the door. The vet stood there, beaming up at Mal in a way that Alp didn't like. Mal was *his* First, not hers.

"I stopped on my way home to check on our star patient," she said, breezing by Mal. She looked around, and her gaze came to rest on Alp. "Oh, you were right. He looks better already."

"Listen, Lydia, I—"

She picked Alp up and turned him over to see his underside. She prodded the residual limb gingerly. "This looks good," she said. "I can tell you cleaned it again. That's excellent." She gently placed Alp back in the cage, then turned to Mal. "Dinner?" she asked, giving him a smile.

"Hm? Oh, no thank you. I'm going to hang out here with the rabbit and—"

"I am *not* hitting on you," she said, giving an exasperated sigh. "You're cute and all, but you're more my daughter's age, and as much as I like animals, I have no wish to be a cougar."

Alp slumped down. She wasn't interested in Mal? That made him a little happier. Though why it bothered him so much that she might, he wasn't really sure.

"With the exception of going away to school, I have lived my entire life in this town. I love it here and have no desire to go anywhere else. That said, I wish the people could understand my love of the animals more, and respected that. You're the only one I know who would rescue a rabbit, spend an obscene amount of money on his care, and then take him to your room to watch over him. What kind of person does that?"

A First, duh! Alp never had one, but at one time, he'd had online friends all over the world who were shifters, and they constantly talked about what it was like to have a First. The caring, the compassion, the... Firstness of them. They made everyone in their pack, clan, gaggle, sleuth—whatever—feel safe, protected, cared about. That was how Alp knew Mal was his First, because he felt all those things when the wolf or the man was nearby. He had since that day Mal had cradled him as he carried him out of the woods.

Alp had to admit, he liked the feelings that filled him. He wasn't so eager to see the world as long as he had someone who cared what happened to him. Not that his parents hadn't, of course, but they'd had fourteen children—which was a small family for rabbits—and Alp felt left behind. With Mal, Alp knew he was seen. It was obvious Mal cared—otherwise Alp would be nothing more than a bit of extra fur on those dead bodies in the woods.

"So, dinner?"

Mal smiled. "Really, I'd like to, but I can't leave the rabbit here by himself."

"That's fine," she said, strolling over to the credenza, where she picked up a binder from the desk and flipped through some pages. "We can order in. We don't have a lot of world-class cuisines, but there's some really good Chinese food if you'd like to try it."

Ooh, Chinese was one of Alp's favorite foods! And now that the doctor had cleared away the mess that Hyde had made—and Alp's mind continued to make—of his leg, his shifter metabolism was revving up again and he was feeling a lot better. Oh, and hungry, and he wanted more than hay. When it came to Chinese food, he loved the seasonings, the tang, the... everything. His mom, bless her, had tried, but she could never capture that authentic flavor. Alp stood, ears perked and peered through the bars of the cage. When Mal noticed Alp wriggled his nose, he grinned.

"Sure, I think some Chinese food sounds great."

Yes! Then Alp realized and thought that bastard had better save him some. Especially the water chestnuts. Ooh, Alp loved those crunchy little morsels.

"Great. Take a look at the book and figure out what you'd like." She made a move toward the door. "I have to go get my phone so we can call it in."

"There's a phone in here."

She waved a dismissive hand. "The restaurant knows my number, and I get a discount because I treat Mrs. Wén's obnoxious cat. Be right back."

As soon as she stepped outside and closed the door behind her, Mal hurried to Alp. "Okay, let me know what you'd like. We'll split it."

Alp let his gaze drift over the page, and when he came upon Buddha's Delight and saw the variety of vegetables in it, his mouth watered. He headbutted the book, and Mal turned it around to see what Alp wanted.

"So you want the beef lo mein?" He wrinkled his nose. "Seems like a weird dish for a bunny, but whatever."

Alp grabbed the bars of the cage in his teeth and rattled them, which made Mal laugh. Seriously, even though he'd just eaten, it was a Buddha bowl!

"Okay, the Buddha's Delight. Got it."

When the vet came back, she placed the order, then sat at the table with Mal and talked. Alp wanted to listen in, but exhaustion swept over him and his eyes fluttered shut. Safe. Mal. Safe. Mal. The two words were becoming synonymous in Alp's brain. He hadn't even realized he'd drifted off until there was another knock at the door. He jolted upright and watched as Mal took the bag from the driver, slipped him some money, then came back to the table and unpacked each of the boxes. Alp's mouth watered and his stomach growled as the room filled with the redolent steam. Mal picked up Alp's dish and put a nice selection of sauced vegetables in it, then put it in Alp's cage.

"Oh, I don't think he'll eat that," the vet said.

Alp snorted. Showed what she knew. He stuffed his face in the bowl and started chomping on what Mal had given him. His first water chestnut sealed the deal. He'd eat the whole damn bowl to show her how wrong she was.

"Well, damn. I've never.... You have a weird rabbit, you know that, right?"

Mal snorted. "You have no idea." He reached out and tapped the bars of the cage with his index finger. "Good food?"

How badly Alp wanted to tell him it was the most delicious thing he'd had in years. Sadly, he meant that literally. The subjects at the lab were given the barest minimum needed to survive, and nothing beyond that. In fact, it was the hunger and the overwhelming fear that drove Alp to attack the person on kennel duty that night. It was an ill-conceived plan at best, but when they opened his pen to feed him, Alp leapt at the man with his waning strength. It wasn't like he could actually have hurt the guy, but throw in enough grunts and snapping, and he could see why the man jumped back, giving Alp enough time to gamely hop for the door.

From there, it was a goddamn maze. He'd had no idea the building was so large. Still, desperation drove him on, because he knew that if they caught him, he'd lose a lot more than a paw. He tried to shift, but there wasn't any strength. He realized that was why they kept them deprived of food. A weak shifter was docile and meek, and only their use of shocks could force the shift.

He'd refused to give in. He continued down the hall, getting weaker with each passing moment. He'd only been out a few minutes when the alarms went off, and he knew he was out of time. The door at the end of the hall opened, and four men rushed in. When they saw Alp, they grabbed batons from their belts and headed for him. Using the last dregs of his strength, Alp bolted for the door they'd come out of. He barely avoided their blows, more out of luck than any effort on his part. The door was the problem. It clicked shut in his face.

"Nowhere to go, little bunny," one of the men said, a sneer on his ugly face.

It was then things went dark for Alp. He didn't remember anything that happened, and the next thing he knew, he was outside, running for his life as the men chased after him. He'd done his best to get deeper into the woods surrounding the lab, but they still followed. And Alp had to admit it. They were going to catch him, and he was more than likely about to die.

Then came his First, bursting through the trees and straight at the men. He remembered the tearing sounds, the screams, the scent of blood, and against everything bunnies believed in—peace and harmony—Alp was glad Mal had killed them.

Now if only he could do the same with Hyde.

CHAPTER 6

"So do you think you can shift today?"

It had been three weeks, and the rabbit was looking much better. He was no longer a sack of bones, and the demands for more water chestnuts amused Mal to no end. At least he was eating. Lydia said she was honestly surprised at how good he looked. The strips of missing fur had filled in, making his coat all gray and glossy. His eyes had lost their haunted look and now were alight with what Mal could only call wonder as he hopped around the room.

It was obvious—to Mal, at least—that the healing shifters were renowned for had finally revved up again and was taking care of most of the worst damage. Except the missing foot. That would never heal, and it saddened Mal.

The rabbit sat up on his haunches and peered at Mal. He seemed to be... asking for something?

"Okay, you've already eaten twice, had a ton of water, and your poop seemed normal."

The rabbit ducked his head, and if Mal didn't know better, he'd swear the bunny was blushing.

He reached out and tapped him on the nose. "Don't look like that. When I was in my First training, I had to deal with all manner of bodily excretions. They don't embarrass me or gross me out. It tells me you're getting healthier, and that makes me happy."

The bunny sat up again and, Mal would swear, preened.

"Yeah, yeah. You're a cute bunny."

That seemed to make him insanely happy, as he dashed around in circles on the bed.

"Can I ask you something? Did you lose your paw a while ago?"

The bunny nodded.

"Yeah, I figured from how easy you could move without it. I'm still sorry it happened."

The bunny rubbed against Mal, who absently stroked a hand over the soft fur. Then it came to him. The rabbit might not be able to *tell* Mal what he wanted, but there were other ways.

"Why don't you show me what it is you want?"

The rabbit walked to the edge of the bed and appeared ready to jump down.

Mal snatched him up and put him gently on the floor. "You're not healthy enough to jump off the bed, ya silly thing. Now go on. What is it you want?"

The rabbit stood and hopped toward the door. Then Mal got it. He'd been cooped up in the room for weeks, without having a chance to go out and see the sun. There was a lake not too far from the motel, and it gave Mal an idea.

"You want to go outside."

The rabbit nodded, then turned his gaze back toward the door.

"What would you say to taking a ride down to the lake? You'd have to stay near me, but—"

Once again, the rabbit started spinning in circles. Mal had apparently made him happy with the suggestion.

"Fine, let's go do that now, then."

He stood and picked his jacket up from the back of the chair, then shrugged into it. Next, he picked up the rabbit off the floor and tried to figure out what to do with him. He wasn't a normal rabbit, which was shown by his propensity for Chinese food, so Mal didn't want to stuff him in the saddlebag again.

"Okay, if I put you in my jacket, do you promise not to move around? I don't want us to have an accident, and sure as hell don't want you slipping and falling."

The rabbit's eyes widened, but he nodded. Mal took him out to where the bike was parked, then proceeded to put the bunny in his jacket. He was surprised when it snuggled in, just his head up over the top of the leathers.

"I'll go slow," Mal promised, not wanting to scare the rabbit.

The rabbit seemed to have other ideas. He nudged Mal, then kinda bunny scowled at him.

"You want me to open it up? We can go pretty fast, so you need to be absolutely certain."

Oh, hell yes, Alp was certain. He hadn't minded the motel room, but after a few days, nothing changed. After a few weeks, Alp was tired of being cooped up. The smell of the cleaners they used were cloying, the air stagnant. Alp wanted to get out in the worst way. When Mal suggested going to the lake, Alp could scarcely contain his excitement.

And then he had the audacity to say he'd go slow? Screw that.

Mal mounted the motorcycle, then asked once again if Alp was sure about this. He thumped his back feet against Mal's chest, trying to get him to go, damn it!

A snort, then the rev of an engine had Alp's heart thumping hard. When Mal put the bike into gear and pulled away from the motel, then opened up the engine? Alp peeked up over the top, watching as the road zoomed by them. Alp had never gone this fast in his life, and it was scary and exciting as hell. Hell's bells, Alp wanted to shriek, but wasn't sure if it was fear or excitement or both.

Then Mal tipped his head down and smiled as Alp looked up, and he had his answer. Definitely both.

In the rabbit community, same-sex attraction was seen as a normal thing, just like heterosexual relationships. Bunnies, after all, would pretty much hump anything that would stand still long enough. Hell, sometimes it didn't even have to stand still, if the rabbit had good enough balance. For Alp, coming out wasn't a thing. He told his parents he wanted to marry Jed when they were both five-years-old, and it was met with a fervent hope that it would last.

It didn't, but by then, Alp had wanted to marry at least three other classmates. With every announcement, his parents wished him the best. Never once did they try to talk him out of it, or tell him he'd be happier with one of the does in the warren. By the time Alp was sixteen, he'd fallen in and out of love with at least a dozen different boys. Things took a horrifying turn when Lars, one of the oldest members of the warren, came out and Alp's parents tried to suggest maybe he and Lars should get to know each other. They figured that Lars's maturity would help to tame Alp. The problem for Alp? Lars was in his sixties and hardly ever left his house. Not that Alp had anything against older men, because they could be downright sexy in that gruff sorta way, but he didn't want to be a home bunny for anyone.

"We're here" came the rumbling voice from above.

Alp snapped his gaze up and marveled at the crystal-blue water, with the sun riding the waves to shore, lapping at the smooth rocks that dotted the sand. The day was awesome. A little chilly by human standards, but for Alp it was bracing. Mal put Alp down gently, and Alp did something he'd been dying to do for years. He lay on his back in the dewy grass and rolled around. It was cool and refreshing and, Maker, Alp wanted this moment to last forever.

"It seems you like that," Mal said, chuckling.

If he only knew how long it had been since Alp had touched real grass. Not counting the day they met, when Alp was so terrified, he hadn't even registered the fact that he was even in the tall stalks. Now?

He grabbed several blades and munched them, delighting in the snap of flavor. He'd missed this so much. Mal came closer and sat on the edge of the grass, right where it met the trail they'd apparently come down. Alp hobbled over to him and crawled into Mal's lap. Sure, grass was nice, but feeling safe with Mal was way better.

"I can't wait for you to be able to shift so we can talk. I'm going to warn you now, though. I have questions. Lots and lots of questions."

And Alp couldn't wait to hear them. Maybe... maybe Mal would know what to do about Hyde. Maybe he would even be willing to help Alp to shut the bastard down, and—no. He couldn't ask Mal to do that. He'd already said that he didn't want the headaches that came with being a First and that was why he'd run.

"See, the thing is, I don't know a lot about rabbits, but I have to say, I have never in my life thought they could think so hard." He slid a finger between Alp's ears, stroking slowly. "It's a day to relax, so try to let your problems go, at least for a little bit. Enjoy the area, explore, get some fresh water from the lake. Do something you'll remember, because I don't know when we'll be able to get out here again."

And Alp did. He slid off Mal's lap and went to stick his nose everywhere it would fit. The scents, so crisp and clear, intoxicated him. Way better than the lab, with its putrid concoction of chemicals and body odor and sweat and... death.

No, Mal had said to put it out of his head, and Alp would do his best to listen to his First. His First. Just thinking the words gave Alp a tingle throughout his body.

He continued his exploration. He hopped toward the water, wanting to lap something cool and clean. The first taste was sweet and exhilarating. It was weird, but since he'd gotten out of the lab, stuff in the world seemed so much sharper, more focused, more... everything.

It was then Alp felt it. Deep in his core, a spark of energy flashed. It radiated from inside him, pushing outward. He knew what that was, and he welcomed it. He turned and hobbled back to Mal, who sat with his head cocked.

"You okay?" he asked.

Better than! He lay at Mal's feet, urging that power to spread throughout as Alp remembered having hands and feet, that little pug nose that his parents told him was adorable, the blond hair on his head that could best be described as artfully messy, until he tamed it with about a gallon of gel, the blue eyes his friends said spoke of mischief. Long, slender fingers ending in nails that begged to be pampered, thin, elegant toes that had nails that demanded equal time, all as part of a frame that people had told him made him look like a swimmer, all toned and neat. A powerhouse stuffed into a compact five-foot three-inch body.

"Oh Maker," Mal gasped, putting a hand atop Alp's head. "You can do this. Trust in yourself, feel the energy and—"

"Shut up," Alp rasped, his vocal cords unused to doing anything other than screaming or crying.

As soon as the shift was complete, Alp lay on the ground, exhausted, his chest heaving as he tried to draw breath back into much larger human lungs. The shift had taken everything in his reserves, and now that tank was truly empty once more, but he was human again. He was about to say something, when Mal manhandled him up and wrapped the leather jacket around Alp's form. It was easy to see that Mal was far bigger, because Alp was practically swimming in the garment that he was now bundled up in. And it was a good thing, because with no fur, he could feel the cold. It permeated his body, causing him to shiver violently. Only when Mal pulled Alp in and held him to that powerful body did Alp stop.

"Hi, little one. I'm Mal," he whispered into Alp's ear, the warmth tickling the hairs.

Funny how his voice sounded so different when Alp was human. A deeper timbre, with notes of concern that wound its way into Alp's mind, setting up residence there.

"I'm Alp," he said, tears streaming down his cheeks. He never believed he'd be able to be human again. He feared he'd die as a rabbit. After they amputated his hand, Alp was left in his cage, never to shift again.

He wound his arms around Mal's waist and sobbed.

"It's a true pleasure to meet you, Alp the Bunny." He sniffed the top of Alp's head, then rubbed his cheek against it. "We should get you back to the room. Wouldn't want you getting sick, especially after all the work Lydia did to make you healthy again."

Alp could only nod. He wasn't ready for Mal to lift him from the ground as though he weighed nothing. Or for him to carry Alp to the bike and set him on the seat.

"You need to hold on to me, okay? Just hang on and let me do the work. We'll be back home shortly."

Home. Funny how that word took on a different meaning when Mal said it. He clambered onto the motorcycle and waited until Alp slid his arms around... oh. Shit. The tears sprang anew as Alp looked at the residual limb where his hand had been. The skin was no longer inflamed, but seeing the damage was more than Alp was ready for. He thought he could deal with it, but he couldn't.

Fucking Hyde had taken Alp's hand, maimed him. Forever. Sure, the damage had healed, leaving the pink skin all smooth, but his hand? That would never heal. He sobbed into Mal's shoulder, devastated by the loss. He was sure he was prepared, but he wasn't. How could one ever be ready for something like that?

Before he knew it, Alp was lifted off the bike and carried back to the edge of the woods.

"What—?"

"Shhh. It's all right. Trust me?"

As Alp watched, Mal stripped off his clothes and shifted into his wolf form. He leaned close and sank his teeth gently into the cuff of the oversized coat, then pulled Alp down to the ground, where Mal proceeded to wind around him. Alp wanted to protest, to say he was fine, but he wasn't. He needed Mal, again. Only Mal could make things better.

"Thank you, First."

And with those words, Alp mourned his lost limb, his lost years, his lost family.

His lost life.

CHAPTER 7

MAL'S STOMACH tightened as he held Alp. What had happened to the man that had scarred him so? Or, more importantly, who had done it? He wanted to ferret out every bit of information, but now was not that time. Alp was grieving, and Mal needed to be patient. Right now, he wasn't even sure Alp knew they were back in the motel room. He'd been sobbing since they'd been at the lake. It had been near impossible to get him back on the bike, but he'd managed it. Once he got them both into the room, he slid the jacket from Alp's form, then lay him down on the bed and drew the covers over him. The shivering didn't stop until Mal lay behind him and wrapped his arm around Alp's waist.

More importantly, Alp had called Mal his First, and for some reason, it didn't chafe as much as Mal thought it should. He cared for Alp, both as rabbit and as human. When he told Alp he wanted to be his First, he'd thought only in the short term, but now? He could see Alp being part of his pack. All two of them.

"First?"

The word didn't freak Mal out as much as he once thought it would. "Yeah?"

"I'm sorry." Alp's voice cracked. "I know you didn't want this, and I—"

"Are going to shut up now," Mal insisted. "I told you, I wanted to be your First. And my wolf wants it too."

Alp choked a laugh. "Are you sure he's not just fattening me up to make a meal out of me?"

It was a joke, and Mal knew it, but his wolf took offense. "No, most definitely not. He—we—care about you."

"I know. It's just... I'm such a fuck up. My own stupidity got me taken to the lab, and—"

"Lab?"

Alp tried to sit up, but Mal put a hand on his shoulder and held him down on the bed.

"Talk to me. Let's get it out, so it stops having power over you."

Alp waved his arm. "They're always going to have power over me. They're the ones who took my hand."

Mal's wolf roared up. "Those fuckers! I'll kill them all," Mal vowed.

"You can't," Alp said, panic in his voice. "There's too many of them. They've got a whole complex full of labs and doctors and—"

"Dead men," Mal snarled. "Every one of them. They can't get away with hurting you."

Alp rolled over and buried his face in Mal's chest. "Not just me. They have dozens, maybe hundreds of shifters there. They like experimenting on the young because they bounce back the fastest. They can do whatever they want, and the shifters will heal the damage." He sighed as he looked down at his missing hand. "Most of it."

"I will kill them," Mal said again. "It doesn't matter what it takes —I will gut them all and leave their corpses to rot."

Alp blew out a breath. "I want him dead. Not just for what he did to me. He hurt so many. Killed a lot too. They can't go unavenged."

"And they won't," Mal promised.

They lay quietly for a few moments. "Can I... I mean, do you think it would be okay if...?" Alp blew out a breath. "I was taken the day after I turned sixteen. I... might have helped myself to the family car, because I wanted to get out and—"

Mal chuckled. "A rebel bunny. I like it."

Alp hung his head, his voice dropping to barely a whisper. "They took me, and my parents never knew what happened. I want to call home, but I'm worried they'll be angry or hate me or hang up on me and—"

Mal reached out and gripped Alp's shoulder. "Hey, stop that. Bunnies love their family. It's how they're built. If you want to call them, we can do that."

"We?"

"I won't leave you to face them or the people at the lab or anything else ever again. You're my bunny, my pack. I will protect you unto my dying breath."

Alp gripped Mal's arm. "Let's not go that far."

It seemed right, being here with Alp. Being his First. Guiding him. Protecting him. Keeping him—aw, shit. These were the lessons First Walker was trying to instill in Mal. To show him that everything within the pack came from him as the center. Without him, the pack would fail. And now, here he was, swearing to Alp that he'd be there, keeping him safe, and that he'd go into this lab and do what he could to get the shifters out of there. First things first, though.

"Let's call your parents."

Alp nodded, then stood and crossed the room to the phone. He picked up the receiver and stared at it a long time.

"What do I say?" he husked.

"Start with, 'Mom? Dad? It's me, Alp.' Then take it from there. No matter what happens, I'm here with you."

Alp pressed a few buttons, and Mal could feel the fear and nervousness rolling off him. He stepped up behind Alp, put his hands on the slender shoulders, and rubbed gently. Mal could hear the phone ringing, and for a moment, he wanted to bundle Alp up and run away, but he needed to be there as Alp faced the issue. When a woman's voice answered, Alp tensed.

"Mom? It's me, Alp."

And the tears rolled down his cheeks, big and fat. He scrubbed a hand over his eyes as he gasped for breath. Mal would protect him from anything, but this was something even he couldn't fix.

～

"ALPIN? IS IT REALLY YOU?" Her voice, brittle and harsh, broke, and the pain in it weighed on Alp.

"Yeah, Mom." He stepped closer to Mal, who slid an arm around his shoulder. "I'm... sorry."

"Alpin Dawkins, where the hell have you been?" she shouted. "We've been worried sick about you."

How could he explain it to her? How could he tell her about the men who'd taken him, kept him in a cage, cut off his goddamn hand? Mom was a gentle soul, and she didn't deserve this kind of stress.

"I'm sorry, I shouldn't have called," he whispered, ready to hang up.

"You hang up that phone, and I will bust your ass!" she cried out. "Alpin, please, I'm begging you. Don't disappear on us again."

As much as Alp didn't want to burden her, he couldn't help it when the story tumbled out of him. "I didn't want to, Mom. They took me. They kept me locked in a cage. They did things to me, and...." He sobbed. "Mom, they cut off my hand."

She gasped. "Who? Who did this?" she demanded.

"A doctor. He wanted to see if I could regrow it, and... I couldn't, Mom. I couldn't do anything. They strapped me down, and I had to watch as they... as they...."

Mal took the phone as Alp turned and threw his arms around Mal's stomach. "Mrs. Dawkins? Hi. Alp is a bit emotional now."

Emotional? Sure. That sounded about right. Alp could hear his mother on the other end, her voice strident.

"Who is this? What are you doing with my son?"

"My name is Mal. Malachi Kurian. I'm the one who found Alp."

"Found him? What do you mean?"

Alp couldn't let Mal deal with this. He reached up and took the phone back. "The men who took me? They were chasing me through the woods. I would have died that night, but Mal saved me. He's... he's a wolf, and he killed the men who were hurting me."

"A wolf?" she said, the horror in her voice evident. "You can't trust him!"

"He's the only one here I do trust!" Alp shot back. "He saved my life. He took me to a vet who helped to fix me. He's been feeding me and taking care of me. Without him, I would have died." He blew out a breath. "Mom, I'm part of his pack. He's my First."

He could feel Mal tense, but that didn't stop him from leaning down and rubbing his cheek against Alp's hair.

"Your First?" she said softly. "What do you mean?"

"Mal's taking care of me, Mom. He's making sure I eat, keeping me healthy. Hell, he's even watching my poop to make sure it looks okay. The vet taught him what to look for. He's pack, Mom. I need that from him."

"Alp, these men who hurt you, I—"

Mal snatched the phone away with a growl. "They're dead men, Mrs. Dawkins. I'm going to kill every one of them. They're holding shifters, many of them children. I can't—won't—let them live."

Alp figured his mother would be horrified. Like his dad, Mom was a pacifist. He was shocked when she heard her say, "Make it hurt."

Alp took the phone back. "Mom? You don't mean that."

"Maker help me, I do. They maimed my son. They kept him away from his family for six years. I want to say we need to move on, but I can't. I won't. If your.... If your First says he's going to kill them, I need that from him." Her voice dropped. "Are you coming home?"

He wanted to, so badly. "No. I'm going to help Mal."

"Alpin?"

"I've changed, Mom. I can't let them get away with this. I can't unhear the screams, the pleading, the dying. I can't just walk away."

"Then let us come see you. Please. I can't... I have to see you."

Alp turned to Mal. "She wants to come see me."

He gave a terse nod, then turned away, his expression solid granite.

"They brought me to Oregon, Mom. Mal and I are in a town called Swenson."

"I'm booking tickets now."

"Just you and Dad. Don't bring anyone else. It would be too hard to protect you all."

"O-okay. Only the two of us." She paused a moment. "Alpin, are you really okay?"

He looked down where his hand had been, and the anger and helplessness he'd felt for the past few weeks roared to the surface again. "I'm not now, but after they're dead, I will be."

MAL WATCHED as Alp spoke with his mother. There were more tears, so much anger and hurt, and a sense of vengeance that even chilled Mal. These men had to die, but as a bunny shifter, Alp shouldn't be part of it. Still, he was proud that Alp was stepping up, even if Mal had no intention of taking him into the war zone. When Alp hung up the phone, he slumped in the chair, looking weary.

"She told me to thank you," he said softly.

"No need," Mal assured him. "You're my pack, which means you're my responsibility." He moved closer and reached out to tousle Alp's hair. "But when I go in, you're not coming with me."

Alp's head snapped up. "The fuck I'm not!"

"Listen to me. I know you're angry, and I understand it. What they did to you was monstrous, and I can get wanting revenge. But you're a rabbit shifter, and you aren't cut out for things like this. Leave it to me."

"Oh, screw you!"

Mal arched his eyebrows. "Excuse me? Did you forget who's First here?"

Alp waved his residual limb. "Did you forget what they did to me? I want to look Hyde in the eye before he dies. I want him to know I'm not afraid of him. And I want to be there when he pisses his pants, knowing that he's about to draw his last breath."

Wow. Mal's little rabbit was pretty bloodthirsty.

"You can't take this away from me, Mal."

"I won't take you with me, and that's final."

The scowl was instant, but then it changed and became something darker, more fearful. "You're not coming back." He jumped out of his chair, nearly knocking it over. "You son of a bitch, you're planning on going in there to die!"

Mal grabbed his shoulders. "I won't let them hurt my pack!" he snarled.

"What do you think dying will do? Huh?" He jabbed Mal in the chest with two fingers, actually forcing him to step back. "What do you think's going to happen?"

"You'll go home with your parents and—"

Alp let loose with what Mal could only call a disgusted grunt. "And again, fuck you. You are the most thick-headed person I've ever met in my life. My folks are coming, and they're grabbing clothes and stuff for me. I don't intend on going home. When this mess is all over, I'm still going to be here. They'll come to visit, and bring my siblings and their kids to see me. Mom doesn't like it, but she understands I need to be here." He drew in a breath. "With you, ya big, dumb fucker."

There was no way Mal wouldn't admit Alp didn't have a cast iron set of balls on him. But he also wouldn't admit how adorable he looked with his chest all puffed out, hair spreading out like straw, breathing hard as he stared Mal down. In another life, another time, maybe Mal and Alp could have had something together. He liked Alp, both as rabbit and as man. Maybe.... He shook his head. Now wasn't the time to deal with flights of fancy. Besides, predator and prey? How the hell would that even work?

"There's no one else," Mal said, trying to get Alp to understand the gravity of the situation. "It's just me, and I won't let you be in harm's way. You can hate me all you want, but that's the way it is. Now, say, 'yes, First,' and let it go."

Alp's eyes narrowed. "Fuck you, *First*."

Before he could twist away, Mal grabbed him by the shoulder. "You don't talk to me like that. I am your First. You've sworn to me, so you'll do as you're told."

Alp shrugged him off. "Not when my First is being an idiot, I don't. Fine, we're a pack of two, but we *are* a pack. Where you go, I go. There is no way around that."

What the hell? No one had ever argued with Mal before. They all did as he expected. Why the fuck was he letting Alp get away with it?

"You will do as I say. This isn't a democracy. We don't all get a vote here."

Alp flopped back onto the chair, his gaze locked on Mal. "Then you'd better figure out another way, because I will be going with you, even if I have to run after your motorcycle on foot." He waggled his arm. "And you're going to look awfully stupid with a three-legged rabbit chasing you."

Alp's words jolted something in Mal's brain. Something his First had tried to instill in him, which Mal rejected. Family. Pack. Joined. The precepts of a pack sprang from the heart and bound the people together. It was forever, unless someone shattered the bonds on their own.

Like Mal had done. He'd run like a coward in the night because of the expectations that were going to be on him. He was too young to be saddled with the needs of a pack. He didn't want to be responsible for anyone but himself. Only now he'd taken up Alp's burdens as his own. How could he protect Alp, especially if the bastard wouldn't do what he was told?

A knock at the door startled him. He sniffed and groaned when he realized Lydia was there.

"You need to shift," he whispered urgently. "We can't let her see you."

"And why is that?" Alp demanded.

"You're right. Here, Lydia, let me introduce my one-handed friend who, oddly enough, is missing the same limb as the rabbit, which isn't here right now."

"Oh." Alp frowned. "I suppose that makes sense."

But Mal could tell Alp didn't like it. And truthfully, neither did Mal. Still, when Alp stripped out of the sweats Mal had given him, he couldn't help but stare at the pale ass, the slender lines of his back, and the soft curve of his cock. Mal shook his head. Why was he thinking about Alp like this? They'd only known each other a few weeks, but he seemed to have... oh, fuck no. No, that wasn't possible. It wasn't something that happened across species. Was it? The thing was, it would explain his need to sniff Alp's hair, to rub his cheek against it, ensuring Alp carried Mal's scent. He was fucking marking Alp, so that any shifter or animal who got close to him would know that he belonged to Mal.

Motherfuck! He'd marked Alp. He'd done more than accept Alp into his pack—he'd made it so no other shifter would come near him without Mal's approval. Worse still, with his scent mingling with Alp's, Mal had wended Alp into his life. Because of that stupidity, Mal needed to keep Alp close, ensure he was protected at all times. He'd seen the First do it with his wife and children, marking them so it would settle him. Son of a bitch, he'd fucked up this whole mission already, because now he wouldn't be able to walk away from Alp.

Ever.

CHAPTER 8

ALP LAY in the corner of his cage, staring at the vet as she chatted with Mal. That insane jealousy roared through him again, and even though he tried to quell it, the heat continued to rise. What was up with that? Even though it had been all he'd wanted, why had he told his parents he wouldn't be coming home, choosing instead to stay with the grumpy werewolf? And why, even weeks later, did his rabbit —and Alp—seek out comfort from Mal?

Sure, he was a First, but that shouldn't have any meaning for Alp. They didn't have any leaders, and yet he acknowledged to his mother that he followed Mal.

"How's my favorite patient doing?" Lydia said, sticking her face near the cage.

Alp wanted to turn and kick the bars. Maybe, if he got lucky, he'd nail her in that smug face of.... *Stop. Just fucking stop. She saved your life. Why are you*—no. It wasn't her he was mad at. It was Mal, who sat there, laughing when Lydia said something, putting a hand atop hers, giving her that smile that Alp thought was just for him. What the fuck was he doing? Couldn't he understand you didn't do stuff like that?

Unless.... Did Mal like her? Is that why he was always smiling at her, when it seemed he only scowled or shouted at Alp? That had to be it. It was the only logical explanation. Alp's anger surged. Well, fuck Mal if he thought Alp was going to sit here and watch the two of them screw. He grabbed the bars in his teeth and yanked hard on them, rattling the whole cage.

Lydia stepped back, her eyes wide. "What the hell?"

Mal was up and to the cage in a heartbeat. "Hey, what's wrong?" He opened the cage, reached in, and made a grab for Alp, who side-stepped him. "Alp, stop," he commanded.

Alp froze. Mal lifted him out of the cage and cuddled him to his chest. Alp didn't want this. Didn't want to feel like this. Didn't want.... Didn't want to lose Mal. Not like this. He needed Mal, probably more than he needed air. Mal was the center of his world, and he couldn't stand the thought he'd walk away, leaving Alp behind.

Lydia was nattering on about something, but Alp only had eyes for Mal. Only needed Mal. He had to be closer. Shit, if he could burrow under Mal's skin, that still wouldn't be close enough. He was safe in Mal's arms, always safe.

And then Lydia gasped. "What the fuck?" she shouted.

Mal let go of Alp and turned, shielding Alp from—oh, fuck. In his fear and panic, Alp had shifted! She'd seen him do it.

"Don't look at him," Mal growled.

"No, no, of course not," Lydia barked. "I mean, it's an everyday occurrence for something to be a rabbit one second, and then be a naked man the next, right? How silly of me to be surprised." But she didn't sound surprised. She sounded... excited.

Alp peered around Mal, who continued to try to stand between him and Lydia. In a swift move, he reached down, grabbed a blanket from the bed, and whipped it around Alp. When he finished, he snarled at Lydia.

"I don't want to hurt you, but if you tell anyone about Alp or what you saw, I'll—"

"So your name is Alp?" she said softly, taking a step closer. "I'm Lydia, and I am so very delighted to meet you. Well, I guess the other you."

"You're not freaked out?" Alp asked, his voice a hoarse whisper.

"Of course I am. I mean, who wouldn't be? But I have to be honest, I'm more amazed than freaked." She peered up at Mal. "I'll never tell anyone about Alp, I swear it."

Mal relaxed slightly. "Humans can't know," he said. "If they did.... If they did, they'd do to others what they've done to Alp. What they're probably already doing to more shifters."

"Shifters? Is that what Alp is?"

Mal drew in a breath, then reached for Alp's hand. "Not just Alp. I'm a wolf. I'm his guardian."

Alp's heart swelled when Mal said it. He leaned in and put his head on Mal's arm, staring up into his eyes, which earned him that smile he'd come to love so much. The one where everything faded away and he seemed to actually *see* Alp.

"Now this whole thing makes so much more sense to me. No one would ever spend that kind of money on a rabbit, especially one missing a foot. And no rabbit could have survived what Alp... I'm sorry, is it okay if I call you Alp? I don't want to be forward."

"Sure, Alp is fine."

Fucking surreal. Alp's parents had warned him repeatedly to stay away from humans. Hyde and his assholes had enforced those beliefs. But Lydia? She actually asked Alp if it was okay to call him by name.

"What were you so angry about, little one?" Mal asked, brushing a hair out of Alp's eyes.

"You were... I mean... I...." Well, shit. *I was a jealous bastard? I hated seeing you so happy with someone else?* "Nothing important. I just got annoyed because I hate being in the cage."

"I'm sorry," Mal said softly, continuing to touch Alp's hair.

"I have a question," Lydia said, breaking Alp's focus. "What really happened to your... well, I guess it's your hand, isn't it?"

In this instance, he would defer to Mal. "First?"

Mal's nostrils flared. "Thank you." He turned to Lydia and started the story from the moment he heard the gunshot, how he'd rescued Alp from the men—glossing over the part where they were now being feasted on by flies in the woods—and about taking Alp to Lydia. Then he turned to Alp. "Can you fill in the rest?"

He didn't want to. Alp was so ashamed that he'd been too damn weak to defend himself. Still, he told his tale. It started out hesitantly, but as the anger burned within him, it came out harsher, raspier.

"Someone knew what you were, and they did that to you on purpose?" Her horror was easy to hear. "Who the fuck? No reputable doctor or scientist would ever experiment on a person."

"Hyde doesn't think we're people. Well, not entirely. He believes we're animals that somehow learned to mimic human behavior. He thinks we emulate people in order to fit in."

Lydia's eyes went wide as she regarded Mal. "Is that the truth?"

Mal shook his head. "Yes and no. Shifters predate Homo sapiens. We're genetic offshoots of humans, as much as Homo sapiens are of Homo erectus. We're a divergent genetic line, nothing more, nothing less. Yes, we've evolved, but we've always been a type of human."

She nodded sagely. "How many shifters are there?"

That got a shrug. "No one knows for certain. There are a lot, that's for sure." He smiled and rubbed Alp's head. "Bunny shifters are pretty prolific, you know."

Alp snorted. "I have thirteen siblings, and we're one of the smaller families in our area."

"Fascinating." She quirked a brow. "I have to ask, if rabbits, even shifters, have such large families, how have you been undetected for so long?"

"Our communities—our warrens—are large tracts of land. In most ways, you'd probably think we were more Amish than anything else. Big families that keep to themselves."

"That's... amazing," she breathed out.

"Okay," Mal said, breaking contact with Alp. "Why are you not more freaked out?"

She shrugged. "I'm a doctor, so science is a huge part of my life. I understand divergent DNA, and what you're saying? It makes absolute sense to me. A part of me wonders if I've gone crazy, but the rest?

I suppose if I sat back and thought about it, I'd start asking the questions that would make my head spin, but after hearing Alp's story, I find that I can't worry enough about the why and wherefore to care. Whoever hurt him is an inhumane son of a bitch."

Mal cleared his throat. "Um... I'm going to be honest with you. My plan is to take them down. Hard."

Lydia cocked her head as she stared at Mal and Alp, and then her eyes widened and her nostrils flared. "You're going to kill them."

If Alp thought Mal would deny it, he apparently didn't know his First.

"Yes," he hissed, his expression dark. His body shook with an undisguised rage, the muscles in his neck tight, his face a twisted caricature of the one Alp knew. "They tortured Alp and who knows how many others. According to Alp, they've killed us, mutilated us, and I won't stand for it."

As her gaze lowered, Lydia blew out a long, slow breath. "I have to admit, I'm conflicted. I mean, I look at Alp and keep seeing Dinah's face. What would I do if they hurt her or someone else I care about?"

"Imagine if it's hundreds of someones," Alp said. "I was there for six years. They kept a lot of shifters to test their crackpot bullshit on. I've seen the bodies of those who didn't survive the experiments. I lay in my pen at night and heard the screams."

The blood drained from Lydia's face. "And you can't call the police, because they'd know what you are then. And once your secret is out, who knows how many others would try the same thing." She shivered. "Shit. I can't approve of killing them, but I can't deny you have every right to protect yourselves either."

"If you have an alternative, let us know," Alp said, hopeful that they could stave off the coming conflict that Mal had decided Alp couldn't be part of.

"I wish to God I did," she replied. "I look at history and see all the peoples whose only option was to fight back. They declared war on you, so how can you not take the fight to them?" She spoke the words, but trembled and her voice cracked.

"I'm sorry," Alp said.

This time Lydia's eyes widened. "For what? Tell me, Alp. What are *you* sorry for? You were a goddamn child, and they cut you up. Why on earth would you be sorry?"

There was such anger in her voice, and Alp was surprised that it wasn't because of him—it was *for* him.

Alp shuddered. "Because if I hadn't lost control, you never would have been dragged into this."

"Well, I suppose there is that," she said, a teasing lilt in her voice. "I'll be honest—if I had to choose between remaining ignorant and knowing that there are horrors being perpetrated on your kind? I'll always choose to know."

That meant a lot to Alp. Finding out that not all humans were monsters helped.

Lydia folded her hands in front of her. "So, how can I help?"

MAL BLINKED. "WHAT DO YOU MEAN?"

"I want to help you. I need to do this."

Mal sat back, keeping a hand on Alp's bouncing leg. "No. No one else is going with me."

She frowned, and then her expression morphed to one of anger. "Oh, I see. It's a suicide mission," she snapped. "You know, I took you to be a smart man. I'm sad to learn I was wrong."

Mal scowled at her. "What? Listen—"

"No, you listen," she shouted. "If there are that many shifters, how will they get out if you're dead? Who's going to let them loose from their pens? They'll starve to death, or be crushed if they shift back. And how many have injuries that might kill them?" She tilted her head toward Alp. "It's obvious you heal faster than normal, but like with Alp, sometimes you need another person to help make things better."

Alp crossed his arms and sat back, a smug look on his face. "Don't hold back, Lydia. Maybe he'll listen to you, since he can't seem to hear what I'm telling him."

"I can't protect you," Mal snarled. "Don't you fucking get it?"

She arched her eyebrows. "Do I look like someone who needs protection?" She blew out a breath. "I won't kill anyone, but you need me to help those shifters who are injured. I mean, I'm not a human doctor, but if they're in their animal forms, I can give them aid."

Mal stood, his posture rigid. He hated that she was right. If he went in there and died, then all the shifters left in the building would probably die too. He had no problems killing the humans who'd vivisected the shifters, but he couldn't see his way to condemning the people they'd held captive. Still, he was only one man, and he had no backup.

"I can't take you in with me. There's no one else to help."

"My parents are coming," Alp reminded him.

"Bunnies aren't fighters. I won't have you lose your folks."

Alp snorted. "My mom is so pissed, she'd probably take them all on at once. You don't hurt any of her babies."

Mal pinned Alp with a harsh stare. "Be honest with me. Do you want your mother in a room with murderers? Do you want her to see their blood as it pours out from their mangled bodies? You good with her being in a building with corpses that have been torn apart?"

Alp paled. "N-no, I don't." Then he turned his gaze up at Mal. "But I can't lose you either."

The ache in Alp's voice made Mal smile. "Okay, what if I promise to come back to you? Will that keep you home?"

Home? When had Mal started thinking of Swenson as home?

Around the same time you found Alp, don't you think?

There was a small handful of places that Mal had been where he'd stayed more than three or four days, and none of them could offer anything to make him hang around. Once he pocketed the cash from the pool game, Mal was out of there. This time, he had a reason to stay.

"No," Alp replied, his tone showing Mal this conversation was far from over. "Because you'd lie to keep me out of the way."

"To keep you safe, you dumb bunny!"

Alp's lips curled up, and then he and Lydia snorted. "Dumb bunny? Really? That's the best you can come up with? At least I called you a big, dumb fucker."

Mal reached out and stroked Alp's hair. Soft, silky strands slid between his fingers. Alp pushed against his hand, and Mal was lost. He'd never had a reaction to anyone like this. Fuck 'em and get gone. That was the best way to handle these things. But he found that with Alp, he wanted to stick around. To run the woods together, to lay down by the lake and sun themselves on a lazy Sunday. He wanted....

"Mal?"

He turned to find Lydia staring at him. "Sorry, what's up?"

"Do you know where these people are?"

Mal gave a shrug. "The way Alp was the day I found him, they couldn't be far from there. He was falling over, stumbling, and—"

"I was fucked up. I think we get the point. Can you move on with your story?" Alp bitched.

Unable to stop himself, Mal reached out and ran fingers through Alp's hair. "Sorry." He turned back to Lydia. "The men were on foot too. I figure the best way is for me to go back to the area and nose around."

"And you mean that literally."

Mal gave a shrug. "Pretty much."

"Alp, do you remember anything that might help?"

His face scrunched up. "Stairs. Lots and lots of them, going up and down. There were elevators too, but I couldn't get into those."

"Can you guess how far you ran?" Mal asked. "Maybe what direction you were coming from?"

Alp shook his head. "I'm sorry. I was so scared, I just ran until I couldn't." He sighed. "I wish I could help."

But he had. "At least we know the area you were in. It has to be there somewhere."

Lydia frowned. "I've lived here my whole life, and I don't know any buildings large enough to house the kind of labs you're talking about. I mean, the instillation would have to be massive."

"Maybe it looked that way because I'm so small."

"No," Mal said firmly. "It's exactly how you saw it, I'm certain." When Alp yawned, Mal stood. "I think that's enough for now. Alp needs rest."

Alp pursed his lips. "I'm fine."

"And I say you need rest." He narrowed his gaze. "Or are you going to argue with me?"

A quick swallow, followed by a turn of his head. "No, First."

"What's a first?" Lydia asked.

"It's a designation for wolves. First means the one that leads, the protector."

"Oh, I see." She blew out a breath. "You know, when I woke up this morning, the only thoughts in my mind were getting some lab results back for one of the dogs at the clinic. Now?" She held up her hands an mimed an explosion. "Mind blown, man."

Alp snickered as Mal walked Lydia to the door. When they got there, she turned and gazed at Alp.

"I'm sorry they did that to you. I know it has to make you not trust people, but I swear to you, I won't ever tell anyone about you. Or any shifters."

"Thank you," Alp said, and the reverence in his voice told Mal that Alp had made a friend.

As soon as the door closed, Alp stripped off his clothes. Mal stood there and stared. Alp was tiny, sure, but he was well toned, and his skin was all sleek and shiny. Mal swallowed hard.

"Did you want me to shift so I can get back into the cage?" he asked, a teasing lilt to his voice.

"No, just get in bed."

He went over and crawled across the mattress, then slid beneath the comforter. When he turned and peered up at Mal, his lashes fluttered.

"Can you sleep with me?"

"Sure, I can do that."

Mal toed off his shoes, then yanked off his shirt and finally slid his pants and underwear down, then stepped out of them. He squatted, ready for the change, when Alp called him.

"I don't want the wolf. I... want you to sleep with me."

Oh. Shit.

CHAPTER 9

ALP NESTLED DEEPER into the blankets. He shouldn't be so happy. He'd run and left all the others behind. He knew there wasn't anything he could have done, but it still didn't set well with him.

"You're shivering," Mal said, reaching up and stroking a hand over Alp's hair. "Are you cold? Do you want me to get another blanket?"

"No, I'm okay."

"You're crap at lying, I hope you realize this. Come here, little one." Mal slid an arm over Alp and tugged him closer. It was so different sleeping with Mal than it had been with the wolf. Where the wolf was big, Mal was massive. His body dwarfed Alp's by more than a bit. As he lay there, held close to Mal, Alp could feel the steady beat of Mal's heart thudding against his back. Mal's hand was fanned over Alp's chest, his fingers splayed so the whole area was covered.

Unable to stand it anymore, Alp turned in Mal's arms and buried his face in the hairy chest. He had no idea what he was doing. The most he'd ever done with another guy was hold his hand, and that was helping Mr. Welling cross the street when he was eleven. Beyond that? Not one thing. Tentatively, Alp reached out and stroked a finger over Mal's chest, shivering at the way the skin rippled. He leaned in and inhaled, a calm washing over him as Mal's scent filled his lungs. When a large hand cupped the back of Alp's head and pulled him in tighter, Alp went with it. He nibbled the skin, pleased when Mal groaned.

"Alp" came the husky plea. "You need to stop."

The fuck Alp did. He scooted down farther in the bed, planting kisses on every piece of exposed skin he could. Throughout it, Mal seemed to not know what to do with his hands as he alternated between pushing down on Alp's head or trying to move him away. It was funny, he thought. Here he was, a tiny little rabbit, and he was making the big wolf whimper and plead.

Lower still. By now, Mal's erection was standing tall and proud. Alp couldn't believe the size, but then, why shouldn't he? Everything about Mal was larger than life, and had been since the day he burst into the clearing and killed the men who would have dragged Alp back to hell.

A tiny droplet of moisture beaded on the head of Mal's cock. Alp leaned in and sniffed, then tentatively stuck his tongue out and swiped it over the slit.

"Ooh, fuck! Alp, no. Don't do that."

Alp ignored him and opened his mouth wide to get more of the syrupy goodness that Mal was making. He closed his lips around the head and hummed as he was rewarded with a sweet and tangy surprise. Now Mal seemed to have made up his mind, as he put both hands on the back of Alp's head and pushed him down.

"For fuck's sake, Alp. Stop," Mal whimpered. "Please."

It was a dichotomy. Mal's mouth said stop, but his hands made it known that no way in hell was that an option. He pressed harder, and Alp opened wider. He knew he couldn't take the whole thing. He doubted there was anyone who could. Alp wrapped a hand around the straining shaft, and Mal seemed to understand. Instead of trying to get Alp to take more or thrusting up, he held Alp steady so only the head was in his mouth.

"Suck me," he begged.

It took a little work, but Alp found a rhythm, stroking a hand up the shaft as he slid his mouth down. By now, Mal was gasping for breath, and Alp's name became a litany as he whispered it over and over.

"You need to stop. I'm going to cum," Mal said, as he pushed Alp away.

Screw that. Alp had worked too hard for this, and he wasn't going to be denied. He gripped the shaft harder and sucked for all he was worth. A few moments later, Mal groaned, and the first spurts of his orgasm squirted into Alp's hungry mouth. He swallowed greedily, delighting in the musky-sweet flavor. When Mal was spent, he collapsed against the bed, an arm over his eyes.

"You shouldn't have done that, little one," he rasped.

Alp didn't care what Mal said. He'd done it, and he loved it. Oh, and he wanted to do it again. He ran a hand over Mal's chest, now glistening with sweat. He loved the feeling of the muscles beneath his hands, the raw strength they held. He wanted to feel those amazing fingers on his body.

"You didn't like it?" Alp asked, unable to suppress the smirk.

Instead of answering, Mal lurched up and grabbed Alp around the waist. Alp yelped, not afraid, but surprised. In a very efficient move, he had Alp on his back and was hovering over him, his eyes glinting in the light.

"I told you to stop," Mal said, his voice low, a threat in his words.

"And yet you liked it."

Mal scowled, and Alp found it insanely hot. "You.... You...."

He reached out, slid a hand beneath Alp's neck, and yanked him up. When Mal slotted his mouth over Alp's, he could have wept. He'd wanted a kiss forever. He'd seen enough porn to know what to do. He opened his mouth, allowing Mal to maul him. The combination of tongue and teeth, of sucks and nips, had Alp achingly hard. When Mal drew back, Alp shuddered. His eyes... they were dark amber.

"Mal?"

"I tried to stop you," Mal said, his voice guttural. "I never wanted this."

The words stung Alp. "You didn't want me?"

"No, you little idiot. I didn't want to bond with you anymore than I already am. My wolf is demanding we take you, hard and fast. He wants to claim you, to give you our bite. To make you ours."

Well, that didn't sound too bad. "O-okay."

"It's forever, Alp. For as long as we live, we'll be soul-bound. Nothing but death can break that bond. I'm trying to hold him back, but he wants you so desperately."

"And what about you? Do you want me too?"

"Yes!" Mal hissed. "You know I fucking do. Why do you think I keep touching you? I love the feeling of your hair, of your skin beneath my fingers. When you're asleep, I lay there and listen to your heart beating, and that's the only thing that'll relax me enough to follow you."

Soul-bound? To be with Mal forever? To feel as safe as he had since the day Mal rescued him? Alp didn't see a downside.

He tilted his neck, offering it to Mal. "Okay, go ahead. Bite me." He sucked in a breath. "Please?"

～

MAL COULDN'T BE HEARING RIGHT. The buildup of testosterone had to have blocked his ears, because no way was Alp, the tiny bunny, asking the wolf to bite him. It simply wasn't possible.

"Do you know what you're asking me to do?" Mal snarled, tightening his grip on Alp's shoulder.

That earned him a sweet smile. "Yes. I'm asking you to keep me safe, to protect me, to be part of me forever. I don't see the downside here."

"When this is all said and done, I was planning to leave."

Alp smiled up at him, and damned if Mal's heart didn't thump a little harder. "Life on the road? Sounds great. I love riding on your motorcycle."

Mal leaned in a little closer. He could smell Alp's blood just beneath the surface. The rush of it through his veins called to Mal, demanded he take it. But this was Alp, who'd already lost so much. What would happen if Mal was to die? No, he couldn't.

"I—I can't," he said, drawing away. It was agonizing, not claiming Alp. The wolf was going nuts, but Mal was more than an animal.

Soft hands pressed to Mal's face. "You can. You will. I want this. Want you."

"It's only been a few weeks. You can't possibly want me."

He tried to move away again, but Alp tightened his grip.

"My mom and dad got married the day after their first date, and they've been together nearly thirty years now. Rabbits know when it's right. It's like a gift we possess. And this? You and me? I know it's right." He let his head fall to the side, exposing that creamy skin. "Bite me, Mal. Make us forever."

Unbidden, Mal's canines dropped. He didn't want to do this. Didn't want to cause Alp any more pain than he'd already suffered, but he nuzzled Alp's neck, tasting the sweetness of his skin. He opened his mouth, and one of his fangs nicked Alp's neck, which caused him to arch his back with a hiss.

"Alp," Mal pleaded, sniffing the tiny droplet of blood that had pearled where his tooth had hit. It was earthy, sweet, and strong. Nothing else Mal had smelled even came close. "Please, get up and walk away. I promise I won't stop you."

Alp slid a hand around Mal's neck. "You're presuming I want to go anywhere. I'm very happy where I am right now, thank you." He smirked and tapped the side of his neck. "Let's go, man. Make with the hickey."

A growl rolled out of Mal. Why was Alp doing this? And why, dear Maker, was Mal so powerless to resist?

"You know, if I could, I'd bite you," Alp said, clearly unafraid. He drew his hand from Mal's neck and brought it to his own, then ran slender fingers over his skin. "Take a nibble, Mal. Taste me."

But that one insignificant drop of blood was already lighting up Mal's every sense. It inflamed his desires, and he hungered for more. He moved in closer and opened his mouth wide.

"That's it. Bite me. Make me yours." Then Alp whispered, "I love you."

And that was it. Mal struck, driving his fangs into the soft flesh.

Alp squeaked and reached out to claw his fingernails over Mal's back. Fearful of hurting him, Mal tried to pull away, until Alp moaned.

"Harder."

That one word, breathed out on a husky exhale, let Mal know this was okay. This was right. Alp was his now, and would be forever. He bit down harder, and blood flooded his mouth. Never before had Mal been so filled with energy. With Alp pinned beneath him, with his blood dancing on Mal's tongue, Mal believed there was nothing he couldn't do.

Even something as hard as falling in love.

Damned rabbit.

HOLY MOTHER OF THE MAKER! Never before in his life had Alp had an experience like that. Pure, white-hot agony flooded him when Mal bit him. It was far worse than anything Hyde had done, even when he'd cut off the hand. Alp felt as though his body was being torn apart, sundered atom by atom, and each one of those had been dipped in acid before it was set on fire.

Then the next instant his body exploded with wave upon wave of bliss and joy. He wasn't sure how it felt for Mal, but Alp knew his mind was being... reconfigured. Mal was pushing his way in, setting up residence, letting Alp know he was no longer by himself. The spark in his mind became a flame as his and Mal's minds merged, becoming one. It was the most intense and life-altering thing Alp had ever experienced. When Mal slumped on top of him, Alp stroked his hair and crooned softly in Mal's ear, letting him know he'd never be alone again.

He tried to put the enormity of it all into words so that he could make Mal understand how everything in his world had turned on its axis. Things he'd believed were scorched away and replaced by the seeding of new thoughts and ideas. New pathways opened for Alp, especially as Mal's presence in his mind settled in, filling Alp with a warmth that he never experienced before.

"Alp," Mal ground out, his lips against Alp's neck. "I'm sorry. I tried so hard to stop—"

"Shut up," Alp whispered, hugging Mal tighter. "For the first time in my life, I'm... settled. I loved my family, but was always one among many. Then I wanted to get out, and I was too alone. Now? I'm one with you. I'm not by myself, and I'm not lost in the crush of others. You can't know how that feels."

"I do," Mal corrected. "When I left my pack, the link between us was severed. The voices I heard, the emotions I sensed, all of the things that made us pack? I allowed them to be ripped away. For weeks, I had to force myself not to go back and beg to be allowed to return. My head was empty, and it scared the crap out of me. Now? I have this twinkling light in there, shining like a beacon and calling to me." He kissed Alp's neck, again lingering on the bite. "I'm no longer adrift."

He rolled, dragging Alp with him. This moment was right, and Alp knew it. Nothing could be more perfect, at least as far as he was concerned.

"Sleep, my bunny," Mal ordered, stroking Alp's hair, and this once, Alp was happy to comply.

"Alpin?"

Alp tried to open his eyes, but he was so warm and comfortable. And why the hell did Mal sound like his mother?

"Alpin Dawkins! I know you're here."

This time he jerked awake. No way! It couldn't be them. He sniffed and let loose with a whine. "It's my mother."

"Your... oh, shit." Mal pushed Alp aside, bouncing him off the mattress and onto the floor. He landed with a grunt and a death glare. "Get dressed," Mal hissed.

"Why?" Alp whined. "I wanted to sleep. Tell her to come back later."

He squeaked when strong hands jerked him up from the floor. "Get dressed. I am not telling your mother you're in bed when she came all this way to see you." His voice softened. "And you know you want to see her."

He truly did. Alp put on Mal's clothes quickly, then flew toward the door of the room. He jerked it open and found his mother peering up at the building, her hands cupped over her mouth.

"Mom," he said upon laying eyes on her.

She squinted against the bright sun, and then her eyes went wide. "Alpin?" She dashed for the door that led to the room and launched herself at him, wrapping him in an embrace. "Oh, Alpin," she cried, burying her face in his neck and inhaling deeply. "I never thought I'd see you again." She kissed his cheeks. "They told us you'd abandoned the car and caught a ride with someone else. We wondered what we'd done to make you leave."

"No, Mom. It wasn't you, I swear to the Maker."

"Alp?" His father's voice, older. Wearier.

"Dad?"

And then another round of hugs, where Alp wanted nothing more than to sink into the warmth that only his family could provide.

"Alp? I have coffee started. If you and your parents would like to come in and—"

His mother's eyes widened as she took in Mal's form. If he thought she'd be wary, he was wrong. She stalked up to Mal and jabbed a finger in his chest. "What have you done to Alpin?" she demanded.

Mal glanced over at Alp, then back to his mother. "Nothing that the two of us didn't want," he said, his voice hard.

"I can smell you all over him."

"Because I was all over him, Mom."

She whirled on her heel. "You what?"

"I wanted him to claim me." Alp pulled the collar of his shirt down, showing off where Mal had bitten him. He stroked a finger over what was now a scar. "I'm his."

She puffed up her chest, then spun back toward Mal. She fixed her gaze on him, her nose twitching. "I want you to remember one thing, wolf. If you hurt him, we bunnies know how to bite and kick."

"Mom!" Alp cried.

A slow smile spread over Mal's face. "I swear I will do my best to never hurt him," he promised.

"Good." She reached out and patted his shoulder. "Now, what flavor creamer do you have for the coffee? I'm partial to vanilla." She clutched Mal's hand and took a few steps toward the door, then glanced over her shoulder. "Are you two coming or what?"

After the two of them entered the room, Alp turned to his father. "What the hell just happened?"

Dad smiled. "I think your mom just welcomed a wolf into the family."

Alp wasn't sure if he was excited or scared to death.

"Alpin! Get your fuzzy butt in here," she called out.

Scared. Definitely scared.

CHAPTER 10

THOUGH HE WASN'T sure what he should expect, Alp's family was unlike anything Mal could have dreamed up. He was curious why his mother hadn't said anything about Alp's hand, but the moment she was behind closed doors with him, she turned and pulled Alp into her arms and wailed.

"My poor baby," she kept repeating. "Oh, Alpin."

His father stood behind her, a steadying hand on her back, as he stared at the residual limb where Alp's hand had been. His foot began to tap, harder and harder, until Mal feared he'd break something. His eyes were wild, and he began chittering. Mal knew rage when he saw it, and Alp's father was deep into his.

"Sir?"

He turned toward Mal, his eyes wild. "You're going to kill these fuckers, right?" he snapped. "If you're not going to, you can't be with my son. No one would let his mate be injured and not do anything about it."

Mal blinked. "His... what?

Alp's head snapped toward his father. "Dad? What are you talking about?"

Mother and father exchanged a look. Then his mom nodded and turned to Mal. "You two are mated. How do you not know this?"

Mated? Was that even possible?

"No, I gave him my First's bite, something that makes us pack, that's all."

Her eyes widened. "No, no, no. You.... You seriously don't understand mating?"

Apparently Mal didn't, and now it bothered him. "It would seem I do not," he admitted.

She gestured to the table, and he and Alp took a seat. She gazed at her son, and Mal felt unworthy of seeing the love that shone in her eyes. His father stepped up behind Alp and put his hands on those slender shoulders, rubbing gently. If they hadn't claimed him as part of their family, Mal would be biting their heads off for touching Alp.

"When a First bites a pack member, that's all there is to it. A quick bite, and then their thoughts open up to the First, allowing him to sense their emotions and general well-being. When a First gives a bite to his mate, it's given along with the exchange of...." Her cheeks flushed. "Semen."

Mal turned to Alp, whose face was crimson. "But we didn't—"

Oh, Maker. Alp had swallowed his seed. He'd opened a connection between the two of them, and Mal had sealed it with the bite.

"Mated?"

His mother smirked. "I did say I could smell him on you."

Alp's head snapped in Mal's direction, his eyes filled with worry. "Mal, I'm sorry!"

"Why?" his mother asked. "A mating is a joyous thing."

She drew down the collar of her Psychedelic Furs T-shirt, and Mal couldn't miss the two tiny punctures there.

"You've mated with Mr. Dawkins?"

"Whoa, hold on," Mr. Dawkins said, holding a hand up. "You're practically my son-in-law. I think Deacon is a lot better."

"And I'm Nura. We're happy to have you as a member of our family, Malachi."

Mal's head was spinning. Thankfully Alp jumped in.

"I don't understand. I thought I was supposed to hate wolves?"

Nura's cheeks flushed. "Most wolves aren't to be trusted," she replied. "Your aunt Marie found that out when someone she thought would be her mate stole everything she owned. He was a wolf, and we always rally around family, so we decided wolves couldn't be trusted." She fixed Mal with a stare. "But knowing that a wolf is responsible for saving my son? Keeping him safe from... from...."

Her lip wobbled and her tiny face scrunched up. A moment later, Mal found himself with his arms full of a sobbing woman.

"Alpin was such a willful child," she said. "He was constantly wanting to get out and explore. His brothers and sisters were perfectly happy staying near the warren, but not Alpin. I can't tell you how many times we had to ground him when we found him in places that we thought were too dangerous."

Deacon came around and lay his head on Nura's shoulder, then pulled her close when she turned and sank into his embrace. "We looked everywhere we could think he might have gone. Then the police called and said they found the car. They told us that they thought Alpin went off with some other people, and we couldn't say it wasn't true, because he was forever going off with others and getting into mischief. We figured he'd come back in a day or two. But then it turned into weeks, then months, and finally years. Nura believed we'd been horrible parents, and that we'd driven our son away. She—"

"Stop it! Just fucking stop!" Alp shrieked, pulling at his hair. "I wanted desperately to come home. Every night I lay there, wishing I could be with my family. Hell, I even thought about Andrew and his giggle farts. I would have given anything to be there with you." He threw himself at Mal, who caught him in midjump and pulled him up and to his chest. "I swear to the Maker, I thought I was going to die, but the only thing—the *only* thing—that kept me going was the chance to see you and tell you how much I love you."

And just like that, three rabbit shifters came together in hugs and kisses. Mal stepped back, wanting to give them space. Nura looked up, then reached for his hand and pulled him into the hug.

"We owe you everything, Malachi. There's nothing you can ask for that is too outlandish. We would sell everything we own in order to pay you back for bringing Alpin home to us." She squeezed Mal's shoulder. "He couldn't have chosen a better mate."

The word still whirled around in Mal's head. "You owe me nothing," he replied. "And for the record, the men who were chasing him are dead. I left their bodies in the woods for the scavengers. They were useless in life, but maybe they can provide something with their deaths."

Nura sniffled. "It's wrong of me to feel glad that they're dead, but Maker help me, I am." She nuzzled Alp's hair. "My Alpin was willful, but he was the sweetest child. He'd get into mischief, but he would never intentionally hurt anyone. It took him being gone for me to realize how truly special he is." She drew in a breath. "It's that, and what he said to me on the phone yesterday, that tells me he's finally found somewhere to settle down. Maybe raise a family."

A family? For fuck's sake, Mal had just found out he was mated, and Nura was already talking about a family?

"Don't put the cart before the horse, Mom," Alp said, smiling wide as he was hugged between his parents. "I don't know that I want kids."

"Oh, Alpin. We're bunnies. Kids are a big part of who we are."

"Yeah, no. I'm not sure about Mal, but after having been one of fourteen kids, I'm happy having it be just me and Mal."

His mom clucked her tongue. "You'll see," she said. "One day, your house will be bursting with children."

Mal shuddered at the thought.

THE EVENING WAS... well, amazing. Alp's parents told stories of their family, and they were so vivid, Mal could have sworn they were his memories too. He especially liked the ones about Alp when he was a child, and how headstrong he was, and how he never *ever* backed down from a challenge. Like all good things, though, the night had to end.

Alp cried when his parents said they needed to head for home.

Apparently a few of his siblings had new litters, and they needed to be there to help out. Alp was bereft, but brightened considerably when Nura suggested they huddle together for the night. When it was time for bed, they shifted and jumped up onto the sofa.

They'd spent the night, in shifted form, snuggled together. Mal stood guard over them, his bunny and the parents who'd seemed to accept him without qualms. No one would get near them without going through Mal first.

His heart melted when Alp pushed deeper into the bunny pile, his nose wriggling. It was plain to see how much it meant to him. This was the man he'd mated. The one he was coming to love. How could he take Alp or Lydia into danger? How could he keep them out of it? Was he really willing to join hearts and souls with Alp, only to go into some lab and probably die?

"I can feel you, you know," Alp whispered in his ear.

Mal spun, shocked out of his thoughts. "I'm sorry?"

"The link between us goes both ways." He slid his fingers through Mal's hair. "I know you're afraid, so why don't you save us both a lot of 'no I'm not, yes you are' back and forth and tell me what's going on in that amazingly gorgeous head of yours."

Mal snorted. Alp was... Maker, he wasn't shy at all. He reminded Mal of the First's wife. She was a force of nature. Instead of being the shy, demure First mate, she had no problems with getting in the trenches and sullying her hands. The man who was in charge of the entire Forest Walker pack would take one look at his mate, and he'd melt. When it came to his kids, no father was more nurturing than the First. Mal never saw that in himself. He wasn't made to settle down, and it was that fear that crept inside him that had caused him to leave.

Now he was responsible for Alp. He wanted him as happy as the First's wife had been. He needed to ensure Alp would never want for anything. To never doubt he was loved. It sent a thrill through Mal to know that he had the opportunity to make Alp his family, and the two of them would be happy together. Hell, he might even go back to Alp's warren and meet his kin. Wasn't that a dynamic shift?

"I'm just thinking." Mal turned toward Alp and cupped his chin. "You were right."

"Of course I was." He cocked his head. "About what?"

"I'm stuck between a rock and a hard place here. I can't take you and Lydia into a dangerous situation."

Alp opened his mouth, but Mal rushed on.

"And I can't leave you out of it. You, in particular, have every right to be there. You need closure, and the only way to get it is by being certain it's done."

A terse nod. "Thank you. I have to be honest with you, though. It's not revenge I'm thinking about."

"Oh?"

"Yes. I remember the razors, the knives, the injections that burned like fire, but what I remember most is the screams. Humans think animals don't have feelings, but those screams will haunt me forever. I need to try to get them to stop. To put them to rest. That's why I need to go. I still want to see Hyde before he dies, but it's for all of us, not just me."

Mal stood there, staring at Alp. He'd always thought of rabbits as flighty, but Alp and his parents showed Mal that nothing could be further from the truth.

He grabbed Alp and drew him in. "You know, you've taught me a lot in the short time we've known each other. I look forward to a lifetime of learning with you."

Alp's eyes widened. "Really? You're not just saying that?"

"No, I most certainly am not." He leaned in and kissed Alp, delighted when his bunny opened for him. Mal swept his tongue inside, tasting every corner of Alp's mouth. If Mal thought Alp would be submissive, however, he was wrong. He gripped Mal's hair in his hand and dragged him into an even deeper kiss, his own tongue now wrestling with Mal's.

"Look, Nura. They're in love," Deacon purred. "It reminds me of us when we were that age."

Mal tried to pull back, but Alp wasn't having that. He tightened his grip on Mal's neck and hauled himself up, locking his legs around

Mal's waist. He continued to plunder Mal's mouth, and after a few moments, Mal sighed, wrapped his arms around Alp's back, cupping his ass, and carried him toward the bathroom.

Nura snickered. "Remember when we went to the club to see that Stones cover band and you dragged me into the bathroom? I think that's the night Jessup was conceived."

The words must have been like ice for Alp, because he sighed into Mal's mouth, then slid back down to the floor. "Really, Mom?"

She blinked. "What?"

"I do not want to think about my parents having sex," he said firmly.

She waved a dismissive hand. "Psh. We have it at least once or twice a night," she shot back. Then she took hold of Deacon's hand and gazed fondly into his eyes. "And lemme tell you, sex is like a fine wine—it gets better with age."

"Make them leave," Alp whimpered. "My poor ears are probably bleeding now."

Mal couldn't help but laugh. He knew that Alp was teasing and that it was going to kill him to see his parents head home.

"How about if I give you some time alone?" Mal asked, nuzzling Alp's ear. "I won't go far, so don't even think about running away from me."

Alp shuddered. "I would never," he said, with so much sincerity in his voice. "I could never leave my pack."

"I know, little one. I couldn't stand to see you go either." A quick kiss, and then he turned to Alp's parents. "It was truly an honor to meet you both," he said, extending a hand. They both looked at him as though he was nuts, then pulled him into a hug.

"Please take care of Alpin," Nura whispered in Mal's ear.

"I will give my life for him," Mal vowed.

"No," Deacon insisted. "We need you both. You are our family, and to rabbits that's the most important thing. Don't do anything stupid and get yourself killed."

And those words, the promise of family, the need to be with Alp, finally told Mal what he needed to do.

"No, sir. I've got plans." He leaned in and kissed Nura's cheek. "Thank you for Alp. It's only been a few weeks, but never has anything in my life been more important to me."

She kissed him back. "We're trusting the two of you to take care of each other," she insisted. "Is it okay if we come back with the family?"

"Absolutely," Mal replied. "I can't wait to meet them all."

She reared back in horror. "Oh, no. We're only bringing a few next time. We have 238 nieces, nephews, grandkids, and cousins that live within five miles of us. A lot more farther out. Do you know how much bringing everyone here would cost?" She shivered dramatically. "A few at a time. We'll have to draw straws, because everyone wants to see Alpin again."

"Then I can't wait," Mal said honestly.

He turned to Deacon, unsure if he should shake with him or hug him. That choice was taken from him when Deacon pulled him into a tight embrace.

"You've given us back a part of our world," he said, his voice dripping with emotion. "We'll never forget that."

"Well, if it helps, you've actually given me a world, so I think it's me who owes you."

He nudged them in Alp's direction, and the three of them went to the table, the remainder of the bag of freeze-dried fruit in front of them, and talked. Mal stepped outside and walked over to what was probably one of the few remaining payphones left in the state. He fished out a handful of coins, then lifted the receiver. Once he dropped his payment in, he dialed the number he'd committed to memory years ago.

"This is Damon" came the gruff reply.

Just like that, Mal was transported back to his youth, when the First needed nothing more than his voice to bring pups to heel.

"Hi, First." Mal wasn't sure what else to say, so he went with the social skills he ordinarily lacked. "How are you?"

There was a sharp intake of breath. "Malachi? Is that you?"

"Yes, sir. I'm sorry I waited so long to call. I.... I need your help."

CHAPTER 11

"Let me see if I understand this, whelp," Damon said, his voice dripping with bitterness and anger. "You snuck out like a fucking polecat into the night, and now you're going to call and ask me for help?"

"Yes." Mal wasn't going to be cowed. He needed this if Alp was going to survive. "If you don't want to help, that's fine. Say so, and I'll find someone else."

Even if there wasn't anyone.

Damon was quiet for several long moments, but then he sighed. "Why did you leave, Mal? I thought you wanted to be a First."

"I thought so too, sir. But then I watched you, every day, tending to the pack. Never having time for yourself. Never having a chance to just be. The pack grew fat and happy and lazy, and why? Because you were out there busting your ass every single day for them." He swallowed. "For us."

"Oh, Mal. That's what a First is. Our lives will never be our own. We belong to the pack—we will live and die for the pack."

It was something Mal was coming to understand. "I've recently become aware, sir."

"Tell me."

Even though he was no longer Mal's First, Damon Walker was a powerful man. His voice reverberated through Mal, letting him know it wasn't a request. So, Mal told him everything, starting from the night he'd gotten off his motorcycle, to finding out he'd claimed Alp.

"A bunny? You've mated a rabbit?" Walker burst out in peals of laughter. "Oh, that's too rich."

"Fuck you!" Mal snarled, his grip on the handset tightening. "Don't disrespect Alp, you son of a bitch."

The line went quiet, and Mal feared he'd done something irrevocable by telling Damon off.

"You've learned," he finally said, sounding oddly happy. "It doesn't matter who I am—all that matters is your pack. You're willing to throw down against me to protect them. Well, him. You've finally figured out what it means to be a First."

A deep sigh rolled out of Mal. "Yes, sir. I guess I have."

"Then you've learned the lesson I don't know that I could have ever taught you. My father did the same to me. He threw me to the wolves, pretty literally. I had to sink or swim, so I chose to swim. Even though it was against a raging river, I fought every fucking day to make it a little farther. At first, I hated the people in the pack, because they were a stone that had been chained to my ankles and were slowly pulling me under."

Damon had never spoken of this to Mal. He'd only told him of how important the pack was. "I... didn't know."

"No, you didn't. But the thing is? As I settled into my role, I discovered that it wasn't me who gave the pack strength. It was them who infused me with it. Their commitment to me and to each other is what made the difference. And it was a lesson you had to learn on your own."

What he said slammed into Mal. "You knew I'd leave."

"Yeah, I knew. You have the potential to be an amazing First, Malachi, but you needed to figure out your place in the world before you could be a leader. And I'm proud to learn you've done that, even though it took a lot longer than I thought it would. Now, tell me, what can I do for you?"

"I need an army," Mal said, not caring that it sounded ludicrous. "I want to kill every one of those sons of bitches for what they've done to Alp. What they're still doing to others. I can't sit back and let them continue. They have to die."

"Do we have any idea of their strengths? Their weaknesses?"

"No, sir. I'm going out today to see if I can find where they're operating from."

"So we'd be walking in blindly. This could well be a suicide mission."

"It could, sir. I won't be upset if you refuse to help me. I know this is my fight."

"I'll tell you right now, Mal. One of the lessons we have to learn as Firsts is when it's okay to ask for help. This is something the old you would have rushed headlong into without a second thought for what you were leaving behind."

"I... was going to do that," Mal admitted. "When I look at Alp, see his missing hand, I want to storm in there and slaughter them all. But now that I understand Alp is not only my pack, but my mate? I can't do that to him. I need to be smart about this."

"Yes, you do. Let me talk to the pack. I will gather as many volunteers as I can, and we will come to assist you."

"Thank you, First."

A throaty chuckle. "I'm no longer your First, Mal. Call me Damon." He sighed, like he was settling in. "Now, tell me about this mate of yours. It sounds like a wild story, and I want to hear it all."

Talk about Alp? That was something Mal was more than happy to do.

A HEAVY HAND settled on Alp's shoulder, giving a firm but gentle squeeze as the car pulled away, with Nura sticking her hand out and yelling to Alp to behave himself.

"Is it stupid I miss them already?" he asked, as the car vanished from view.

"No, not at all," Mal replied. "Believe it or not, I kind of miss them too. I like how your mom can embarrass you so easily."

"Ha. Ha. Ha. You're so funny." He turned and stepped into Mal's embrace, laying his head on the broad chest. "She brought me clothes, so I can stop wearing yours."

"Hey, I like you in my clothes," Mal whispered in his ear. "I love how your scent mixes with mine. It gives me no end of pleasure." He kissed Alp's neck. "Hello, mate."

Maker, the word made Alp shiver. He was fucking mated to someone.

"You owe me an orgasm," he blurted out.

Mal snickered. "You wanna cum, my little bunny?"

"Oh, Maker yes," Alp moaned. "As much as I enjoyed what we did, I never got off."

"That's a lie, and you know it."

Fine, sucking Mal had caused Alp to shoot off without touching himself. But he longed to know what it was like to be touched, to have actual sex.

"Mal," he whined. "I need you."

"And I need you. Always." He hefted Alp into his arms, smiling when Alp wrapped his hand around Mal's neck. "Can I claim you tonight, Alp?"

"I thought you already—oh, you mean.... Um, you're kind of, you know, big."

"I am, but I swear to you I'll be gentle. At least until you're begging for more."

Alp raised his brows. "Rather high opinion of yourself, yeah?"

"No," Mal replied, squeezing Alp. "The only opinion of me that matters is yours."

It was a good thing Mal had a grip on him, or Alp would have melted into the grass.

"Sure, we can try. Promise me, though. If I ask you to stop, you will."

"I will do my best to never hurt you. Didn't you hear me promise your mother?"

He had, and Alp knew it wasn't in Mal to lie. "Okay, let's do it."

As soon as Mal had him inside, he nudged the door closed with his heavy boot. If Alp thought Mal would toss him on the bed, he was mistaken. Mal leaned over and placed Alp on the mattress as if he was the most precious thing on earth. He briefly wondered if he could ever be worthy of a First.

"You are... simply stunning," Mal breathed out. "I'm in awe of your sea-green eyes, so much different from your rabbit's. And your hair, which is as yellow and soft as spun gold." He stroked a hand down Alp's side, raising goose bumps. "But this? It's as beautiful as anything I've ever seen. It takes my breath away."

Laid bare by the searching gaze, Alp slid his residual limb under the comforter.

"What are you doing, little one?" Mal demanded, spearing Alp with a sharp stare.

Alp turned his head away. "I'm sorry," he whispered, his cheeks warming. "I know it's awful to look at, and—"

When Mal leaned over and pressed their mouths together, Alp whimpered. He chased Mal's lips when he stood back up.

"You are stunning, Alp. You are incredible. You are mine. Your hand is a symbol of your strength. Many would have given up, but you fought. You proved yourself stronger than those who held you. I couldn't ask for a more amazing mate."

Certain there was untruth in the words, Alp stared into Mal's face. What he saw made him gasp. Not only did Mal mean it, but love shone in those eyes. It took his breath away to have someone looking at him the way Mal did.

"I love you, little rabbit."

And to his core Alp believed *that* was the truth.

"Now, slide your skinny ass over and let me in the bed so I can proceed to ravage you properly." He winked. "I want to be with you, Alp. In whatever way you're comfortable with."

Never in his life had Alp felt cherished. Sure, his parents and his family loved him, but again, one of many. Right now, he had Mal's full attention, and he couldn't believe this First wolf was his.

"This isn't a dream, right?"

Mal grinned as he reached out and gave Alp's nipple a twist. Alp hissed and arched his back. It wasn't painful, but fuck, it was erotic.

"You like your nipples touched? Noted. What about this?" Mal asked, leaning in to nibble on Alp's neck.

"Oh, fuck," Alp gasped.

As he licked and sucked, Mal's hand slid over Alp's chest, down to his stomach, and finally nestling in his pubic hair. Then a hot, rough hand encircled Alp's shaft.

"Oh, Maker!" Alp cried, as the first hand to ever touch him sent indescribable feelings through him.

"Do you like me touching you, Alp?"

"Yes, oh Maker, yes." He squeezed his eyes shut, unable to look at Mal. "Please, don't stop."

"Oh, no. You and me? We're just getting started."

Alp wondered if he could die from pleasure. Mal's hands were everywhere, touching everything. He let them slide over Alp's hip, his shoulders, his face, his neck. And damned if every time he did, Alp whined.

"It seems to me your entire body is an erogenous zone," Mal said with a chuckle. "Though there are still a few places I need to check."

Alp took a deep breath waiting for the next onslaught of feelings and emotions. When something warm and wet brushed over his cock head, Alp snapped his head up to find a grinning Mal swirling his tongue over Alp's heated flesh. He now understood why Mal hadn't seemed to know what to do with his hands. All Alp wanted was to grab Mal's ears and thrust deep, but he lay there, his chest heaving as he tried to draw a steadying breath.

A man—his mate—was sucking Alp's cock. And it was *way* better than his hand had ever felt.

"Oh, fuck. Mal, please."

Please? What? Don't stop? Stop? Harder? What did Alp want? That was easy. He wanted to join with Mal in the most intimate way mates could. He swallowed hard.

"Mal?"

Mal lifted his head, and Alp peered into inky depths of blown pupils. "Yes, mate?"

Another shudder. Alp would never tire of hearing that word. "I want to try. Can we?"

"Not only can we, we need to." Mal smiled. "I'm not sure I could survive without being inside of you." He laved Alp's cock again. "It's going to hurt. I'll be as gentle as I can, but I won't lie."

"No, I know. It's just... I trust you."

Mal's eyes widened. "Then if you want this, we should see about prepping you properly." He got off the bed and went to his bag. He reached in and pulled out a bottle of lubricant. He brought it back to the bed and placed it beside Alp.

"If you're scared or nervous, just say stop. I won't force anything, I swear." He kissed Alp. "Are you certain about this?"

Was he? A glance down at Mal's thick, heavy, straining shaft had Alp biting back a *no*, because he really did want this.

"Yeah, I'm sure."

Mal turned Alp on his side, then got down behind him. Alp tried to lift his head, but Mal dropped that heavy hand on Alp's shoulder, holding him in place. Then he leaned in and the tip of his nose touched Alp's ass a moment before his tongue speared Alp's hole.

"Oh my Maker, what the fuck!"

Mal didn't answer, just pushed in farther. Alp writhed on the bed, the feelings overwhelming. In all the porn he'd seen—mostly his brother's—Alp had never known people did this, and now he wanted to find out what else they did.

A bit of cold zipped through him, and Alp shivered as something thick and blunt slid slowly into his ass. At first he pushed back, wanting to expel the invader.

"Do you want me to stop?"

Yes! No! How the hell was he supposed to answer that? "I don't know," he whined.

"Does it hurt?"

Alp scrunched his face, then jolted when the finger brushed over something in his ass that sent jolts of pleasure through his body. "Holy Maker! That was... oh, damn," he groaned.

Mal chuckled. "That's your prostate," Mal said, and Alp couldn't miss the smugness in his voice. "It's the G-spot for a man."

For a man? "Have you... been with many people?"

"Yes," Mal answered, and there wasn't any teasing or anything in his voice. "But now that I have you? I'm never going to want another. You are everything—and I do mean *everything*—I could hope for in a partner."

As he spoke, Mal kept up his ministrations, and as far as Alp was concerned, whatever Mal was saying was nothing more than babbling. He was lost in a haze of feelings like he'd never dealt with before, riding a crest of euphoria. It took several long moments for him to realize that Mal had added a second finger and was now pressing them in hard and giving them a twist.

"Ooh, Mal," he whimpered.

"I'll always take care of you, Alp," he whispered, before adding a third finger. "Always."

His heart ready to burst from emotions he'd never felt before, Alp grabbed Mal by the back of the neck and dragged him down into a fierce kiss. It was tongue, teeth, gnashing, crashing together as Alp rode the never-ending waves of emotions. Mal continued to take him ever higher, until Alp thought he'd either scream or pass out from pleasure.

"Please, Mal, please," he whimpered, his head thrashing side to side. "I'm ready."

But Mal didn't listen. Instead, he engulfed Alp's cock in that amazing mouth of his, and Alp couldn't help when his hand tightened in Mal's hair and yanked him down.

"Sorry, I'm sorry," he sputtered, but he couldn't control it anymore.

When Mal lifted him off the bed and flipped him over, then pulled him up to his knees, Alp didn't have the energy to protest. Mal could do whatever the hell he wanted right now. Alp was too buzzed to say no.

Two pillows were slid under Alp, and then Mal lowered him onto them. He giggled as he pictured himself, face down, ass up, waiting to be fucked by his mate.

"Are you sure about this?" Mal asked. "We don't have to do this now. I mean, we can take time and loosen you up the right way. Toys would help stretch you, I think." His voice broke. "I can't bear the thought of hurting you, my little bunny."

"You said it would hurt. I'm ready to try."

"Please, baby. If it hurts, you have to tell me." He ran a hand down Alp's back. "Close your eyes, take some deep breaths. When I push in, you push out, okay?"

Alp nodded, too overwhelmed to form coherent thoughts.

"No, Alp. You need to tell me. I won't do anything unless you explicitly say the words."

Alp snapped his head back. "Fuck me, damn it! Are those the words you want?"

The smirk he got in answer shouldn't have been sexy, but it was. Everything about Mal tripped triggers for Alp. He tensed when the telephone pole nestled against his hole. He quickly closed his eyes and took those deep breaths Mal mentioned. The first press of flesh to flesh had Alp crying out and scrambling to get away.

"Alp? Oh, fuck. I'm sorry!" Mal clutched Alp and pulled him into a fierce hug. "Maker, please forgive me. I'm sorry."

It stunned Alp when he felt hot tears on his neck. Was Mal seriously crying?

Over him?

CHAPTER 12

THE SCREAM TORE through Mal as Alp jerked away from him, and he panicked. He'd never really given much thought to the comfort of the people he slept with. Sure, they weren't virgins, but they hadn't normally been with a First wolf.

"Alp? Oh, fuck. I'm sorry!" Mal grabbed Alp and pulled him into a fierce hug. "Maker, please forgive me. I'm sorry."

A moment later, a hand patted Mal's back. "Are you... crying?"

Mal shook his head. Of course he wasn't. Firsts didn't cry. "I told you I didn't want to hurt you. I'm so fucking sorry."

"Hey." Alp kissed his neck. "Look at me."

But Mal couldn't. The thought of seeing anger or pain on Alp's face had him wanting to hide away.

"Mal, look at me."

Slowly, Mal pulled back until he could see Alp's face. There was no censure, no anger. And when Alp leaned in and kissed him, the fears he'd somehow screwed this whole thing up went *poof*.

"You warned me, okay? You said it would hurt. You tried to get me to calm down, to prepare myself. I... thought you were exaggerating." He gave Mal a peck on the lips. "This is on me, not you."

"No, I—"

"Need to shut up now and listen. I get that you're a First, and you like the control, but you need to understand, I have my own mind too. Sometimes—not often, no matter what my mother said—I do stupid things. This was one of them. You've been nothing but considerate. I need to listen a little more, I think."

"Your mom said you need to listen a lot more. When I went to pour coffee, she followed me, and after another round of complaints about not having vanilla creamer, said I needed to use a firm hand with you, because you were... what were her words? Oh, yeah, a stubborn little shit who thought he knew better than anyone else." He stroked Alp's face. "She didn't understand that it was that streak in you is what I fell for. You're so fucking strong, and I'm honored to be mated to you."

Alp's cheeks pinked. "Can we try this again?"

"Do you think you're ready? I'm fine with blow jobs, because you've got a fucking hot mouth. Or even a hand job, because your hand is so soft." He nuzzled Alp's neck. "Whatever you want, I will always do my best to give it to you."

Alp flipped over onto the pillows again and lifted his ass. "I want you to get in me." He squinted. "But maybe be a little patient if I ask you to go slow, okay?"

Mal couldn't help but smile. When his First had talked about mates, he glossed over how it happened and spoke more about the feelings involved. How it was like two beings merged into one, each completing the other, making them whole. Since meeting Alp, Mal's entire life had done a 180-degree turn, and now he was headed back to the life he thought he didn't want. But having Alp—a pack—suddenly meant more to him than he could verbalize.

"C'mon man, this ass isn't going to fuck itself," Alp whined.

"Well, there are toys, you know," Mal retorted with a wink.

"You're impossible," Alp said, but there was such a bright smile on his face.

After a few strokes, Mal's cock rose to full hardness again. At just shy of nine inches, it was a blunt instrument, one that he'd always loved using. This was different, though. It was Alp, and Mal could feel in his blood that the man gazing up at him was now and forever a part of him.

He applied more lube to his cock, then fingered Alp's hole again, wanting to loosen it again.

"Okay, I'm ready," Alp said, spreading his legs.

"No, not this time," Mal grumbled. "I let you and my desire for you get the better of me before, but now? We go at my pace, so lay there and shut up." He chuckled. "I mean, feel. Stupid autocorrect."

Alp snickered and shook his head. "You're crazy."

"For you," Mal said, with all the seriousness he could muster.

It didn't take long before Alp was a mewling heap, pleading for more. Mal took his time, not in a hurry at all, as he made his mate come apart at the seams.

"Need you," Alp whined. "Mate, please. Need."

And that was what Mal was waiting for. Alp, totally relaxed, undone, spread for him. He didn't say anything, not wanting to break that spell. He notched his cock in line with Alp's hole, and slowly, so slowly, he pressed in. Mal watched Alp closely. Every twitch had him stopping and waiting until Alp relaxed again, then continuing. There were a few times he thought about stopping again when Alp whined, but when he was about to withdraw, Alp grabbed his wrist.

"Stop it!" he snapped. "If I can't handle it, I'll tell you."

So Mal listened and continued his snail's-pace intrusion in the tightest hole he'd ever experienced. If Alp was human, they'd never have gotten this far. But a shifter had better stamina than that. Mal shuddered. The combination of muscle and heat sent lust skittering up his spine, demanding that he go harder, faster. But now wasn't the time. A man always remembered his first sex, and if he wanted Alp to surrender to him again, Mal needed to show him how amazing it could be between them.

It was agonizing, but Mal's cock eventually disappeared inside of Alp's small body. To be honest, he wasn't sure his cock would fit. It was foolish, and he knew it, but he had the horrifying vision of Alp being split in twain, but now that he was fully seated in that delicious heat, Mal would have been content to never pull out again.

"Are you going to move sometime today?" Alp complained, his voice muffled by the pillow.

"Alp...."

He turned and locked gazes with Mal. "It... it doesn't hurt as much. I feel full. I mean, *really* full. But, I don't know. It's kinda good now."

There was tension in his words, but his heart and mind were open, and Mal could tell he meant them.

Mal slid out a fraction, then slowly pushed back in. They had time, so there would be no furious rutting. Instead, he set a slow, languorous pace. It was odd to discover that making slow love could be hotter than a quickie in some skanky motel room.

"Oh, fuck, Maaaaal," Alp moaned as Mal dragged his heavy cock out until only the head remained. Then he pushed in, taking his sweet time, loving the way Alp squeezed him, the way the muscles contracted and milked his length.

"You doin' okay?"

"Oh, yeah. This is so good. I never thought it could be like this," Alp purred. "Can you... I mean, is it all right if you go harder?"

"Are you sure? I mean, I'm really loving this pace."

"Goddamn it, I will kill you in your sleep if you don't move faster! I've seen porn, so I know fucking is harder than this."

"No," Mal insisted. "Porn is fantasy. This is the real deal. Porn has nothing to do with this. I am not fucking my mate—I'm making love to him. Sure, we can go harder, but never confuse the two. Do you understand me?"

Alp's eyes widened. "Yes, I understand." He waved an impatient hand. "Make love faster, then."

Mal shook his head. "You're incorrigible." He winked. "I love it. You'll keep me on my toes, that's for sure."

"Toes, knees. I especially like the knees thing." Alp stroked a finger over Mal's hand. "I love you so fucking much."

"And I love you, my foul-mouthed little bunny."

Alp snapped his fingers. "Now move, slave. Pleasure your master."

"You are such a little shit. Remember, you asked for it."

This time, drawing nearly all the way out, Mal rammed back in so hard, Alp was slammed into the headboard, which then hit the wall with a solid *thunk*. A high-pitched squeak slid out of Alp, and for a second, Mal thought he'd been too rough. Alp leaned forward, dislodging Mal, who was about to apologize, then flipped over and pulled his knees to his chest.

"More!"

Mal blew out a breath. Alp was loving this. For Mal, that was permission to take him hard. He grabbed Alp's legs and jerked them into the air, exposing that beautiful ass. He gripped his cock and notched it at Alp's hole, then thrust hard.

"Oh my fuck," Alp moaned. "Do that again! More!" he demanded.

"Yes, my master," Mal teased.

He held Alp's legs in one hand and twisted him to the side slightly, then thrust over and over, loving every grunt and squeal and plea from Alp's lips.

"I'm going to fuck you whenever I want, do you understand me? You're my mate, and I'm going to have you."

"Yes!" Alp cried. "Anytime, I swear."

He opened his eyes and gazed up at Mal, who stuttered to a stop. In those eyes, Mal saw lust and longing, sure, but he also saw love and trust and... life. His life, with Alp, growing old together, falling deeper and deeper in love with every passing day.

It settled in his chest, and Mal knew with complete certainty he would do whatever he had to if it would only make Alp happy.

THAT COCK. Oh, Maker. That amazing, thick, hard length sliding into him, hammering that spot. Mal had dissolved him into a whimpering mess. Who knew that sex was this amazing? Sure as hell not Alp. And if Mal thought sex was going to happen on his schedule, he was sorely mistaken, because Alp was a bunny, damn it, and they could go for hours and hours and never tire out.

Poor mate, he had no idea what he was getting himself into.

"This is pretty good," Alp said, gazing up with affection at Mal. "Can you put a little effort in, though?"

Mal's lip curled back, exposing his canines. This was what Alp was hoping for. He tilted his neck to the side, exposing the scar Mal had given him. He heard the intake of breath as Mal leaned in and sniffed the spot.

"That's it. See where you've marked me? Imagine how good it would feel to do that again."

Mal groaned and his thrusts increased. He gripped Alp's hair and held his head steady. "Don't fuck with me, Alp," he warned.

"Uh, I think it's you who's fucking with me," Alp reminded him, teasingly.

"Allllp" came the guttural growl.

"Do it, Mal. Mark me again. I want you to."

He thought Mal would protest, but he didn't. He lurched forward, burying himself deep inside of Alp, and latched his teeth onto Alp's neck. As he lay there, licking the blood, Alp thrust up, burying Mal's cock in him again. He wanted this, the two most intense feelings he'd ever had, combined into one.

Mal groaned and thrust in, meeting Alp's upward one. Just when he thought it was impossible for it to be better, it was. He wrapped his legs around Mal's waist and used that to lift himself as Mal thrust in harder than before, the movement rocking the bed. When he started grunting, Alp knew he was close. He reached down and wrapped a hand around his cock, jacking furiously. This seemed to inflame Mal, as he locked his hands on Alp's hips and thrust viciously.

"Alllp." The sound was dragged out of Mal, coming from the deepest recesses of his being, Alp knew. "Never felt like this. Never knew I could."

"I love you, mate."

And that was the trigger. Mal howled when he came, all sense of pacing lost. He rutted hard, deep, fast, and Alp fucking loved it. He squeezed his cock, and it erupted, spewing his load between them, squishing when Mal plunged into him, their stomachs rubbing together. Alp was lost in a haze between the most intense orgasm and the feelings of love pouring from Mal.

The movements slowed, but Mal stayed buried in Alp, still licking his neck. Finally, he rolled over and dragged Alp on top of him. He kissed him then, slowly, sensuously, languorously. Alp was cherished, and he knew that deep to his soul.

When he'd been a young boy, Alp had told his mother that he was going to marry a man. She smiled and said she knew, and that as long as he was happy, that should be all that mattered.

And now? He was mated—not quite married in the human sense —to the wolf who'd won his heart that day, but he had to wonder if it could last. If Mal was going to take the fight to Hyde, would he come back alive?

"Mal?"

"Yes, little one?"

Alp bit his lip to keep from sighing. He loved it when Mal referred to him as little one or called him his bunny. He might not notice the possessive way it was said, but Alp did, and it did the most delicious things to his insides.

"Are we going to get through this? I mean—"

"I know what you mean," Mal broke in with a sigh. "And I won't lie to you. I honestly don't know."

"I want to say we should run, hide away, but I keep thinking of all those people still in the lab, and I can't be selfish like that. I lost my hand. What have the rest of them lost?" He lay his head on Mal's chest, listening to the slowing heartbeat.

"You are the farthest thing from selfish, you know. You are kind and considerate, even when you're angry. That day you were in the cage and Lydia was there? You were jealous, but even then, you wouldn't have hurt her for the world."

Alp wanted to deny it. To laugh it off. "Yeah, I was. She kept touching you, and I hated it. It was worse when you smiled at her. That was my fucking smile, and you were giving it to her!" He sighed. "I'm sorry."

Mal slid a hand over Alp's back and let it come to rest on his ass.

"Do you know in the entirety of my life, no one has ever been jealous of someone touching me? I was convenient for a lay, but beyond that, no one wanted to keep me. I mean, don't get me wrong, I wouldn't have stayed, but it would have been nice to have someone at least ask."

It wasn't something Alp understood. His family expected he'd stay nearby. Only a few people moved away from the warren, and those who did usually came back not too long after. Rabbits didn't do well without others around them, but Alp was determined he'd be the exception.

"If it helps, I am always going to want to keep your stubborn ass." He tilted his head up and kissed Mal's chin. "We have to get through this, because I need you to make my life miserable forever."

The rumbling chuckle vibrated through Alp as Mal drew him closer and wrapped him in those big, strong arms. He kissed the top of Alp's head. "Don't worry, I plan on making you miserable for years to come." He sucked in a breath. "I called for help."

"Oh?"

"My old pack. I know I can't win without help, and I'm well aware I can't keep you and Lydia out of harm's way unless I have someone there to watch our backs. If it wasn't for you, I would have gone in there, metaphorical guns blazing, and died in the crossfire. I can't do that now. I have a mate to think about."

The fact that Mal was admitting these things was astounding enough, but to know he was doing it for Alp?

"Thank you."

"Don't need to thank me," he drawled. "You just need to make sure you keep your ass where I tell you to park it. You can protect Lydia, but beyond that, you don't move from where I say you should be."

"I will," Alp vowed, not meaning a word of it. If Mal was in trouble, then Alp would be there beside him, doing his best to keep him safe.

"I know you're lying," Mal said. "You won't look me in the eye, and your ears twitch."

Damned ears. "My place is by your side," Alp insisted.

"Your place is where I tell you," Mal said firmly. "I am your First, and your mate, and you will obey me."

Alp lifted an eyebrow and stared at Mal. "I'm sorry, did you just say I will obey you?"

Mal sighed. "In this, yes. Don't test me, rabbit. If I have to, I'll put you back in your cage and lock the fucking door. You and Lydia will sit in a place I say is safe, and if you move from there, I'll... I'll...." He blew out a frustrated breath. "Would you at least try to look like you're listening to me?"

"Nope."

"Why are you so stubborn? The mate of a First is supposed to be demure."

That really had Alp cracking up. "Demure?" He thrust out a hand. "I'm sorry, have we met? Hi, I'm Alp, mated to an idiot wolf who thinks I'll take orders. I swear, it's like you never met my mother."

Mal's chin dropped to his chest. "Why couldn't you take more after your father?"

"Dad is the demure one, because he's besotted with my mom. He goes out of his way to make her happy." He put a hand on Mal's chest. "I'll do that for you too, but I won't stop being who I am for anyone."

A quirked lip had Alp worrying, until Mal said, "I wouldn't have you any other way. I do need you to stay with Lydia, though. I've got no idea how many people Damon will find to come here. He knows what's going to happen, and not having any real information, we might not get anyone."

"Then you'll need me to fight at your side."

"You're a bunny—you don't fight," Mal reminded him.

"I'm a guy with a lot to live for. If I have to kick ass to keep it, then so be it." Alp held up his residual limb. "Besides, I'm invested in seeing those bastards suffer for what they've done to us."

"Okay, how about this? You, Lydia, and at least one wolf, if Damon sends them, will stay back in reserve. If things start to go wrong, you'll be there to jump in." He squeezed Alp's ass. "I'm not trying to keep you out of the fight, but we do need backup, and one pissed-off bunny seems perfect to me."

"No."

"Alp, you need—"

"What I *need* is for you to stop treating me like I'm helpless." He huffed a breath, and then it struck him. He lifted his arm. "Is it because of this?"

"Yes, of course it is!" Mal snapped. "They've already taken something from you, and I'm afraid when I think about what else they could take." He rubbed noses with Alp. "I'm terrified I'll lose you."

"Maybe now you understand how I feel about you going in there without me. If I'm fighting alongside you, I'll know that I've done everything I can to keep you safe." He nuzzled Mal's chin. "Please, don't try to take this away from me. You'll waste more energy doing what you can to convince me to stay behind than you will if you accept I am going to be there." He smirked. "Don't fuck with me on this, First. You won't win."

CHAPTER 13

THERE WERE SO many things Mal never imagined in his life. To consider settling down in one spot to take care of the second thing he never figured he'd have, a mate. And what a mate Alp was. So beautiful in his submission to his First, but also so fucking fierce when he refused to back down because he had firm beliefs.

"Alp, I—"

His mate held up a hand. "Not discussing this anymore with you. I'm going, and that's final."

"You're going," Mal conceded, and even his wolf seemed happy with the decision.

"Really?" Alp's eyes were huge. "You'll let me come?"

Mal frowned. "Let you? Could I have stopped you?"

"Sure. You could have said, 'Alp, I love you, and it would kill me if something happened to you, so please stay behind.'"

Mal gaped. "You lying little shit."

That earned him a grin. "Okay, maybe I would have tried to persuade you to let me come anyway."

"Uh, I think you spelled bullied wrong."

"What was it you said to—oh, wait, I remember. 'Stupid autocorrect.'"

And Mal couldn't help it. He burst out with a laugh unlike

anything he'd done in a long time. Since leaving his pack, he'd been a broody loner. Alp dragged him back into the sunlight, showing him that life was still there and was still beautiful.

"We should get up," Mal said. "I need to go scouting. Damon is going to want to know everything there is before he'll commit people to helping us."

"Okay, I'll get dressed, and we can—"

"No."

Alp rolled off him and stood. "No? We're going to start this shit again? What's the problem this time?"

"I've got a lot of ground to cover, and you'll slow me down."

Alp sneered. "Because of my hand?"

Sliding off the bed, Mal towered over his mate. He reached out and cupped the back of his neck, drawing him close. "No, not at all. If it was your hand, I wouldn't be letting you come when we go in to cleanse the place. I'm going to be moving fast, taking in all the scents I can. If you're there, all I'll smell is you. All I'll want is you. I need my head clear, and you will screw it up big-time."

"Then why can I come with you when you go in?"

"Because I'll be fighting for you, and knowing where you are will help keep me focused. I'm not going to want to pull your pants down and fuck you during a firefight. Well, probably not. I'll bring lube, you know, just in case."

Alp pressed his naked body against Mal's and kissed his chest. "You say the sweetest things."

"Can I trust you'll stay here?"

"Oh, of course," Alp said, and his entire expression told Mal it was a total lie. He was nibbling on his lip, his ears twitched, and he kept staring at Mal's chest, refusing to look up.

"Okay, I'm going to take you to sit with Lydia."

"What? No!"

He squeezed Alp's shoulders and gave him a gentle shake. "Listen to me, okay? I get you're strong and brave. I understand you want to be with me. I'm doing this to keep you safe, and I can't do that if I have to move slowly or if I have to stop and bend you over. I wasn't kidding. Your scent drives me nuts. It's all I can do to keep from pressing your face to the mattress and taking you now. You have to let me focus, okay?" He waggled his brows. "I'll come back as soon as I can, and then we can do some more fucking."

"You mean lovemaking," Alp said, his tone letting Mal know he wasn't happy.

Mal squeezed him hard. "No, baby. I mean fucking. I'm going to drill you into the goddamn mattress. We'll put porn movies to shame."

That seemed to satisfy Alp. Or so Mal thought, until he poked him in the chest. "Fine. But you'd better come back. No running off with another rabbit or... or a fucking woodchuck!" he shouted.

"A... woodchuck?" Mal smoothed a hand over Alp's hair, then leaned in and took a deep breath, sighing as his mate's scent filled his lungs. "Where does your mind go?"

"You know, I only have one hand, but I can kick the shit out of anyone who tries to take you—"

"Stop, now," Mal ordered.

Alp crossed his arms over his chest, staring at the ground. He was trembling, but Mal wasn't sure if it was from hurt or anger.

"No one is taking me away from you," Mal promised. "Not any human, shifter, or crackpot doctors. I'm yours, only yours."

Alp's head snapped up, his gaze defiant. "You said you slept with a lot of people. How can I be sure you won't—"

Grabbing him by the back of the head, Mal dragged Alp into a kiss. He loved when Alp whimpered and opened for him, allowing Mal to plunder his mouth. He felt the tension drain from Alp, and then his arms snaked around Mal's waist. When Mal broke the kiss, Alp still hung on.

"Where's all this coming from, little one?" Alp shook his head. "You're going to tell me, and we're going to deal with it. Now, Alp."

It took several long moments, but eventually Alp tipped his head back and stared up into Mal's eyes. "I've never had anything that was mine alone. Everything I ever got was someone else's leftovers. Clothes, schoolbooks, beds. It didn't matter what it was, we all used the same things until they wore out and my folks had to get something new. Even then, it went to the oldest. Then I got you, and I thought maybe, finally, I'd have something I could call my own."

"I am yours, Alp. Now and forever, my heart and soul belongs only to you. I will never in my life love another person like I do you. If you never believe me about anything else, you have to know that, okay?"

A slight nod.

"No, not that. Tell me. Let me see inside your head."

A deep, shuddering breath, and Alp sagged in Mal's arms. "Hyde is a monster. He'd kill you as soon as look at you. I had a nightmare that he captured you, and I had to stand there and watch as he cut you apart, and all the while you were staring, pleading with me to do something, to save you, and I couldn't." He barked a laugh. "The worst thing? I wasn't even restrained. I just fucking stood there and let him kill you. I let him take you away from me."

Huge tears slid down Alp's cheeks, and his sobs tore at Mal's heart. He was foolish if he thought the trauma Alp had experienced at the hands of those fuckers hadn't damaged him, but that made him love Alp all the more, because he came through it strong and sarcastic and sweet.

"Listen to me, okay?" Mal said, tugging Alp back down onto the bed, where he lay his head on Mal's chest. "Do you remember when you and your mom went to the store to get her fucking vanilla creamer and left me here with your dad?"

Alp nodded, his tears still slipping onto Mal's chest.

"I asked him to tell me about mates, because I admit, I'm clueless. I mean, I knew they were out there, but I never figured I'd have one, so why bother learning about it, right? Anyway, he told me that a mate is the missing part of your soul, and that you might not realize it's missing if you don't have it, but once you discover it, you can never be the same again. Being with you changed me, made me hope for a future where the two of us can sit down by the lake and watch as the sun rises or sets. Where we can make love under the stars. Where the two of us can go running together, and explore our home."

"Our... home?" Alp whispered, his voice full of hope.

"I want to make a home with you. It can be anywhere you want, but it has to be with you."

"Can we...? I mean, I don't know how you feel about the place, but...."

He buried his face in Mal's chest hair. "You want to stay here? In Swenson?"

Alp nodded. "I think this is the place I'm meant to be. I don't understand it, but I feel as though I need to be here."

"Then here is where we'll stay. Together. Until the Maker calls us home."

That sounded so good. A dream Mal hadn't even known he wanted.

"You should go."

But he couldn't leave Alp, not like this. "I'll stay. I can go out tonight, after dark."

"No, this has to be done." Alp sighed. "It's weird. We just found each other, but I realize our lives aren't our own yet. We have too many others depending on us doing the right thing here." He sat up and scrubbed a hand over his eyes. "Go. I'll be okay."

Mal stood, peering down. He hated this. His mate needed him desperately, but was telling him to go help others.

"You're the most incredible person I've ever met." He kissed Alp's head. "And I love you so fucking much."

Alp smiled. "I love you too. I'll see you when you get back."

A quick kiss, and then Mal was headed for the motorcycle to find out what awaited them. *Maker, let it end soon so I can go off with Alp.*

MAL GOT OFF THE BIKE, then dragged it down into the woods near when he'd been when he found Alp. The memories of the man who would become his mate, lying on his side, panting in the dirt and grass, assailed him, and he had to bite back a howl. He undressed, folded his clothes, and slipped them into the pack he'd brought.

Once he was satisfied everything was safe, he shifted and plunged into the woods.

When he came upon the clearing where he'd found Alp, he was surprised to find the men's bodies had been feasted on much more than he thought. Large chunks of flesh were torn out, and their stomachs and hearts appeared to have been devoured. One of them seemed to have become a chew toy for a bear, as his skull was cracked open and slivers of bone dotted the ground around what had been his head. Mal didn't bother to check if it had eaten the brains, because honestly? He no longer cared about dead men. He was more interested in the soon-to-be-dead men.

He inhaled sharply, letting the scents of the surrounding area wash over him. Mixed in with the death also came life. New animals, born recently, were in the forest with their parents, learning to hunt or forage, he was certain. He wondered briefly if they'd used the men's bodies as an easy food source.

The sharp tang of chemicals was still present, but had diminished from the last time he'd seen the men. That probably explained why the animals had taken to eating the flesh, which was usually pretty putrid. Humans were, by and large, not all that appetizing. Mal turned in the direction he knew Alp had come from. Though the scent was long gone, the trail was clear. The men had forced their way through, and the broken branches were a testament to their need to get him back.

Mal took off at a trot, headed back the way he believed they'd come, letting the smells wash over him. Thanks to the chemicals, he at least had an idea of what he was looking for. He rushed up a cliff, then down into a gulley. The area was pretty impassable if you weren't a shifter. He wondered where the road was, because no way would humans have been able to kidnap and carry all the shifters Alp had seen through the dense undergrowth.

He ran in ever-widening circles for nearly an hour before the acrid smell was carried to him by the wind. His mind screamed poison. Fear. Death. Mal knew he'd found the spot. He moved quickly toward the area when he caught sight of the first camera.

Mounted high up in the tree, it scanned the vicinity. Keeping an eye on the trees, Mal spotted sixteen more, which he evaded with careful timing. Whoever was here didn't want anyone sneaking up on them.

He crept up a hill and stretched out on the hard-packed earth. There, in a small clearing, Mal discovered a strange structure with what appeared to be a high-tech keypad. It was too small to be used for anything. Barely large enough for a shack, it seemed to be the source of the overpowering smells, but that made no sense.

He moved closer, needing to know what was going on there. Then he saw tire tracks that started from and ended near the building. Just... stopped. As if whatever had driven there had simply vanished. Not one thing about this area made any sense to Mal. He decided to go back up to the hill and watch, to see if there was something else at work here. He climbed up to the highest point where he could still keep an eye out and lay there, amid the dirt and leaves, swishing his tail to keep the bugs off him.

It was just over an hour when his patience was rewarded. A pickup truck, shiny and black, came in from the forest side. It was a pretty treacherous path, but one the driver seemed familiar with, as he dodged trees and boulders to come to a stop near the building. He reached out and tapped a few buttons on the pad, then sat there as though he was waiting for—

The ground rumbled, not in a natural way, but one that sounded mechanical. As Mal watched, the forest floor opened up and a long ramp disappeared into the darkness. The truck rolled forward, until it reached the ramp, then started a descent into the bowels of the earth. Once it disappeared from view, the ramp closed, and Mal could see the seams where the doorway was.

Mal had to decide if he should continue waiting or plunge in after the truck. For the old him, it would have been no question, but Mal had a mate. A man who was waiting on him to come home. Even though he desperately wanted to know what was beneath the ground, he stayed where he was.

Less than ten minutes later, the door opened again, and the truck he'd seen reappeared, only this time it carried six humans. The sun had long since vanished from the horizon, and Mal could sense Alp was going nuts, but he'd come too far to turn back without knowing more.

Over the next two hours, the truck returned, filled with new humans, and every time it departed, it had others in the seats. He counted thirty men and women. He snuck closer, and when the truck left again, he could hear them discussing the tests they'd done today. One of them laughed when he talked about how the shifter yowled when they removed his eyes. It took everything in Mal to stop himself from rushing forward and ripping out the man's throat.

That would come later, he vowed.

When the truck reappeared the last time, totally empty except for the driver, Mal hurried back to his bike. He shifted, dressed, and was on the road in under two minutes, excitement and disgust roiling in his belly over what he'd found and what he'd heard. He'd just pulled into the motel parking lot when the door to their room flew open and Alp dashed out, tears streaming down his cheeks.

"Where were you?" he whimpered, his hands all over Mal.

"I'm sorry, little one. I hadn't intended on being gone this long, but I found out a lot of things. I need to talk to Damon." He bent and kissed Alp, letting his sweet scent wash away the revulsion. "Come with me, please. You can hear what I found, and maybe you can fill in some gaps." He took two steps, then stopped. What if this was too much for Alp to hear? "It's not pleasant."

"I'd be surprised if it was," Alp bitched.

"You don't need to hear it, if you'd rather not."

"Let's just get this over with!"

They returned to the room, and Mal couldn't help but notice that Alp never stopped touching him.

"I'm okay, little one, I promise."

"Yeah, well, don't expect me to believe you," Alp snapped, but then his arrogance vanished, replaced by sadness and desperation. "I'm sorry. I got scared," he whispered, turning away.

"No, don't hide from me," Mal said, reaching out to take Alp's chin. "No one ever worried about me, and I'm not used to thinking about others. Know this, however: when I was there, the whole time I was thinking about you. When I had to choose between waiting and running in—"

"You did not go in there!" Alp shrieked, balling his hand into a fist. "I will kick your fucking ass if you did something so stupid."

"No, baby. I didn't go in there," Mal crooned, pulling Alp in and enfolding him in an embrace. "I wanted to, but I knew I had a mate waiting at home, and I needed to come back to him."

"You... did?"

Mal leaned in, sniffing Alp's hair and letting the calming scent wash over him. "Yeah," he breathed out. "I'm not a lone wolf anymore, so I have to make smarter choices. I find myself asking, 'What would Alp do?' Then I try to do the exact opposite, because that seems the smart option."

"Hey!" Alp shouted, smacking his hand on Mal's chest.

The chuckle felt good. After what he'd seen and heard, he needed it. "I'm kidding. I ask what you'd do, and then I try it that way, because I know it'll make you happy." He kissed Alp's hair. "And for the rest of my life, that's what I want to do. Make you happy."

"Yeah, just keep doing that, and we'll get along fine," Alp said, snuggling in closer to Mal.

Screw it. Damon could wait a little bit longer. His mate needed him, and Mal would never disappoint him.

CHAPTER 14

"THIS COMPLICATES MATTERS," Damon intoned. "Best guess is that there's an underground complex, but we'll have no idea how far it extends or how it's manned. You should have gone in."

"No, he should not!" Alp shouted. "Don't even try to lay this on Mal."

It was quiet for a moment, and then Damon chuckled. "You weren't kidding, Malachi. He's a riot."

Alp's cheeks warmed. "I'm sorry."

"No, never say that," Damon said. "My mate would never apologize for standing up for me, and you shouldn't either. It's a sign of love and respect. And you're right. If Malachi had gone in, we might have lost him, and anything he learned would never have made it back."

The hackles were back up in an instant. "And we would have lost Mal, or did you forget that part?"

"Alp, he's being—"

"A dick!" Alp snapped. "Look, I care about everyone down there. I do. And I get that at some point we're going to be risking our lives trying to save them, but I'm not willing to lose Mal because of stupid choices. Or don't you understand that."

"Oh, he knows about stupid choices," said a woman's voice. "Hi. Your name is Alp, right?"

"Um, yes?"

"I'm Cecilia, this one's mate. The thing to remember when dealing with Firsts is that they're all arrogant and egotistical and pigheaded. And thinking before they speak? Not really something they're good at."

"Cece," Damon growled.

"But they're also fiercely loyal to what's theirs. What my less-than-communicative mate is trying to say—stop that, ass!—is that Mal learned valuable information, and he's grateful he was willing to risk himself to get it." She snorted. "Now, isn't that what you meant, Damon?"

"Cece, I—"

"Is that or is that not what you meant?" she growled, her tone showing she expected nothing less than agreement.

"Yes, my mate. That's exactly what I meant." A deep sigh. "Forgive me, Alp. I chose my words poorly."

It was all Alp could do to keep the laughter from bursting out. He liked this woman, and she'd given him a good lesson in how to deal with Mal when he got stubborn.

"I could try to go back, and—"

"The fuck you could!" Alp ground out. "They took someone's eyes, Mal. His eyes. My hand was bad enough, but this person will never be able to see again. You're not going in there alone. If you try, I will fucking neuter you."

Cece laughed. "By George, I think he's got it."

Alp huffed a breath, doing his best to tamp down the anger. What was it with wolves? Were they all like this, or had Alp and Cece drawn the short straws with theirs?

"Alp?"

"Yeah?" he replied, turning back to the phone as if Cece would be able to see him.

"You and I? We need to be besties. Can you imagine what these guys would be like if we got together?"

"Cece, we're in a meeting, do you mind?"

She scoffed. "We'll talk later, I promise." Then she said, "Damon, I'm going to go check on the kids."

"Okay." Soft footfalls leading away faded into nothing. "Don't worry about them getting together, Mal. We're on opposite ends of the country."

"We have phones," Alp reminded them.

"Screw phones. We have a jet," Cece called out.

"Shit," Damon murmured. "I am so going to pay for that later."

"Probably sooner than you think, my *First*."

"Can you please check the kids and leave me alone?" he grumbled.

"For now. I need time to think of a suitable punishment anyway."

"This is on you, Mal," Damon whined. "Now I'm going to have to grovel to get back in her good graces."

"That's okay. Mal's going to have to do the same here," Alp said, a wide grin on his face.

"Can we please focus?" Mal snapped.

Alp realized he was playing too much for the seriousness of the conversation. "Sorry."

"Come here and sit on my lap," Mal said.

Alp scampered over and did as he was asked. Mal leaned in, and Alp knew he was sniffing him.

"Okay, I talked to the pack last night."

Mal tensed, and Alp knew he needed comfort, so he reached up and massaged Mal's neck. The soft smile he got made it well worth it.

"Should I even ask?"

Damon growled. "Do you believe my pack would abandon you? Is that what you think of us?"

"No, First," Mal said quickly. "I apologize. That wasn't what I meant at all."

A chuckle rolled out of Damon. "Even as a First yourself, you're easily brought to heel. Alp will have much fun with that. Anyway, when I explained what we believed was happening, there was no end of volunteers. The members who knew you before you left? They were among the most eager to help. There will be sixty-three of us coming."

"Sixty-four," Cece shouted.

"You are not going, and that is final!" Damon yelled back. "You need to be here for the kids."

Fast footsteps sounded as Cece returned. "You did not just say I wasn't going."

"You're not. We talked about this, and I told you that you were staying here. I need someone I trust to watch the children."

"Okay, let me call your mother and let her know you don't trust her to take care of the kids. I'm sure that'll go well for you."

Damon sighed, and Alp wished the call had been on Skype. He'd love to sit with a big tub of buttered popcorn and watch the shitshow that was about to drop on Damon's head.

"That is not what I meant, and you know it."

"But it is what you said, isn't it? Who here is a better fighter than me? Huh? I can take down two of your enforcers at the same time."

"That's not the point. You are my mate. They are not. I am First, and you ob—um, should listen to me."

"You were going to say I obey you? Seriously?" She huffed an exasperated breath. "Mal, Alp, we're going to be getting our gear together. We'll see you in two days, with a contingent of people. In the meantime, *First*, you and I are going to—"

The call was disconnected, and Mal chuckled. "I'd hate to be in his shoes right now."

Alp glowered at him.

"Oh. I am in his shoes right now, huh?"

Alp huffed, hand on his hip. "Why do you have to be the perfect mate?"

Those eyes widened. "I'm sorry, what?"

He wanted to put his feelings into words, then realized how impossible that was. There weren't enough words to express how much Alp had come to love Mal.

"Cece isn't wrong. Firsts, including you, are stubborn and opinionated." He blew out a slow breath. "But you're also kind, caring.

And you're loyal to a fault. I'm sorry I thought you might leave me for someone else. It's just—"

"Never had anything of your own, I know. So you're not used to having something you don't have to give away or worry that it's going to be taken from you. Am I right?"

Alp nodded, unable to speak. Mal saw him clear to his core.

"We are always going to be together. A pack of two. Not needing anyone else to make us complete. We can set up our home here, but the open road is available to us, if we want to go somewhere. I can take you to see the Statue of Liberty, or the Golden Gate Bridge. We could go to Kings Canyon National Park and run in the forest of sequoia trees, or go to Vermont when the weather is getting cooler and look at the beautiful leaves as they turn from green to gold. If you like music, we can go to Colorado and check out Red Rocks Amphitheatre. Plus, there are so many other places I'd love for you to see. But, that's your choice."

Years ago, travel had been high on Alp's list of things to do. Now? It sounded good, but so did settling down with Mal.

"How about we play it by"—Mal tweaked Alp's lobe—"ear."

"You're a funny, funny man," Alp muttered, even though he was secretly pleased that Mal thought playing with him was fun.

Mal waggled his brows. "You have no idea how funny I can be. Just wait until you see my impressions."

Alp curled up beside Mal, not looking for a repeat of the sweaty times they'd had a short while ago, but for comfort.

And Mal gave that in spades.

MAL LAY PERFECTLY STILL as a sleeping Alp inched his way across the bed and onto Mal's chest. Even in sleep, Alp sought him out. He couldn't even begin to guess the demons that still haunted Alp, and probably would for the rest of his life. He'd undergone horrific things in the last six years, and that had to change a person.

Oh, Alp said he was fine, but Mal knew better. When he thought

Mal wasn't looking, Alp was nervous, twitchy, and scared pretty much all the time. He was fierce, though, and Mal truly believed that if push came to shove, Alp would bury that fear and do what needed to be done.

"Mal. No, not Mal. Don't..." came the whispered plea and a quick jolt, which was followed by a soft snore.

As he ran his hand over Alp's back, trying to get him to slip deeper into sleep, Mal knew he'd never be able to walk away from this man who wore his bite. Not that he wanted to. He'd started falling in love with Alp when he was still just a bunny. That core of strength he displayed rivaled the strongest of shifters. Then when Alp shifted and Mal got to smell the man? It was all over for him. Mal had fallen under the rabbit's spell and was finding it wasn't as terrifying as he thought it would be.

"No! Mal, run!" Alp sat bolt upright, his eyes wide, his skin slick with sweat. His head jerked side to side, as though he was looking for something. "Mal! Mal! Where are you?"

"I'm here, Alp. Right here." He soothed a hand over Alp's arms. "Look at me."

But whatever had a hold on Alp wasn't letting go. He was screaming, pleading for Mal to run, to live. Mal clutched him tighter, his heart breaking over the plaintive cries. When someone in another room shouted to quiet the fuck down, Mal wanted to go pull their intestines out through their nose, but instead ignored it.

Then the sobbing started. "I'm so sorry, Mal. I'm sorry. I'm sorry."

He shook Alp gently, uncertain if it was safe to wake him, but not willing to let him suffer like this. When Alp's eyes, those beautiful sea-green eyes, settled on him, Mal was grateful.

"Mal!" Alp cried, doing his best to climb into Mal's lap. "Mal, you can't go. You have to stay behind. They're going to kill you."

"Hush, sweetheart. It's okay, we're both safe."

"No, you don't understand. Hyde knows."

"What does he know?"

"He knows," Alp repeated, and his body went slack in Mal's arms.

"Alp?"

Nothing. He shook Alp, needing him to wake up. When his eyes opened, Mal leaned in and kissed him softly.

"You okay?"

Alp buried his face in Mal's chest and shook his head.

"Wanna talk about it?"

Another soft shake.

"Okay. How about we lay back down, and you can snuggle with me?"

That got him a nod. He pulled Alp back to the mattress, his head tucked under Mal's chin. A few moments later, dampness matted the hairs on his chest.

"Alp?"

"He's going to kill you. He knows."

"What does he know?" Mal asked gently, not wanting to rattle his precious mate.

"I'm not sure. It's just a feeling. He's going to kill you, and I'm going to see it. There'll be so much blood."

His words, dead and cold, sent shivers through Mal.

"There'll be dozens of us. We're going to take them all down."

Alp shook his head. "Not before he kills you."

"Listen to me. I'm going to promise you something, okay? I am not going to die today, tomorrow, or anytime in the foreseeable future. I am a First. I'm stronger than other wolves. It would take something far greater than a human can muster to kill me. You're stuck with me for decades to come." He slid a hand up Alp's neck and tangled his fingers in the collar-length hair. "Get used to it, bunny."

Alp nodded, but Mal knew he wasn't believing it. What kind of dream terrified a person so badly?

You idiot. The kind that comes from six years of torture. Of hearing other shifters screaming as they died. Of never knowing if today was the day you'd finally meet the Maker.

The only thing Mal could do was to help Alp get over it. Maybe see a therapist. That was far more likely to help than any platitudes Mal could come up with.

"Baby, I—"

There was a knock at the door.

Mal sniffed. "Lydia is here."

Alp slid off the bed and dressed. There wasn't any of the normal hyper energy that Mal was used to seeing, and that bothered him. He wanted to send Lydia away so he could tend to Alp, but she was going to be risking her life for them.

Another knock.

"One sec," Mal called out before he turned to Alp. "I can tell her we'll talk later."

He shook his head. "We need her help. I'm fine."

Mal stared at Alp, knowing he was anything but fine. "Alp, I—"

"I'm fine, I promise. Let's see what Lydia has to say."

He trudged to the door and pulled it open. Lydia stood there, with several bags in her hands. She stepped into the room, a bright smile on her face, but it quickly dimmed when she looked at Alp. "What's wrong?"

Alp shrugged, then turned and went to the other room, closing the door behind him.

She locked gazes with Mal. "What's going on?"

A deep sigh slid out of him. "Alp had a nightmare. He's been having them more often lately, but this one seems to have rattled him."

"Does he remember what it was?"

"My death."

"Oh." Lydia flopped onto the couch and let her head drop back, so she was staring up at the ceiling. "Did he say how?"

"He's not sure. He only knows there was a lot of blood. He's angry with himself because, in this dream, he watched Hyde kill me and did nothing to stop it."

"But it was a dream. He can't take that kind of stuff to heart."

Mal sat beside Lydia and took her hand. "Alp was held for six years, and during that time, they did unspeakable things to him. Hyde is the monster who haunts his dreams. He's literally Alp's bogeyman. And now, he's watched Hyde take away the one thing he feels is his."

"That sucks," she said quietly.

"Tell me about it. I want to help him, but I don't know how." He put his head in his hands. "I'm thinking, after this, he needs to see a doctor, but how can he tell them the truth?"

For several long moments, Lydia said nothing. "When Dinah was younger, like thirteen, she went through a long bout of depression. Everything was closing in on her, she told me. She didn't want to be queer—she only wanted to be normal. I talked to her until I was blue in the face, assuring her that however she was, whoever she was, that was her normal. Nothing helped. I took her to see a doctor, and he wanted to put her on medications. She flatly refused, saying she didn't want to become dependent on them.

"Doing nothing wouldn't work either. She got worse, spiraling deeper into anger and pain. Finally, she accepted that she needed help and has been on antidepressants since then. They've worked wonders for her, and she's no longer hating life or afraid to live it."

"What does this have to do with Alp?"

"The FDA has allowed some medications to be given to pets." Before Mal could say anything, she pushed on. "I know Alp isn't an animal, and I honestly think it might be better for him to see a human therapist, but it'll be hard to explain about his lost hand without telling them the whole story." She gave a soft smile. "I can look for someone, but not sure I can tell them about Alp without mentioning the other things."

"No, we can't do that."

"I know, and I do get it. Really. I wish I had other options, but I'm operating in the dark here."

As if Mal wasn't. He needed to get back on familiar ground, so he cleared his throat and turned his attention back to Lydia. "Did you need something?"

"Oh, yeah. I was coming to tell you I've placed a big order for things to treat animals, so if there are other shifters in that place, I can help you out."

"The place is there, and we believe the shifters are too. I couldn't go in, because of Alp. I won't leave him alone."

"Then you're a good man. If he's already suffering, you shouldn't compound it. That doesn't mean he has to fight, of course."

"And what about you? Will you come with us?"

She nodded. "Yes. I won't hurt anyone, but I will come with you to help out where I can. Do you have a plan?"

"We have something better. We have an army."

CHAPTER 15

TWO DAYS LATER, Alp stood outside with Mal and Lydia, waiting for the arrival of Damon Walker and his entourage. Alp had finally come out of the room, exhausted, despite all the sleep he'd gotten, but the remnants of the dream still clung to him. When he and Lydia broached the subject of antidepressants, Alp scowled, but when Lydia told him about her daughter, his stiff posture relaxed and he listened intently.

"How about this?" he offered. "When this is over, we can revisit it. Right now, I can't even be sure it would work for me. Our metabolism burns off most things, especially after a shift." He reached for her and placed a hand atop hers. "I know you're both worried about me." His gaze flicked to Mal. "And I appreciate you more than I can say. Right now, though? We have a job to do." He drew in a breath. "When we're ready, I'm going with you, Mal."

Mal nodded. "That'll be fine. I prefer to have you with me," he replied with a smile.

The thrum of the first vehicle echoed off the cliffs surrounding the motel. A frisson of excitement wound its way through Alp, starting in his stomach and zipping out to all areas of his body. He was about to meet the man that his First called First. Not that it was at all confusing, of course.

When the trucks came around the corner, Alp murmured, "Oh my Maker." This was no covert operation. Sixteen semitrucks, ten Hummers, cars, vans, and other assorted vehicles chugged toward the motel, dark smoke plumes visible for as far as the eye could see.

The lead Hummer came to a halt, and the rest fell in line behind it, winding down the highway. The door opened and out stepped a man who could only be Damon. He was bigger than Mal, with a broad chest and arms and legs thick with muscles. Next to him, Mal seemed tiny. The rest of the people stayed in their vehicles, which were now all silent. It was rather unnerving.

He didn't speak as he strode to where Mal, Alp, and Lydia stood. He locked his gaze on Mal and clomped toward him. The man was awe-inspiring. A TAC vest strained to contain the immense power that radiated off Damon. Mal lowered his gaze and dropped to a knee before him.

"First, welcome to Swenson."

"Coffee," Damon growled, which became a jaw-popping yawn. "I need it, like, now."

"Of course." Mal rose. "I'll make some right away."

Damon shook his head. "My people will all need it. We drove straight through, stopping only to water a few trees along the way. They're going to need plenty of food and coffee."

"I already anticipated that," Alp said, smiling at Mal. "The guy who owns the diner was sure I was messing with them when I ordered a hundred burgers with fries, a hundred fried chicken with mashed potatoes and gravy, as well as twenty steak dinners, thirty meatloaf and fries, and fifty of their allegedly famous rib sandwiches. We went and put down a deposit, so he'd know we were serious."

Damon's tongue darted out, swiping over his lips. "Did you get mozzarella sticks? I would kill for some."

"And onion rings, cheese curds, and quesadillas."

The smile he got drained some of the tension Alp was feeling. "Introduce me, Malachi."

"First—"

"Damon, please," he reminded Mal.

"Damon," Mal said, his tone still reverent. "I would like to introduce you to Alpin Dawkins, my mate."

Damon leaned in and sniffed Alp. What was it with wolves and the sniffing? When he brushed his face against Alp's, the stubble scraping his skin, Alp gasped. He'd never been near any wolf beside Mal, and as much as he thought Mal was power personified, he was a candle next to Damon's roaring flame.

"It is my pleasure, Alpin Dawkins," Damon said. "You are a wonderful First's mate. Instinctively you cared for us, even though you had no idea who we were or what we were like. Mal has chosen wisely." He then stood and turned to Lydia. The smile that had graced his face, handsome in a rough, craggy way, slipped. "A human?" he snarled, his gaze snapping to Mal. "You told a human about us?"

"No, Damon. She was the one who helped to save Alp. She worked tirelessly to mend his broken body. She found out by mistake, but I trust her, and I ask that you do the same."

"Attend me, human," Damon growled, which sent a chill up Alp's spine.

Lydia stepped forward, and Alp couldn't miss the wariness.

"Tell me why you're here," Damon demanded.

Lydia cleared her throat and stood straight, but still didn't make eye contact. "To help where I can, Damon. First. Uh, I'm not sure which I should call you, sir."

"And how will you help us?" Damon asked, his tone still brittle.

"I'm a veterinarian. I ordered supplies to help any shifter in need. I can't work on their human counterparts, but I can tend to any wounded animals." She nodded. "Like Alp was. When Mal brought him in, I wanted—needed—to try to heal him. It's what I do."

Damon's lip curled up, showing off a rather large fang. "Humans were never meant to know about us," he ground out, the menace in his voice unmistakable.

Alp stepped between them. "She saved my fucking life!" he shouted. "I'm not going to have you browbeating her for my mistake."

"Your mistake?"

Alp sighed. "I was... angry at Mal. I needed him, skin to skin, and he was dealing with something else. When he held me, I tried to get closer, and in my need, I shifted. Lydia was there, and saw."

Damon rubbed a hand over his eyes. "A shifter who can't control himself is a threat. He could expose us all."

This time it was Mal who stepped forward, pushing Alp and Lydia behind him. "If you try to touch them, I swear to the Maker, I will gut you where you stand. No one threatens my mate or our friend."

Tension filled the air as the two Firsts glared at one another. Alp wasn't sure what to do, but then a voice rang out.

"Stop the posturing, for fuck's sake. Mal, he wouldn't harm a hair —" She snickered. "On your hare. And as for the human, we are pleased to have an ally such as her."

A moment later, three people got out of the same Hummer Damon had. Alp was struck by the woman. She was tall, her shoulders wide. The muscle shirt she wore showed off her powerful arms, and her narrow hips were hugged by the black jeans she wore. Her auburn hair was pulled back into a harsh ponytail, exposing her face, which Alp found to be expressive, with eyes that were rife with mischief.

This had to be Cece.

"Damon, stop being a dick."

He flushed and turned his attention back to Lydia. "I'm sorry," he said, and it sounded sincere. "My mate is right. With the changes going on in the world, we need all the allies we can get. Please forgive my stupidity." He leaned in and sniffed her, then brushed his face against hers. "You are welcome among us."

Lydia looked like she was about to fall over.

"There. Much better. See? We can all be friends."

It was easy to see Cece wasn't one to take lightly. Two men flanked her, both with their hands crossed in front of them as they scanned the area. They were tall, their features harsh and angular. They seemed to be wound tight, ready to spring into action. Their harsh buzzcuts and deep, dark eyes sent a shiver through Alp, because he couldn't read them at all.

"Hey, Alp. I'm Cece." She opened her arms and wiggled her fingers. "Come gimme some sugar."

Alp smiled and raced toward her, but the two men stepped in front of her, barring his path.

"Seriously?" she snapped. "Did you not fucking hear me call him to come over to me?"

The men didn't move, their eyes locked on Alp. Cece stepped around them, her face like a thunderstorm. Someone was about to get smacked down.

"Damon Walker, tell me you did not order Tweedledum and Tweededumber to keep me safe!" She huffed out a breath. "I can beat them both, so how are they supposed to protect me?

"I will make no apologies for that!" Damon snapped, obviously annoyed, but Alp saw it. The love in his eyes as his gaze settled on Cece. "Had you stayed home—"

"Don't start this again. I'm here, I'm not leaving, get over yourself." Her head swiveled back to Alp as she once again held up her arms. "As I was saying, baby, come give mama some sugar."

He stepped to the side, then closed the gap between them. He squeaked when Cece snatched him off the ground and brought him into a crushing hug.

"It is so good to meet you," she whispered in his ear. "You and I? We're gonna be such good friends, I can tell." She put him down, then turned to Mal and gave him a warm smile. "A pleasure to see you again, Mal."

"And you, First mate," Mal said, dipping his chin respectfully.

Cece rolled her eyes. "What is this shit?" she barked. "You know my name. We've been friends for years."

Mal frowned. "It's a matter of respect, and—"

"Have you ever, and I mean *ever* known Cece to care about respect?" Damon asked, his tone grumpy. "Do you know she actually did call my mother and tell her I didn't trust her with the kids?"

"Because you were being a dick and saying I couldn't come with you," she shot back. "I'm your best backup, and you damn well know it."

"But the kids need their mother! If something happens—"

Cece gave him a soft smile. "Then your mother will raise them, as she did you. Wiley will make a fine First when he comes of age—you made sure of that." She slipped an arm around Alp. "And I had someone I was dying to meet."

Alp cleared his throat. "I'm going to go get the food."

Cece snickered. "Where's your car? I'll come with you."

"You should stay with me," Damon said, his tone letting Alp know it wasn't a request.

"And you should go get some coffee and chill out." She gripped Alp's hand. "Your car?"

Oh. Shit. "Mal?"

He sighed. "I forgot too." He turned to Damon. "Could we borrow one of your vehicles? I've got my bike, and—"

"You have a cycle?" Damon asked, his eyes wide and sparkling. "What kind?"

"A 1951 Vincent Black Shadow," Mal said proudly. "I restored it myself."

If Alp didn't know better, he would swear Damon was drooling. He tossed a set of keys to Alp, who snagged them in midair. "Cece, go with Alp and get the food. I'll stay here."

"And just like that, thrown over for a motorcycle. Great." She chuckled. "C'mon, let's go before he realizes what he's done."

They them walked off, with the other two men following close behind.

"I wanted it to be the two of us, but my shadows won't leave until Damon says it's okay."

Alp sniffed. "They don't smell like wolves."

"They're not," she told him. "They're Ursus arctos middendorffi, otherwise known as Kodiak bears." She pointed at one. "This is Ivan, and that one is his brother, Teddy." She snorted. "I do get such a charge out of Teddy the bear."

Alp gaped at her, and she laughed. For such a big person, it was a soft, delicate sound that Alp liked immediately.

"I'm not just a pretty face, Alp. I've got brains, charm oozing out of my pores, and looks." She nudged him with a shoulder. "Baby, I'm the whole package."

"They're bears, and you can beat them?" Alp whispered, realizing the two men would likely hear him.

Cece turned to her bodyguards. "Who won in our last fight?"

The one man's—Teddy—cheeks flamed. "You did, ma'am."

"And did I take only you on?"

The other one cringed and toed the soil, clearly uncomfortable. "No, you beat us both."

"Uh, you're forgetting the best part."

"At the same time," they echoed, and it was easy to see they were trying hard to not roll their eyes.

"And it wasn't just once," Cece said with a cackle.

They got to the vehicles, and she pointed to another truck. "You two take that one and follow us."

"But we're supposed to—"

"Follow. Us," she said, clipping her words. "There's going to be a lot of food, and I don't want to make more than one trip."

Dutifully they got into one of the 2020 Chevrolet Silverados. Cece slipped into the driver's seat of theirs, then held her hand out. "Keys."

Alp passed her the keys.

She started the truck and asked Alp where they were headed. Once he told her, he scowled.

"I can drive, you know."

"Really? Cool. Show me your license." She smiled. "I know all about you, Alpin Dawkins. I even spoke with your mother. She's a lovely woman. I'm going to fly out to see her next week so we can go shopping. If you want, I can swing by and pick you up."

"You talked to my mother?" Alp was a little offended. "What gives you the right?"

She reached out and patted his arm. "I protect what's mine, sweetheart. If you think I would let Damon go off without knowing the people he was going to be dealing with, you're sadly mistaken. I'm sorry if it hurts your feelings, but my mate comes first in every situation."

It made sense. Alp would do the same for Mal. "I'm sorry," he muttered.

"Don't be. You have every right to know. I might bust his balls, pretty much constantly, but I love Damon with every fiber of my being. That's why I wasn't about to let him come here without me. He might not like to admit it, but he knows in a fight, I would kick his ass, just like I did the Tweedles. If I wanted to be First, it wouldn't be hard."

Alp could see that. She had the swagger and cocky attitude down. "Why don't you?"

A soft smile tugged at her lips. "I love my life. I'm a mother, the First mate of one of the wealthiest packs in the country, and I have a husband I would give my life for. I'm content."

That was how Alp felt about Mal. Well, except for the rich part.

"You really have a jet?" he asked, steering the conversation away from uncomfortable topics.

She shrugged. "Sure. It's not a huge one, more like a lear jet, but we make do."

Make do? Alp couldn't imagine having that much money.

When they got to the diner, a sign in the window said they were closed for a special event. Alp opened his door and slid out of the behemoth vehicle. He went and knocked, and a few moments later, a harried older man opened for him.

"Good afternoon. I called in an order?"

The man shook his head. "Do you know you wiped out every last bit of our inventory. I think we might have a bucket of pickles left."

"Ooh, I love pickles," Cece said, coming up beside Alp. "Let us have those too. And give Alp back his deposit, because I'll be paying for this."

She held out a credit card, the likes of which Alp had never seen. The owner of the diner's eyes widened, but he snatched the card away and hurried back inside.

"What was that card?"

"Hm? Oh, it's an Amex Black Card." She shrugged. "It's nice for small things."

"Never heard of it," Alp told her. "We were going to pay cash."

"I know, and believe me, we do appreciate your hospitality. But you shouldn't be put out because of us. As for the card? You have to be invited to get one. We had been offered another, and it was a lot better, but it came from a courier for the Dubai royal family. When Damon saw it, he handed it back to the man, thanked him, and told him no way was he interested in something from a country that treated women and gays poorly."

Alp was floored. "I thought most wolf packs weren't cool with the whole gay thing?"

"We adapt, my darling. Our son Wiley is gay, and Damon announced it at the last gathering of the packs. When someone like Damon tells you he's not going to take shit, you change that shit to something he's going to accept, or you lose out on any hope of partnering with us on projects. Most packs fell in line quickly. The holdouts soon learned that Damon's reach is as deep as his pockets, and they came around. Sure, there is still some grumbling, but they're smart enough to do it out of earshot of the man who worships his family. And I have to admit, a lot of them really seemed to have embraced the changes and have admitted they have gay family members too."

The whole exchange made Alp feel like he was dealing with shifter royalty.

A few minutes later, the door to the diner opened up again, and six young men, loaded down with boxes of food, came out. The two men with Cece grabbed the boxes and stacked them into the trucks. It was funny watching them lug all the boxes it took the six guys to carry without breaking a sweat.

In no time at all, everything was put away and ready to go. The owner presented Cece with a receipt, which she signed and added a tip that made the guy's eyes bug out.

"Thank you!" he practically shouted. "Thanks to you and your friends, we're making more in one day than we have in the last nine months."

"You and your employees did us a great favor. It's the least we can do."

"If you need anything else, let me know. I'll do my best to get it for you."

"I will likely take you up on that," Cece told him. She then turned to Alp and wrapped an arm around his shoulder. "Let's go feed our boys."

The ride back, she and Alp didn't speak, but it wasn't an uncomfortable silence. More like being with a good friend, without having to constantly fill the quiet with meaningless conversation.

As they approached the motel, Cece put a hand on Alp's leg. "You doing okay?"

"Sure," he replied.

"Maybe I didn't phrase that properly. Are you doing all right? And don't lie to me. I'm a wolf, so I can sense it."

Alp sighed and stared out at the forest zooming by them. "I'm scared," he admitted. "I just got him, and I'm having nightmares about losing him."

Cece squeezed his leg. "Can I let you in on a little secret?"

"Sure."

"Part of the reason I insist on going with Damon is that I have those dreams too. I know I can't let him go alone, because I have to be with him to keep him safe."

"But he has bodyguards."

"And no matter how I tease them, they're amazing men. They're incredible at their jobs, and they would take a bullet for my mate. But they're not me. They're loyal because Damon gave them a home, but he gave me a family and a life." She shook her head. "I know it sounds stupid, but if something is going to happen, I need to be there."

But it didn't sound stupid at all. In fact, it warmed Alp to know that someone understood what he was feeling.

And for the first time in days, Alp blew out a relieved breath. Things would work out. They had to.

CHAPTER 16

"SO... A BUNNY, HUH?" Damon asked as he ran a hand over the steel and chrome of the motorcycle. "This is an amazing bike," he muttered.

"Yep, a bunny. A sweet, sarcastic-as-fuck rabbit."

"I can see why you mated him. Anyone who would stand between me and you is someone you need to keep in your life. And to have you threaten me? That speaks volumes about how you feel for him."

"I won't let anyone touch him," Mal vowed.

"Good man. You should always protect your mate, even when they tell you they don't need it and make your life miserable because of it." He slid a hand over the leather seat. "You feeling confident about going into this place?"

Was he? "I'm not sure. I don't like us not knowing what's waiting on us, but I couldn't chance going inside."

"No. I don't say this often, and if you tell anyone I did, I'll tell them you're lying. I was wrong when I said you should have. Yes, I want to know, and yes, I want my people safe, but not at the expense of a friend."

Long moments passed while Mal tried to figure out how to broach the subjects on his mind.

"I need a favor," he finally said.

"Another one?" Damon teased. Before Mal could continue, Damon said, "If something happens, we'll take Alp home with us. Cece has already told me she'll care for him until he's okay, and then she'll either welcome him to the pack or take him home to his family."

"You would take a rabbit into the pack?"

"No, I would take your mate into the pack. We have a couple of bears too."

This wasn't the Damon Mal knew. He was always going on about wolves and their place in the shifter society. How they were the vanguards, the ones who set the rules.

"I've been an idiot," Damon said. "And, of course, it took Cece to show me. Our son, Wiley? He's gay. Honestly, I thought at first he was defective. There had to be something wrong with him, because a true wolf would find a mate and create strong pups to strengthen the pack. But Wiley? He's not like that. He's strong, but kind, and I can't see him any other way.

"One night, when he was six, he showed us something he'd drawn. It was a picture of him and his best friend, hugging each other. I went ballistic and railed at him, telling him wolves didn't hug friends. We were strong, fierce warriors and...." He sighed. "Cece dragged me out of the house and she threw me against one of the outbuildings. I'd never seen her so angry. She told me if I *ever* talked to her son like that again, she would take him and Micah, and she'd leave me. It didn't matter to her that the mate bond would tear her heart apart, she'd sever it to protect our sons."

Mal listened with rapt attention. He'd always liked Damon, but for the longest time, he'd been cold, aloof.

"Wiley is seventeen now, and I swear to the Maker, I have never been so proud of anyone in my life. It was him who showed me what a leader could—*should*—be. That caring about his people was more than a job—it was a calling. I hug both my sons now. I tell them how much I love them. I will forever stand between them and the cruel bastards of the world, not because they're my sons, but because my family is my world."

"But the pack—"

"Will go on for a few days without my input. I have advisors now, and if they can't handle a problem, they'll come to me. I'm still involved, of course, but now I'm overseeing things to make them better, not trying to do it all myself. Cece again. She reminded me that our sons needed us both in their lives. She instituted mandatory weekend family time. From the moment I leave my office on Friday until eight on Monday morning, it's just us, unless there's an emergency." He snorted and his features softened. "And I watch them now, you know? Can you believe it took Cece to make me pay attention to my own kids? Wiley and his friend? I think they're waiting to become of age to mate. He's been a fierce protector of the boy since the picture he did when he was six. I came to see that no matter what anyone says, it's love, and it fucking humbles me, because in my arrogance, I could have missed it."

Wow. He'd grown a lot since Mal last spoke with him.

"Now let's talk about you."

Aw, hell.

"You're not the same man I knew, Mal."

"I could say the same."

Damon sighed. "Personal growth, it's a thing. When I was training you to be a First, you seemed so eager, but I knew you weren't."

"Then why did we continue?"

"Because you needed to go out and discover who Mal was and who he wanted to become. The only way for me to do that was to make you so miserable, you left."

"You never made me miserable," Mal said, wanting Damon to know that he wasn't to blame.

"I did. I forced interactions between you and the pack. I was hopeful that maybe one day it would sink in they were your people, but your heart was never there. It was always somewhere out here," he said, gesturing to the wooded area near the motel. "And I get that. This place? It's pristine, beautiful, and wild. It calls to my wolf too."

"Then we should run. See the trails and hills, the lake. The area is teeming with wildlife, so food is plentiful if you want it. Tonight, after you and your people have had some rest, we could go out and have some fun."

"Because tomorrow we may die?"

"Something like that," Mal admitted with a shrug.

"Then we'll do that."

"Mal?" Lydia called. He turned to face her and found her with a soft smile. "Alp is back."

He'd known it, of course. He could feel Alp no matter what. He occupied a sliver of Mal's mind, and Mal was always aware of his mate.

"Thank you, Lydia," Mal said, standing. "Are you staying for lunch?"

She chuckled. "Cece said I was staying, so apparently I am," she replied, turning to go back to the rest of the group.

Damon shook his head. "My mate. Thinks she's in charge of everything."

"Don't worry, I won't tell her you know she is."

That got a chuckle. "Thanks. I appreciate that." He turned to Mal. "And though I never said it, I appreciate you. You've always been a damn good friend."

"But I left, and—"

"A true friend is someone you don't need to see every day, but they're still in your heart. That's you."

The words humbled Mal. "Thank you."

Damon waved a hand. "Don't thank me—that's what Wiley says. I think you're a dick." He cuffed Mal on the chin, then followed in the direction Lydia had gone.

Mal stood a few moments, wondering at the changes in Damon and in himself. They weren't the same people as they'd been when Mal was part of the pack. He'd always liked Damon as a First, but now? He liked him just as much as a friend.

～

ALP WAS WATCHING the wolves tear through the food, aghast. There were a lot of belches, more than a few farts, and quite a bit of cursing. If he hadn't told Rebecca, the owner, they were having a family get-together, she probably would have called the sheriff long before now.

The thing was, they were a family, and that was easy to see. Even the bears were part of the pack. Now that they were off duty, they laughed and joked with the wolves. Through it all, Cece and Damon kept a watchful eye on their people. If things started getting too rowdy, they'd step in and calm the situation with a couple words. When nothing but a few crumbs remained, the wolves all pitched in and helped clean up the area, then one by one came over to Alp and thanked him for his hospitality.

"I never expected that," he admitted to Mal.

"Cece would have had their heads if they hadn't shown their gratitude." Mal leaned in and kissed Alp breathless. "And that's mine. You didn't have to take care of the pack. You could have simply told them to go into the woods and fend for themselves, but you didn't."

"I would never," Alp said firmly as he crawled into Mal's lap, wanting his warmth to chase away the chill that had settled in ever since that dream. "These people are your family, and that makes them mine. I'm not a wolf, but as a rabbit, I know that family is always going to be the most important thing." He kissed under Mal's chin. "And besides, we made the guy who owns the diner *very* happy."

"I've no doubt. That's cutting into our money, though."

"Oh!" Alp bounded from his spot, then hurried to grab his pants. He took out the wad of cash and handed it to Mal. "Cece and Damon paid for it. She said that they wouldn't let us go broke by buying their food." He resumed his spot, curling an arm around Mal's neck. "And she's got a black credit card!"

It didn't sit well with Mal that they were coming to help he and Alp and then paying for everything, but he had to admit, no way did he have the money to pay for sixty-four hungry wolves and bears, especially if they'd be here a few days. He worried how they were going to deal with the next several.

"Are you doing better?" he asked, giving Alp a squeeze.

He nodded. "Some. I talked with Cece, and she let me know I wasn't alone in how I felt." He kissed Mal's neck. "I'm still scared. I have no idea how I got out of there, but my head is screaming to never go back again. Something awful is going to happen, I can feel it." He rested his cheek on Mal's chest. "And it's going to happen to you."

"I won't say nothing will go wrong, but it was a dream, and you can't let it control what you do."

"It wasn't a dream," Alp insisted. "It was real, and even now I feel it in my heart."

"Then stay here, and—"

"Fuck you!" He leaned back, his eyes dark. "I'm not staying alone. I'm going with you to save those people. Those kids. Don't even try to talk me out of it."

"I wasn't, I swear."

There was a knock, and Alp sighed. "Is it going to be like this from now on?" He clambered from Mal's lap, and went to the door. Damon stood there, a tight T crossed over his massive chest. Alp could almost hear the seams pleading to be allowed to relax a few minutes.

"Are you ready?" he asked Mal.

"I...," Mal peered at Alp. "I should stay here."

Damon nodded. "Okay."

"Wait. What's going on?" Alp asked, his gaze flitting back and forth between the men.

"I told Damon we could go running tonight, but I think you need me more."

A run? Alp hadn't had a real run in ages. He stood and moved to where Mal was. "Let's go."

"What? Are you sure? What about your foot?"

He shrugged. "It's not going to grow back, so I have to learn to use what I still have. And a run sounds great."

"Damon?"

"You have my word, none of my wolves will bother him. In fact, they'll ensure no one gets near him."

That got a smile. "Alp? Let's go running."

They went out and joined the rest of Damon's pack. Men and women, each who'd come to help rescue shifters they'd never met. This is what having friends felt like. Someone who always had your back and would never let you sink.

"Damon?"

He turned from Cece. "Yes?"

Alp went to him and slid his arms around the broad waist. "Thank you to you and the pack for doing this. For helping us to save these people."

"Hey, nothing was more important than this. They hurt you, and that makes Cece angry. And we don't like it when she's angry."

She snorted. "Work on that humor, hon." Then she put a hand on Alp's back. "We want to make this Hyde guy pay. I don't care what he thinks we are, he's committed murder and we won't let that go." She slid her fingers through Alp's hair. "And lastly, he has to pay for what he did to you."

When Alp glanced up, he was taken aback. Cece had tears in her eyes, which he never expected from her. She seemed so strong and put together, but now she was crying?

"Are you okay?" he asked.

She held up a finger, and a second later, Damon was there, his arm around her, pulling her in.

"Cece is fine," he said. "When she looks at you, she thinks of our sons and how this could have happened to them."

"I'm sorry," Alp said, sadness churning in his gut. "I don't mean to upset you."

Damon blinked and then burst out laughing. Alp was about to snap at him, tell him he sucked as a mate if he could treat Cece like that, but he held up a hand and closed the distance between them. When he got to where Alp stood, he smiled down at him. "Oh, Alp. No, no, no. She's not sad. She's angry, and this is her way of venting some frustration without having to hurt anyone."

Both bears came and took positions beside her. One put his hand on her shoulder, and Alp was surprised to see her lean into him a little.

"Anyone but us. The last time she was upset, she got me and Ivan out on the mat and reminded us not to mistake tears for weakness," Teddy said. "She's a devil bear, this one." He grinned. "But she's also the fiercest and kindest warrior we know."

His brother joined him. "Cece is... how do you say it? Our boss. Damon is in charge of the pack, but Cece is in charge of us. She works with us, spars with us, and makes us better than what we are. One day we hope to beat her."

"Keep dreaming, Ivan," she snorted, then turned and hugged him. He wrapped his arms around her and put his chin on her head. He was the picture of contentment as she held on to him.

"We will kill this man for you," he vowed in a low growl. "Do not worry—we will not fail you."

"Yeah," his cohort replied. "We haven't killed anyone in far too long. It'll be good to flex those muscles again." He cracked his knuckles. "And if we save some babies while we're at it? So much the better to get back in the Maker's good graces, right?"

At first, Alp thought they were teasing, but one look at the pain etched on their faces told him it was anything but. Whatever they were thinking about nearly gutted them.

He reached out and put a hand on Ivan's arm. "Are you okay?"

Ivan gave a sad smile as he reached up to squeeze Alp's shoulder. "Yeah, fine."

But his words didn't match his expression. There was both sadness and anger showing on his face, plus the tightness in his posture and the pain in his eyes. Ivan's gaze flitted in Alp's direction.

"I'm fine, but thank you for your concern."

"He is fine, Alp. I make sure both of them are," Cece assured him, straightening and scrubbing a hand over her eyes. "I think someone promised us a run, and I for one have energy to work off."

Damon arched his eyebrows.

"Don't even think about it, horndog," Cece chastised. "Once was enough to tell me that position ain't comfortable."

When Damon's cheeks pinked, Alp bit back a laugh.

A thought struck him. He hadn't prepared for their arrival nearly as well as he'd thought. "Where's everyone sleeping?" The motel didn't have nearly enough rooms for the whole pack, and it was the only place in Swenson, beyond the B&B, that rented rooms.

"Outside," Damon replied, his tone indicating the answer was obvious.

That made sense. They were wolves, for Maker's sake. "Oh, I forgot you're used to it. Sorry."

Cece stared at Alp as though he'd grown another head. "Used to it?" She pointed to a long black truck. "Sweetheart, that one has our tents. Ain't none of us sleeping out in the open air with the ticks and the flies and mosquitoes." She shuddered. "That's crazy talk. We're wolves, not animals. We rented the space beside the motel. The owner was more than happy to let us do that, especially if it meant she didn't have to do the laundry."

Damon smiled at his wife, so obviously besotted with her. The two of them were meant to be, just like him and Mal.

Now he just had to ensure they both lived through what was coming.

CHAPTER 17

MAL FLOPPED down on the mattress, his breathing ragged.

"You okay?" Alp asked, sitting down beside him and stroking a hand over his leg. "Didn't wear you out, right?"

He snickered. "It's been years since I've been on a pack run. Damon didn't take it easy on me. I forgot what a bitch some of those hills could be."

He rolled to his side and lifted his arm. Alp slid in beside him and sighed when Mal embraced him.

"Thank you for coming along."

Alp snorted. "Thank you for carrying me most of the way. You guys were amazing. My legs are built for bursts of speed, not long distance. And you're right about those hills. I think I'd still be on the first one, if Cece hadn't nudged me up it."

It meant the world that Alp fit in with Cece and Damon. If something happened to him, at least he knew Alp would be surrounded by people who cared for him.

"You ready for the morning?"

"You mean, five hours from now? Yeah, I am," Alp said, but he heard the wobble in his own voice.

"Damon laid out a good plan. Groups of six, each splitting off and going in different directions, taking down humans as they go."

"But...."

"What? Tell me what's on your mind?"

Alp sighed. "What if some of these people are innocent? Who knows what Hyde told them they're doing."

The thought had occurred to Mal, but then he'd come to a real- ization. "The one guy knew he'd taken a shifter's eyes," he ground out, the anger bubbling up. "He fucking laughed about it. I wanted to jump into the truck and rip his throat out. He said it in front of everyone with him, which tells me they all know. The other factor is, we have to protect ourselves, and that means they've got to die."

"I guess."

Mal grabbed him by the arm, his grip tight but not painful. "No, don't guess. You have to be committed to this, or you'll be the weak link in the chain we need. Remember what they did to you. You weren't a rabbit when they cut off your hand—you were in your skin. There's no way they're innocent." He tightened his grip on Alp a bit more, holding him closer.

"No, you're right," Alp breathed out, his breath hitching. "We have to do this."

"The operation is going to take all day," Mal reminded him. "We figured that the trucks coming and going means the people were housed somewhere and brought in for their shifts. Damon is going to let a few of them escape so he can track them back to wherever they go, and then wipe them out there as well. None can remain."

"How do we know if anyone who worked there before left? I mean, this opens a whole spiderweb of possibilities."

"Damon has people—other shifters—who can remotely access the computers once we get into the complex. They'll be able to tell us who needs to be silenced."

Silenced. Such a sanitized word, especially when it really meant killed. Murdered. "Mal...."

He tugged Alp to him. "I know. I hate it too, but we can't let them expose us. We can't let what happened to you happen to other shifters."

The words still didn't settle the disquiet in Alp. To hear his own mother tell Mal to kill them had shocked him. It was made worse by the fact that Alp had harbored the same feelings. But now that anger was about to be given form, to be made real?

"You can still stay here," Mal murmured, his lips against Alp's ear. "No one will think poorly of you."

Fragments of the dream came back with crystal clarity. Mal, laying on the floor, his sightless eyes forever staring at nothing. Never again to let Alp see the warmth they held, not crinkling in the corners when Mal smiled at him. Not open wide when he was in the throes of orgasm.

Just... dead.

The visions steeled his resolve. Even if he didn't like the idea of killing them all, he wouldn't allow Mal to die. At least not if he could prevent it.

"No, I'm going," he said, his voice strong and steady.

Mal kissed him, deep and claiming. Then he held Alp against him. "Sleep, my bunny. Tomorrow will be here sooner than either of us thinks."

MAL WAS grateful when Alp finally succumbed to the inevitable. He'd lain there, squeezing Mal's hand, trying to force himself to remain awake. Mal had noticed what he was trying to do and grabbed Alp's ankles, then pushed his knees to his chest and fucked him until Alp clutched at Mal's neck, trying his best to pull Mal into a kiss. When he'd bent and given Alp what he wanted, his bunny came, crying Mal's name into his mouth. Afterward, Mal told him to stay where he was and cleaned the cum from Alp's chest and stomach. Then, finally sated, Alp drifted into slumber with Mal's name on his lips.

If only Mal could be so lucky.

In a few hours, he would have to fight a war while ensuring that Alp wasn't hurt. In his mind, it didn't matter to Mal if he died, as long as Alp lived a long, happy life. Sure, he'd prefer it was with him, but if not, then he had options open. Whether it was with Damon's pack or back at home with his family, that wasn't the point. What was the point was that his fluffy bunny would be surrounded by love where he could heal.

He leaned in and sniffed Alp's hair, then brushed a cheek over his head, marking him with Mal's scent. He really shouldn't be doing it. If something happened to him, Alp would need to find someone else, and having Mal's scent on him would keep shifters away.

But... he couldn't help it. They'd bonded and shared a soul now. Mal would do whatever he could to make it back to Alp, to help him become whole again, to love him until the Maker called them home. That was the wish that Mal kept buried in his heart. To never be parted from Alp, to love him for the rest of their days.

He nuzzled Alp again, the intoxicating scent of sweet grass and dandelions and dew permeating every cell of Mal's body. How had he fallen so hard, so fast? What made Alp different from anyone else Mal had ever been with? It wasn't that he was passive, because Alp was anything but. He stood up to Damon, for fuck's sake, and Mal had no reason to believe that he wouldn't have thrown down with the First.

There was an intricacy to Alp. So many parts that seemed incongruous, but somehow slotted together to create one amazing, but tiny, whole that Mal was wild about. He would gladly stand between Alp and the world for one of his smiles. The caress of his hand on Mal's face. The look in his eyes as Mal slid into him. They all screamed to Mal that he was loved, and for a lone wolf, that was a heady thing.

But you're not a lone wolf anymore.

And that was the truth as well. Mal thought he could never be happy being part of a pack. He relished not being responsible for anyone or anything but himself. Now? This man nestled in his arms had turned Mal's world on its ear. He'd taken everything Mal had believed about himself and held it up to the light to show it was all a lie.

Mal wanted his pack. He wanted Alp. He fucking wanted to live so he could continue to make Alp happy, because going to be with the Maker and watching as Alp found new love wasn't an option.

Leave him here. Go on without him. It's the only way to keep him safe.

Maker, but Mal wanted to do that. He'd thought about pleading with Damon to have one of his people take Alp far away, keep him out of the coming fight, but he'd made a promise, and if he wanted to prove himself worthy of Alp's love, he had to keep it, as much as everything in him screamed it was a bad idea.

The rap at the door pulled Mal out of his thoughts. He glanced over at the clock. It was already four. Time to get ready.

"Alp?"

The only answer was Alp snuggling in deeper, burying his face in Mal's chest.

"Sweetheart?" He kissed Alp's head. "We have to get ready."

"Five more minutes" came the whimpered voice.

No way could Mal hold back the smile.

The knock sounded again, followed by a whispered, "Mal." It was Cece.

Mal disentangled himself from Alp, then pulled the covers up to his chin. He smiled down at his mate when he snuggled in the warmth. Maker, he loved Alp so.

He went to the door and pulled it open. Cece stood there, dressed for a fight. She wore a dark T-shirt, a belt around her cargo pants that held two guns, a TAC vest that covered her from chin to belt. She had goggles strapped around her neck. One thing was certain: she was ready for war.

"What's up?" he asked.

"It's time to go." She peered over his shoulder at Alp. "I really think you should leave him here. This won't be any place for him."

She wasn't wrong, but.... "I'd give anything to keep him out of the fight, but he deserves to be there. He needs to see this through, to find out that the man who tortured him is dead and that I'm the one who killed him. I can't keep this closure from him."

She gave a grim nod. "I understand. It's just... he's so sweet and pure. Even after everything, he's innocent in so many ways. We're not. We're wolves and warriors. We will kill with no compunction, then go out and have some beers and celebrate the slaughter. Alp might think he wants this, but—"

"But he does," Alp said, sitting up. "I want—*need*—to see Hyde pay for this," he exclaimed, holding up his arm. "To see the Maker punish him for what he's done to her children. I know you're all instruments of that retribution, and even though I hate it, I'm sure it's what has to be."

"I could make you stay," Cece said, her eyes flinty gray.

"You could try," Alp tossed back. "I won't be left behind." His gaze flicked too Mal. "Not for anything."

She sighed "You're a stubborn brat," she told Alp. "Why is it everyone in my life does what I tell them, except you?"

Mal threw his hands up. "Welcome to my world. My mate won't do a damn thing he's told." He strode to Alp, who'd sat up and was pulling on his clothes, bent, and kissed him on the neck, delighting in the squeak. "And I wouldn't have him any other way."

"Then let's go," she said. "We have to get ready."

Mal dressed and followed behind her, with Alp bringing up the rear. As soon as they exited their room, they saw the sea of shifters, all checking one another to ensure they were set to go.

"Are you all using guns?" Alp asked.

"No, sugar," Cece replied. "This fight is personal, so the weapons of choice will be claws and teeth. The guns are there in case we need them. Our people can fight in either form. If something happens, they'll shift to start repairing the damage, but then they'll swap to the guns so they can continue. We'll have a central hub of operations where we'll leave the gear, but for now, we're ensuring everything is as it should be.

"Plus, we have some noncombatants who will have weapons should they need them. They'll be setting up a triage station to deal with any injuries that come in. We'll leave two guards with them, but in the expected chaos, anything could happen."

Alp swallowed hard. Mal could tell he was conflicted about taking Lydia into this. "Can't we leave Lydia behind?" Alp asked, obviously worried for their friend.

"We could, but we only have one healer, and Lydia would be a great asset. It's up to Mal how we proceed. She's his, so what he says goes."

"No," Mal replied, putting a hand on Alp's shoulder. "He was there. He's seen what they've been doing. I have to trust in him to guide me in this."

Alp pressed into Mal's touch. "Thank you, First," he said, his voice cracking. "I don't want to take her, but Cece is right. We need everyone we can, and as much as I hate the idea, Lydia wants to go, and we will definitely need her help."

"Okay, then, let's ride," Mal said, slapping his hip. When he saw how Alp and Cece were staring at him, he grinned. "What? I've always wanted to say that."

Cece shook her head and led the way to where the gathering was taking place.

Mal drew in a breath.

It was time to go to war.

CHAPTER 18

DAMON CALLED the wolves and bears into a huddle, then gave them their final instructions. Mal listened, wanting to know things were going according to plan.

"I will designate two teams. One is going to trail behind the truck to see where they go. If they've got houses nearby, I want to know. If they're staying together, I want to know that too. Then, after the attack starts, another team will allow a few of them to escape so we know where they go, in case it's somewhere other than their places. Kern and Davis, you'll be the ones who keep watch. When they get to whatever hole they're heading for, you call and tell me. Do *not* try to handle this on your own, unless I tell you otherwise. We don't know how many people they've got, so you're to watch and report. Is that understood?"

"Yes, First," they both replied.

"Where's Lydia?" Alp asked, scanning for his friend.

"They're setting up to deal with casualties. Once we breach the complex and can clear an area, she and our healer will be led to a secure location where we can protect her and our own people." Damon glanced over to Mal. "Malachi? Do you have anything to say before we go in?"

Mal pulled Alp along behind him, striding forward until they got to the center of the crowd. "This is my mate, Alp. We're here to rescue the shifters who are being tortured, much like he was. While we will grieve at the loss of life, we cannot—will not—allow these monsters to hurt anyone else. Stay safe, be cautious, but don't show mercy."

Damon clapped him on the shoulder. "Well said." He faced his people. "Now, if the timetable Malachi gave us from his visit here is still accurate, they should start changing shifts in the next thirty minutes. I want you all to gather your groups and be ready to move as soon as that door opens. Any questions?" One shifter raised his hand, and Damon's brows shot up. "Squire?"

"Yes, sir. I was wondering what we'll be doing for dinner tonight? That stuff we had yesterday was deelish! I especially liked those little burgers."

A laugh rolled through the group, breaking the tension.

"Hopefully we'll have time to eat. We don't know what we're going to find in there, and this might take us days to sort out. I'll have a better answer for you once we get the information." Damon grinned. "If that's okay with you."

Squire snapped to attention. "Yes, sir!"

"Then gather with your groups. Group leaders, prep your teams. Good luck, and may the Maker be on our side this day."

Those gathered broke into smaller groups. Mal could hear the thrum of conversation as they gave out additional orders to their people. Damon pulled Mal and Alp to the side, his expression grim.

"I'm glad you gave us the lay of the land, Malachi. It's going to be tricky getting in undetected thanks to those cameras."

"Agreed, but I like the idea of swarming in. Once we get inside, we can cut any feeds. I still think the element of surprise is ours. I mean, who's going to expect the pack to descend on them?"

"From your lips to the Maker's ears," Damon murmured, glancing around.

"Are you looking for Cece?" Alp asked.

He gave Alp a look that screamed *duh.*

When he placed a hand on Damon's arm, Alp got a narrowed-eyes look. "She's the most competent and confident person I've ever known, beside Mal. She is obviously your other half, and the two of you are lucky to have found each other."

Damon's gaze softened. "Thank you. She and the boys are my world. I always lived for my pack, until Cece showed me there was more to life. Now? I thank the Maker every day I have them, and I would do anything to keep them." He let out a long, slow breath. "I know she's here to watch over me. She's our best fighter, and I feel better having her here, but the thought I could lose her? It scares the crap out of me."

"You want to get a roll of bubble wrap and shove her in it, so no one or nothing can touch her," Mal said, his voice husky, but his gaze locked on Alp.

"Yes," Damon hissed. "I want to rip out the throat of anyone who comes near her. When she approached me about allowing the two bears into our pack, I was against it. She sat me down, took my hand in hers, and explained to me that they'd been assigned to guard their leader's children. They failed. For that, their leader had them beaten within the scantest bit of their lives and left them out in the snow to die. Cece came upon them while she was running, and by herself, she dragged them back to where she'd parked. She wrestled them into the truck and brought them to me."

Mal couldn't imagine anything worse than failing your leader. Then again, he'd done it. He bailed on Damon, and though the man said it had been what he wanted, that didn't soothe Mal at all.

"At first, I refused to get involved. I told her they weren't wolves and she should have left them to die. The look I got from her was so fucking cold, it chilled me to my soul. She told me in no uncertain terms that if wolves were supposed to be the fucking pinnacle as I'd claimed, then we damn well better start realizing that being on top meant taking care of those below us, not abandoning them. She was so mad, I had to...." He sighed. "She told me she couldn't stand to look at me and made me sleep in the spare room. She didn't talk to me for four days, during which time she tended to Ivan and Teddy by herself. Seeing her, watching as she cared for these two men, I came to realize I was wrong and, as always, she was right.

"I marched into that room, took the towels from her, and insisted she go get some rest, because I'd been told she hadn't slept more than an hour here and there while she tended to her new boys. She told me that what their leader did to them was a death sentence and that she wasn't going to have it, so I needed to, and I quote, fuck off, because she wouldn't leave the bears alone. I told her they wouldn't be, that I would care for them myself. She smiled at me, gave me a kiss, and everything in me settled once more.

"Now that I think back on it, I'm ashamed. What good is it for us to hold ourselves as an example, when we—I—was treating people so shabbily?" He blew out a breath. "For six years, they've been exemplary pack members. They do what they're told without hesitation, and they're nothing but kind and gentle with everyone. I could have missed out on that because of my stubbornness."

When Damon's cheeks pinked, Mal knew he'd seen his mate.

"Go on, talk with her. Tell her you love her. If this is the last chance any of us have, the words shouldn't go unspoken."

He nodded, then strode off in her direction.

Mal took the opportunity to pull Alp into his body. He inhaled his mate's scent, pulling the precious smell into every pore of his being. "Alp, I—"

Before he could continue, Alp clutched the back of Mal's neck and pulled him into a scorching kiss. Mal put his hands on Alp's ass and lifted him from the ground, never breaking contact. Alp opened for him, and Mal swept his tongue inside, tasting the sweetness of his mate.

"I love you," Alp whispered. "So very fucking much. If this is our last day, I—"

"This is not our last day," Mal growled. "I won't let it be. Nothing on the Maker's earth will keep me away from you," he vowed, even though he knew it was one he shouldn't be making. He couldn't control what was going to happen. He wasn't even sure the Maker could.

Alp stroked Mal's cheek. "Regardless, I love you," he affirmed. "You are, without a doubt, the best thing that's ever happened to me."

He grinned. "Well, maybe second. My mom makes some wicked carrot ice cream."

They stood there, Mal holding Alp to him, feeling their hearts beating together.

If he was to die, this, this moment, the two of them becoming closer than Mal thought was possible, was worth it.

ALP SAT in the back of one of the trucks, along with a lot of other men. They sat, grim-faced, their gazes locked on the floor. When he looked around, he noticed Ivan and Teddy huddled together, their lips moving. He got up and walked to where they were seated. "You guys okay?" he asked.

Teddy jerked his head up. "Yes, we're fine," he replied, but there was no confidence there.

Alp sat next to them. "You can talk to me, you know."

Ivan shook his head, and Teddy turned away, but not before Alp noticed the sheen of tears.

"Are you afraid? Is that it?"

Ivan snarled. "We are not afraid!"

"Then what?" Alp pushed.

Teddy sighed and looked up at his brother. "Tell him," he said. "If we are to die today, it would be good to get it off our chests.'"

Concern flashed across Ivan's face. "Are you sure?"

A quick nod.

Ivan leaned in, his face near Alp's. "We failed our leader. Because of us, his family died. It is something we can never make right."

"How did it happen?"

A whimper slid out of Teddy's throat, and he squeezed his eyes shut tight.

Ivan wrapped an arm around his brother's shoulder and pulled him in close. "Teddy and I were guarding the perimeter. We watched throughout the night and never knew anything had happened until the alarm was raised. By then it was too late." He sighed. "We were dragged before our leader, who accused us of dereliction of duty. The thing was, we weren't. We never strayed from our post, and we were vigilant throughout the night."

"He had us stripped," Teddy whispered. "Then he forced us to shift into our human forms and beat us. Neither of us cried out or asked him to stop. Our lives were forfeit, and we understood that. He didn't kill us, though. When he tired of the beating, he had his people lock us away in a small room. After what seemed like several days, he came back and ordered them to drag us behind the truck, then dumped us in the forest. We lay there as snowflakes covered our naked bodies, waiting to die. That was where the First's made found us."

"She is a goddess," Ivan said, clutching his brother's hand. "After she made sure we mended, we told her what we'd done, and she said it didn't matter, we were hers now and we were safe. She protected us. She gave us purpose again. She trusted us to look after her sons, her mate. We cannot fail her, not like we did our own people."

"I keep telling you, brother. Cece said we did not fail." Teddy peered up at Alp. "We heard later that someone in our sleuth, angry over something our leader did, snuck in at night and attacked his family. We never detected an enemy because he was one of us."

"It doesn't matter," Teddy moaned, burying his face in Ivan's chest, weeping. "They still ended up dead, and there is no way for us to erase that stain from our past. Cece and Damon have been good to us. They treat us as part of their pack. We owe them our lives."

"I don't think Cece sees it that way," Alp said. "As shifters, we are supposed to care for each other. No shifter, from the tiniest hedgehog to the largest whale, is better than another. That's the lesson she was trying to impart."

"No," the men said together. "We owe them, and we will serve them for as long as we live," Ivan finished. "This is a debt of blood and honor."

"I would never try to tell you otherwise," Alp insisted. "But maybe talk with Cece to see what she expects from you. What you're doing is good and decent, but what about finding someone to love? Raising families of your own? How does that fit into the lives you're planning on living?"

The men looked at each other, and Alp could see the pain and indecisiveness in their expressions.

"Talk to Cece," he said. "Don't put your life on hold for no reason." He gestured toward the front of the truck. "If nothing else, this should show you that tomorrow is never promised, so you need to make the most of what you can today." He stood and patted their shoulders. "Just think about it," Alp said, before going back to his seat.

He watched for a few moments as they talked, gesturing to each other. Alp had no idea what would happen once they got to the labs, but he had given some good advice. He told Mal he loved him, and that was enough. If he had to go meet the Maker, he'd do it knowing he had been a good person—mostly—and lived a—mostly—good life.

And that was enough.

CHAPTER 19

THE NERVOUS ENERGY that rolled off Alp was enough to make Mal's stomach churn. He could feel every bit of the fear that Alp did, and it showed Mal once again how strong his bunny was. If Mal's heart was hammering the way Alp's was, he'd turn tail and run as far and as fast as his legs would carry him. Not Alp, though. Even on the brink of a full-blown panic attack, Alp stayed, and pride swelled in Mal's chest.

"It's nearly time," Cece whispered. "Damon is hidden behind the shack. As soon as the door opens, he, Ivan, and Teddy will go inside to ensure they can't lock us out. Once they're done, we will all rush in and...." She peered at Alp. "Do what we need to."

"Kill them," Alp snapped. "Don't try to sugarcoat it. That's beneath you."

He put a finger in his mouth and nibbled on the nail. Mal took the hand in his and held it tight.

"Alp? Sweetheart?" Cece cooed. "No one here wants to do this. I know you think we're all slavering beasts who can't wait to rip the throat out of these people, but that's not us. We're the mother who is willing to lay down her life to ensure her pups will grow up safe. We're the father who is willing to kill to protect his family. We're the bears who seek redemption for a crime that wasn't theirs. Don't you think we'd all rather be home, curled up in front of the fire with our families? Micah has a thing at school tonight, and I'd much rather be in the audience listening to him sing. He's not talented, but he is enthusiastic.

"And that's what I'd be doing if I wasn't here. Wrapping my arms around Micah, telling him how much I loved his voice. Instead, I'm here, ensuring that his voice will continue to be heard for years to come. I don't kill indiscriminately, but to protect my family, the one I've created from our pack? The one that you're now a part of? Yes, Alp. I will do *anything* for them, including ending the lives of those who threaten them."

Mal shivered to hear the coldness in Cece's voice. He'd never known her to be so strident.

"Cece? What's wrong with you?"

She glared at him "Wrong with me? Not one goddamn thing is *wrong*, Malachi. Do you mean about how different I am? Let me tell you, and then you can say you don't understand. When Micah was born, I held him in my arms. I peered into those beautiful eyes of his, and I vowed I would do whatever the hell I had to in order to keep him safe. Wiley? He's going to be the First, which means he'll have advisors and the shifter council looking out for him. Micah? As the second son, he has me. I'm the one who is going to stand between him and the world, reminding him that his destiny isn't linked to his brother's. That he'll forge a future of his own. And it's not just Micah. I'll do it for any of my pack. I don't care if they're wolves or bears...." Her gaze drifted to Alp. "Or bunny rabbits. Tell me you don't understand."

Her words gripped Mal. Until that day in the woods, he'd never killed a human. Beat the shit out of them, sure. That night, knowing he had to protect the rabbit? He didn't feel a single twinge of regret or remorse. He'd never even wondered why. Now? What Cece said told Mal everything. He was the one meant to protect Alp, to stand for him when the world let him down. The one who would slaughter every human in that lab because they'd dared to touch what was Mal's.

"No, I do understand," he ground out, his throat scratchy. "And

I'm good with going in there and doing what we have to. I don't like it, but you're right. We're protecting what belongs to us." He reached out and stroked a hand over Alp's head, centering himself. "I'm sorry, Alp. I won't let them ever hurt you or anyone else again. Like Lydia said, we didn't go after them, they brought it to us, and we have every right to protect ourselves, by whatever means is necessary."

Alp gave a terse nod. "No, you're both right. I'm not meant for fighting. I'd prefer to run and hide away. That's what I was trying to do the night Mal found me. I was so goddamn scared, because I knew I'd die here. I would never see my parents again or be with any of my family. Now, after hearing what you said, I realize that the others in there have to be feeling the same thing. They need protectors who are willing to make the hard calls and do what's necessary to ensure they can get out of there and see the fucking sunlight again." He winced. "I guess my mom was right. Make it hurt."

"No," Cece said, slipping her arms around Alp's shoulders. "We're not here to inflict pain. We won't make anyone suffer needlessly. We'll do our best to make their deaths quick. Unlike them, we're not psychotic sons of bitches." She grinned. "Well, okay. Damon is a son of a bitch, I guess. So are my boys."

And the chuckle that slipped from Alp made Mal more certain than ever that this was what he needed to do for his mate. Cece was right. They were shifters, but they weren't as cruel as some humans.

Except for Hyde. Him Mal would make suffer and scream for what he did to Alp.

What he'd taken from Mal's mate.

As soon as the ramp opened and the truck pulled out, three shadows rushed inside the complex. With his sensitive hearing, Alp detected the cry of a human that was quickly silenced. Moments later, Damon's head popped up, and en masse the wolves rushed for the opening. It no longer mattered if someone saw them, because they'd be dead shortly after.

"Let's go," Mal said, grabbing Alp's hand.

He led Alp down the ramp, and with every step, Alp's anxiety soared. Why had he said he wanted to come? He should have done the smart thing and listened to Mal. Had he ever done the smart thing? Not that Alp could recall.

They took several turns, Mal leading Alp deeper into the complex. Around them were shouts, screams, pleading, and the sound of flesh and bone being torn into.

They came to one of the labs where two big men stood guard, their pistols at the ready. Mal pushed his way into the large room. Inside, Lydia was putting bandages, needles, and other accoutrements out on trays. She glanced up as they entered, then gave them a curt nod. Her face was pale, and Alp could see she was trembling. He rushed to her and threw his arms around her waist.

"I'm so sorry," he breathed out.

She shook her head. "No, don't be. I signed on for this, and knew what I was getting into."

It was then Alp smelled it. The overpowering scent of vomit.

"Are you okay?" he asked.

"Nope. Won't lie, this is worse than I ever imagined. I keep hearing the growls and the screams and...." She squeezed Alp harder. "How the hell did you make it through this?" she asked, her voice shaky.

"It wasn't easy," Alp admitted. "Hearing all this, it makes me think that I'm back here, stuck in that fucking pen, listening as they conduct their fucked-up experiments."

Before Lydia could reply, a shot rang out, followed by a howl that echoed down the cavernous halls.

"Fuck," Mal grunted. "They've brought out the guns. Alp, stay here."

But Mal was going to die. Alp knew it. He'd seen it.

"No. I'm going where you go. That's what you said, remember? Shift and let's get moving."

A scowl, a terse nod, and Mal stripped out of his clothes. A moment after that, he stood in his wolf form as the two guards came inside, carrying another wolf with blood matting its fur.

"Hind quarters, losing blood. Can you handle this?" the one snapped, his gaze never wavering from the wolf.

"Lay him down here," Lydia replied, pointing at the table as she grabbed her instruments.

"Do you need me to stay?" Alp asked.

She shook her head, her eyes locked on her patient. "You'd be in the way. Go."

Alp did as Mal had and stripped out of his clothes. He shifted, listed a bit until he figured out his balance, then hopped to Mal. The guard opened the door, and Mal was off like a bolt, with Alp doing his best to follow. When they rounded the corner, they came upon two women and a man. He was barking orders at them, and the women were scrambling to obey.

"You two, get inside the fucking lab and find something to barricade the—"

Mal growled, and it went straight through Alp. These people were about to die. Before they could react, Mal was on them. He locked his jaws around the man's throat, the crunch loud in the nearly empty hall. One of the women cried out, turned, and tried to run, but Mal was faster. He was on her, and before she could scream, he ripped out the back of her neck, her spine snapping. When he turned toward the other, she got up and backed toward the corner.

"Please, God, no. Don't let me—"

Those were her final words as Mal surged forward, knocking her to the floor. True to his word, she didn't suffer as he tore open her throat. The spray of blood, followed by the gurgle, lasted only a few seconds before the light went out of her eyes. When Mal faced Alp, his muzzle was coated in the blood of the people he'd killed. Alp hopped closer, only to squeak as a bullet hit the wall near him.

Mal, turning to face the new threat, pulled back his lips and showed off the fangs that were already crimson. The guy who'd shot, his hands shook so bad, he couldn't even aim a second time. He cried out when Mal mowed him down. His screams, echoing in the hall, were cut short.

As soon as the man was dead, Mal shifted even as he turned back to Alp. He picked him up and held him close. "Are you okay? Did he hit you?"

The protectiveness comforted Alp, as Mal rubbed his face along Alp's fur. When he seemed satisfied that Alp was okay, only then did he put him back down. Throughout the corridors, the screams, the gunshots, and the horrific sounds of people being slaughtered continued, but Mal ignored it, instead directing his attention to Alp.

Alp's nose twitched as a familiar scent washed over him. Blood, urine, death. After six years of terror, Alp knew it as well as he knew his own. Hyde was nearby. Alp reeled. In truth, he'd thought he'd never have to face Hyde. Someone, somewhere should have already come across him and taken him out. But Hyde knew the complex inside and out, and probably had a dozen scenarios if trouble should ever arise. As much as he hated it, Alp had to admit, Hyde wasn't stupid.

"Alp?"

Mal's voice pulled Alp away from the thoughts dragging him down. Now he worried about Mal, because his death was coming closer.

Alp shifted and grabbed Mal. "You have to run. Go back to Lydia, or leave this place," he begged, not caring how it sounded.

"What? No, I'm not leaving. What's going—?" His head twisted and Mal glared down the corridor. His features blurred. He was nearing a shift. "He's here, isn't he?" The voice came out low, guttural, dangerous.

"Yes. Please, just go. Let someone else—"

Mal turned back, his face an icy mask of anger and pain in equal parts. "Listen to me. We'll find someone who can take you back to safety while I—"

"No!" Alp cried out, then winced. Too loud. Much too loud. *Be a quiet bunny, Alp. Don't fuss and it won't hurt so badly. Just let us do what we need to, and everything will be okay.*

That voice in his head drowned out everything else. All Alp could remember now was the saw. The pain. His hand as Hyde lifted, so gentle and so careful, before he put it into the specimen container.

"You've done a great service, Alp. Your sacrifice will help so many humans. And when it grows back, it'll help even more."

"It won't grow back," Alp screamed.

"It will," Hyde said, sounding utterly certain. "My research tells me—"

It came out of Alp then. A keening wail that had the others in the room covering their ears. Then the jab in his arm, and the world slowly squeezed down into a pinprick of light. Now the world was floating, and Alp was being taken along for the ride. It wasn't so bad, he decided. This feeling, this euphoria. It was all kinda nice.

Rough hands grabbed Alp by the scruff of his neck and shoved him back inside the fetid cage before the door was slammed and locked. Alp lay there, on the damp cloths, and licked his wounded leg, doing something he'd never done before. Praying for death.

"Alp!"

Mal's voice. No, it couldn't be. Mal was dead. Alp had seen it. Hyde killed Mal. So much blood, and it was all Alp's fault, because he'd brought Mal to this place. *Maker, please don't let Mal hate me.*

"Alpin Dawkins!"

His mother shook him, but she sounded like Mal. She was another person who had to hate him. He'd disappeared and made her and the family worry for six years, all because Alp couldn't sit still. Couldn't be happy with the life he had. Why did he have to alienate everyone? All his siblings were over-the-moon thrilled to be home with their growing families. The warren was full to bursting with love, but Alp had never wanted it. Never felt it like they did. Was he broken because he wanted something else?

Strong hands wrestled Alp from where he was. The scents were growing stronger. Hyde was coming for Alp! He shifted, hoping to run, but he was pushed into a room and the door was almost closed, giving Alp the chance to look out. Instead, he backed into the corner, then lay there, panting hard, knowing that if anyone heard him, he'd die.

Mal would die. Alone. So much blood. So much fear. Too much. Gotta get away. Have to run. To hide.

Mal would die.

Alone.

Mal would die.

And it would be Alp's fault.

CHAPTER 20

EVEN IN THE STORAGE CLOSET, Mal could taste Alp's fear. Why the fuck had Mal agreed to bring him? Alp's heart was hammering so hard, Mal was afraid his mate was about to have a heart attack. He should have forced him to stay behind. He was the fucking First—it was his duty to protect his mate, even when said mate didn't want to be coddled and kept safe.

The acrid scent was drawing closer, and Mal could understand why Alp was finding it so hard to be near it. Even under the layers of soap, the reek of death and decay was obvious, and no amount of soap or showers could hide that fact from a shifter. How many murders had this man committed? How many shifter lives were lost in the name of his perverted science? Even without knowing what he'd done to Alp, Mal couldn't doubt that this man was a monster.

Mal saw him then, scurrying down the hall. In his mind, Mal had built Hyde up to be a threat unlike any other. A creature of monstrous proportions who would fight tooth and nail, leaving the outcome of their battle in doubt. The truth was something far different.

He was a nondescript little man with a rounded belly hidden beneath a crisp white lab coat, thinning gray hair, and a set of glasses he had to keep pushing up on his somewhat bulbous nose. Then Mal noticed it. Despite all the sounds, the scents of the dead, the sheer terror in the air, Hyde seemed mostly unaffected. Yes, there was anxiety, but not the overwhelming dread most of the other humans seemed to be experiencing.

It didn't matter. This man—this monster—was about to die under Mal's jaws. He would rip the asshole apart, limb by limb, and relish the taste of the blood as it spurted over his tongue, the screams of agony that would send jolts of pleasure through Mal, and when Hyde finally died, Alp would be—Alp. Mal had told Alp they weren't monsters. If he killed Hyde, that was one thing. If he took revenge against the man, that would scare Alp, and Mal couldn't have that.

A quick, clean kill. That was what he needed. Something that would put Alp's mind at rest, knowing the dark thing that haunted his dreams was no more. It didn't matter how Mal felt, Alp was the one who'd been hurt, and it was his feelings that were important.

Hyde moved slowly down the hall, casting furtive glances left and right. He obviously hadn't seen Mal yet. When he got near the room, he turned and started to head down the hall. No way was Mal about to blow this chance to get closure for Alp. He yanked open the door.

Hyde spun on his heel, his blue eyes narrowed. "You're one of them," he snapped.

"Gee, what gave it away?" Mal snarled, flexing his fingers, itching to eviscerate the son of a bitch. "The fact that I'm standing here, naked? Or is it the blood covering me? None of which is mine, by the way."

The tensing of muscles let Mal know that Hyde was going to try and bolt, but that wasn't going to happen. He gripped Hyde's lab coat and jerked him back. He should do it now, here in the hall. Snap his neck like a dried twig, then go in, pull Alp into his arms, and let him know the nightmare was finally over.

But Alp had said he wanted to look Hyde in the eyes and let him know he wasn't afraid, and he wanted to see the dawning of his impending death when it hit Hyde. He dragged Hyde into the lab, staying far enough away from the room Alp was hidden in where he could see, but not be seen.

He glanced toward the closet, and in that distracted moment, Hyde struck.

"Mal!"

Alp watched, horrified, as Hyde slammed a needle into Mal's neck, pressing the plunger. When Mal's grip slackened, Hyde jerked away. Mal stiffened a moment, then stumbled. He shook his head and stalked toward Hyde, his lips curled back into a snarl.

"You hurt Alp," he ground out. "What you're doing here is horrifying, but I'm going to kill you because of what you did to my mate."

Hyde scrambled back, keeping just out of Mal's reach. "This is science," he snapped. "We have to make sacrifices."

"Humans—children—are not sacrifices!" Mal shouted.

"If a few animals die for the betterment of mankind, then it's worth it in the end. Your *mate* is no different than any other animal we've experimented on."

Mal slammed his fist into a steel examination table, launching it across the floor where it slammed into a cabinet, shattering the glass and sending the instruments crashing to the tiles.

"Alp is a fucking human being!"

Hyde smirked. "But he's not, is he? None of you really are. You play the part well, but we both know it's nothing but pretend."

Alp noticed that Mal was moving slower now, and though he wanted to do something, it was as if roots had sprung from his feet and were holding him in place.

"I'm saddened that we need their help. I truly wish we didn't have to harm anything, but for mankind to move forward, we need knowledge. And the things we've learned from examining these creatures? It's remarkable. Who knows where this research might lead? We could be able to make medicines to stave off aging, we might learn how to make vaccines that will save tens of thousands of lives, or we could unlock the secrets of how to regrow limbs. In the end, anything we've done here will be hailed as nothing short of miraculous."

Mal howled his rage, and it sent shivers zipping up Alp's spine. He could feel Mal's despair, and the force of it nearly knocked Alp back. It was like a living thing, writhing and slithering inside Mal, tearing him up.

"We are fucking human beings, you psychotic son of a bitch." He moved closer. "Alp is a human being," he ground out, his voice dropping low and getting more gravelly.

"He's a rabbit, nothing more, nothing less," Hyde snapped. "He's no different than the ones cosmetics are tested on. No, I take that back. He's better, because he mimics human attributes."

Another step, and Mal's knees buckled. Hyde gave him a creepy-as-fuck smile as Mal slid to the floor, his chest heaving.

"Oh, I should have mentioned, another thing that we discovered? How to protect ourselves against your kind. That venom? When we heard there were aquatic shifters, that opened up new avenues of research. Marine life is so vast and varied, it was incredible. Then we discovered a box jellyfish shifter, and from his sacrifice, we learned how to bring your kind to heel." He knelt next to Mal and patted his chest. "Hard to breathe, isn't it? The venom's toxins can cause extreme pain, paralysis, delirium, shock, cardiac arrest, and even death within minutes. Box jellyfish are among the deadliest of animals. Each one has enough venom to kill sixty adults. In all our testing, not one of your kind survived. Now, tell me how any creature that deadly is remotely human."

Mal clutched his throat, gasping for air, his skin paling. His gaze, defiant at always, stayed locked on Hyde.

"Consider this your contribution to my experiments," Hyde said. "Will your accelerated healing allow you to survive this? I think the results will be fascinating."

Alp's heart sundered as he watched Mal's breathing become shallower, harsher. Why couldn't he move? When Mal's gaze flicked to him, rage poured into Alp. He couldn't move because he was fucking terrified of Hyde. Of what the man would do if he got hold of Alp again. And while he stood there, useless, Mal was dying.

"No!" screamed Alp, slamming against the door and throwing it open against the wall with a bang.

Hyde's head snapped in Alp's direction, and a slow smile spread over his face. "You came back. I knew you would."

Alp took in the room and saw what he needed lying beside the overturned table. He made a mad dash for it and snatched the gleaming knife from the floor. Fucking Hyde could not have Mal! Not now, not ever!

Alp stood and launched himself at Hyde, who stumbled back. There was fear in his eyes, and Alp relished it.

"You tortured me for six fucking years. You took my hand, and I'm going to have to live with that for the rest of my life. The worst thing? You're trying to kill my mate." He slashed at Hyde, barely missing him. Hyde crabwalked backward, but Alp wasn't about to let him get away. Yeah, he wanted to go to Mal, but if Hyde escaped, he'd be taking shifter secrets with him, which would allow him to start this shit again in another location. Alp knew in his heart that Mal would want him to stop Hyde before anything else.

"Help!" Hyde screamed as he hit the wall behind him.

"Help? Do you know how many times I wanted to do that? To yell for someone to help me? To save me? And those so-called animals? Their screams were the same. They wanted, no, they *needed* someone to come to their rescue." Alp stalked toward Hyde, the surgical blade gleaming in the light. "And that's the ones who could actually speak. The children? How could they understand what was happening to them? Or worse, *why* it was happening."

He stood over Hyde, who now had his hands drawn to his chest, tears sliding down his cheeks. Any other time, Alp might have had sympathy, but that died years ago. He raised the knife and slammed it down into Hyde's shoulder, eliciting a scream that shot through Alp, causing him to let go of the knife and scurry back. This wasn't him. He wasn't a killer. Blood poured from Hyde's wound, and he pushed a hand on it to staunch the bleeding.

It would be so simple to finish the job, but Mal needed him, and

Alp couldn't forget his mate. He turned to find Cece behind him, her gorgeous red fur matted with blood.

"I'm sorry," he whispered, stroking a hand over her face. "I can't kill him. Oh, Maker, I want to. I really do."

She morphed back to human and gripped Alp's shoulder. "We all have a role in the Maker's plan," she said gently. "Yours isn't to take a life." She started to shift, her snout elongating, her fingers becoming claws. Still, she could speak, and that was incredible. "That's my job," she said with a deep snarl. She turned to Hyde. "I've seen what you've done. Found the bodies. The children you've murdered. I know I told Alp we weren't monsters, but this time that's totally what I plan on being."

She was a wolf again, the remainder of the shift so fast, Alp barely realized it. Then she lunged at Hyde, sinking her fangs into his face, pinning him to the tiled floor. The wail that came from the man would haunt Alp's dreams as Cece savaged him, with Hyde flailing as he tried to escape Cece's wolf. She was huge and incredibly fast. Hyde never stood a chance against her. Blood spattered the floor and walls as she bit him repeatedly, viciously. Finally, blessedly, Hyde's screams were silent. And though it hadn't been him who killed the man, Alp still looked at his corpse and found the anger he'd carried for so long now sliding out of him.

"Malachi!" came the growl from behind them.

Alp turned and found Damon beside Mal, his hands on Mal's chest, compressing it. A cold seeped into Alp. He knew Mal was dead. He'd dreamed it. And the blood he'd seen? That was Hyde's. Everything was coming true.

"Alp, get the fuck over here," Damon snapped.

"What can I do?" Cece asked, hurrying to stand beside her mate. Her face was coated in Hyde's blood, giving her a macabre mask.

"Find Gwyneth and that woman vet," he told her. "Tell them Mal needs help."

Cece tore off naked down the hall, calling out for this Gwyneth person. Alp hustled to Mal's side and burst into tears at the sight of him lying there, not breathing. His mate, his only one, was dead.

"Fucking get it together, Alp," Damon snapped. "I need you to pinch his nose and blow into his mouth. You need to count for me. Every thirty, you give him two breaths. Do you understand?"

Alp nodded mutely.

"Goddamn it, Alp! Do you understand, or are you going to be fucking useless? If you can't help me, then get the fuck out of my way."

That snapped Alp out of his daze. Damon was trying to help Mal, and Alp needed to do whatever he could to assist. "No, I can do it," he said.

"Good man," Damon said softly as he pressed on Mal's chest.

When he hit thirty, Alp pinched Mal's nose and puffed air into his lungs. This went on for several long minutes, with no changes. Damon, however, wasn't giving up. He was like a man possessed, and that helped keep Alp focused.

"Damon!" Cece called out, hurrying around the corner with another woman behind her. Where Cece was bigger and wider, the mate of a First wolf, more like an Amazon princess, Gwyneth was a slender woman, with golden hair who seemed to glow with an internal light. She held Lydia's hand, guiding her to the room.

"What happened?" Lydia asked, dropping to her knees beside Alp.

Alp told them what Hyde had said about the toxin.

"The man is—" Gwyneth looked over at Hyde's rapidly cooling corpse, not even flinching at the trauma. "Was an idiot." She reached into her bag and drew out a hypodermic. After taking off the top, she told everyone to step back. When they did, she plunged the needle into Mal's heart, and Alp screamed.

"Oh, hush, you baby. It's adrenaline to help restart his heart," she snapped, her brusque tone standing in stark contrast to her ethereal beauty. She gestured to Lydia. "I need you, the First, and his mate to help hold Malachi down." She peered at Alp. "You need to come over here and put your head on his chest, right above his heart."

"But—"

"Do as I say, damn it!"

Everyone scrambled to follow her directions. Cece and Lydia each took an arm, while Damon knelt on Mal's legs. Alp whimpered as he lay his head where Gwyneth instructed, because there was no heartbeat. No sign of life. How would he explain to his mother that he'd allowed his mate to be killed? That he'd stood there, useless, as Mal took his last breaths. It would have been better if Alp had died, because then Mal would still be alive.

A wheezed breath slid out of Mal, then another, and another. The color was returning to his face. Then Mal was thrashing, the muscles in his thick arms straining. It wasn't hard to see that they were having problems holding him down. Finally, his eyes flew open.

"Alp!" he cried, and it was the sweetest sound Alp had ever heard. He slipped a hand under Mal's neck as he peppered his face with kisses.

"What did you do, Gwyneth?" Damon asked, sitting back, the relief obvious in his voice.

"After giving him the shot, I had Alp lay above Mal's heart, hoping that when Mal started breathing, he'd take the scent of his mate's distress into his lungs, which would speed his healing as he sought to protect him."

Alp looked up and gave her a smile. "Thank you. Thank you all for my mate's life."

Gwyneth smiled at him and stroked long, slender fingers over his cheek. "He's a good wolf, and he's got an amazing mate. Never forget that you are important not only to him, but to all of us. You show that we can live in harmony, no matter what species we are."

Damon smacked Mal on the arm. "Get up, you lazy son of a bitch. We need to start figuring out what to do with all these people."

Though he tried to come off like it was all fine, Alp could hear the tremor in Damon's voice, and he noticed that he was shaking. When Cece came up behind him, Damon flinched, but then leaned into her touch.

Mal tried to sit up but sagged back to the floor. His face, still ashen, crinkled as he winced. "Maybe in five minutes?" he rasped out, his voice sounding as though he'd gargled glass.

Damon traced a finger along Mal's jawline. The gesture was intimate and showed how deep his feelings were for Mal. Not like lovers, but more like a father who cared for his son. Alp was humbled to see it.

"Take all the time you need, kid. We're going to check in with everyone, then get started on the cleanup. Sixty dead humans aren't going to be easy to get rid of, but we'll find a way."

Mal nodded, but then his gaze flicked in Alp's direction. "Alp?"

"Yes, First?" he whispered, too overcome with emotions to hold them in.

Mal tried to raise an arm, but it fell limply at his side. "Lay with me?"

"Of course," Alp said, lying beside Mal and curling an arm around his stomach. "Forever."

CHAPTER 21

THE FIRST THING Mal noticed when he woke was that every fucking part of him hurt. His joints ached and he had a throbbing pain in his head. He tried to sit up, but he simply couldn't work up the strength.

"Mal?" came a sweet voice in his ear.

"Alp," he croaked. "Are you okay?"

A hand brushed over Mal's chest, tangling in the hair as Alp laid his head on top of Mal.

"Is this all right?" Alp asked, his voice whisper-soft and filled with fear.

Mal had to force himself not to wince. Alp's touch burned, the brush of skin on skin more like shards of glass being shoved into Mal, ripping him apart, but it also brought comfort, because this was his mate, who was also seeking comfort from him.

"This is fine," Mal replied. "Though in truth, I can't seem to make my body work enough to hold you in return. However, I love the feeling of you touching me. Of you loving me. And you didn't answer my question. Are you doing okay?"

A sniffle, followed by warmth pooling on Mal's skin. "Honestly? I was so fucking scared. You were dead, and I couldn't do a goddamn thing about it." Alp snorted. "I worried about telling my mom that I'd let you die." Another sniffle. "I stood there and let you die!" he wailed.

Pain seared Mal's muscles as he wrapped his arms around Alp. The need to comfort his mate overrode the sheer agony of moving. "Hey, no. Don't think like that. I was stupid. I figured that Hyde was weak and pathetic and that he knew he was about to die. I didn't think he would have something to use against me. My hubris is what got me.... Well, killed."

"I saw him standing there, and then you went down. I grabbed a knife or scalpel or whatever it was and went after him. I stabbed him, and then I looked into his eyes and saw fear. I wondered if that's how I looked every time they did something to me. Then I realized I couldn't kill him. Even after what he did to you, I couldn't finish the job. You must hate me."

But Mal didn't. Not at all. "The fact that you couldn't kill him makes me love you all the more," he said, inhaling Alp's scent. "What I've noticed about you is you've got a rock-solid core in you. You're amazing and tough. Were you scared? Yeah, but you faced it and stood up to your demons. That says so much about the person you are."

"Cece killed him. She ripped him apart."

At least Mal knew Hyde wouldn't hurt anyone else.

"I should get up," Mal told Alp. "I'm sure there's a lot of work to do."

"The bodies have been removed, and the people Damon let get out have all been tracked down and killed."

What? "How? No way they could have gotten that all done so quickly."

"You've been asleep three days," Alp said. "Except to pee, I haven't left your side at all." He stroked a hand down Mal's chest. "Well, Damon and Cece told me I had to stay here with you, because according to Gwyneth, my scent was helping you to heal. Cece has been bringing me food, but I haven't been able to eat."

"What about the shifters?"

Alp was quiet for a few moments. "There were so many dead," Alp said, and Mal knew his heart was breaking. "According to his notes, Hyde would do his experiments and then kill and dissect his... his victims in order to *learn* even more. Once he was done, he stored the bodies in a freezer in case he needed them again." A snort. "They couldn't even be buried properly. That fucker was a monster."

He was, and Mal found he was unable to work up an iota of sympathy.

"Damon came in earlier and told me that there was an effort underway to get the shifters back to their families, but a lot of them are too young, and there was no real information about where they came from to get them home."

The door opened, and Damon strode in.

"You're awake. I'm glad. We were all worried about you, Malachi."

Mal tried to sit up, and that still wasn't happening. "I'm sorry," he said. "I'm trying to get up, but my body is saying 'no the fuck you ain't.'"

That drew a chuckle. "If you won't listen to your body, listen to your mate and me. No the fuck you ain't getting out of bed. You died, Malachi. I knelt over you as you took your last breath. I watched as Alp fell apart. Gwyneth said if it wasn't for you being a First and having such a strong mate bond, we would not be having this conversation. That toxin is lethal, and by all rights, you should still be... dead."

Damon's lip trembled, and there was a sheen of tears in his eyes. Mal had never seen Damon cry. Alp stood and went to him, taking Damon in his arms. As soon as Alp embraced him, Damon broke down.

"I kept thinking this was on me, because I wanted you to go out and find yourself. That maybe if I had done something different, this wouldn't have happened."

"You'd have taken away something precious to me," Alp said, gazing back at Mal. "I agree this was hard, and I know you and I both feel guilt over it, but there's nothing that can change it."

"I have a question," Mal said. "How is there even a bed in here?"

Alp and Damon both stared down at him as though he was nuts, then looked at each other, and Damon cracked a sad grin.

"Sorry, but he's all yours now," Damon said, patting Alp on the shoulder.

"There are a few beds down here," Alp explained. "This place is enormous."

"I had my guys research it. This used to be a military base fifty or so years ago. They did top-secret stuff here, which is why the townspeople didn't know anything about it. They mothballed it in 1972, and it's sat empty since then. Until Hyde. He wasn't supposed to be here. There was never any record of him having permission to engage in any activity on this premises."

"Which means what?" Mal asked.

"As far as we can determine, Hyde acted on his own. The people he worked with were other doctors and scientists who espoused crackpot theories. He met them online, and they all got to talking. Hyde came up with the idea and found this base in a list of decommissioned properties."

"Where'd he get his money from?"

Damon sighed. "He had money. Before he went off the deep end, Hyde was a respected researcher. He had several patents, which pulled in decent residuals, and could have lived a happy and comfortable life. Then something went wrong. He started talking about people who were really animals. He claimed to have proof, but no one took him seriously. At least no reputable person."

"So what happened?" Alp asked.

When Alp leaned into Damon's space, Mal didn't like it. His mate should only be concerned with him at the moment. Then he tamped down the anger, because this was Damon, who'd helped to save Mal's life. That was a debt that could never be repaid.

"He found likeminded people on the internet. He ventured into some very dark cesspools, and the people there ate his claims up. Over time, Hyde fell in with a group there, each of them former academics who were fired for either unlawful experiments or for promoting antivax, antivirus... hell, antianything. Hyde told them he had plans and promised these others that if they joined him, they could do whatever they wanted, with no government oversight and no moral gray areas because, his emails said, the subjects weren't human."

This time Mal couldn't hold back the growl, but Damon held up a hand to stop him.

"I know, believe me. The only saving grace was the fact that Hyde kept meticulous records. He truly believed this was going to get him back into the esteemed halls of academia—his words, not mine."

"Wow," Alp murmured.

Damon heaved out a sigh. "It gets worse."

That caught Mal's attention. "How the fuck could it get worse?"

"The one who betrayed shifters to Hyde? It was a shifter himself."

"WHAT? NO!" Alp shouted. "That's a sacrosanct rule. No one tells humans about shifters without getting approval from their leader."

Damon winced, and Alp understood.

"Oh. The person *was* a leader. But... why?"

"He wasn't a good leader. He gambled away most of the money he was supposed to be using to run the pack. In the end, he was desperate and made a deal with the devil."

"Who would be so driven to such lengths?" Mal demanded, and Alp could hear the simmering anger in his words.

"I sent Cece home," Damon replied. "She took Ivan and Teddy with her."

"Okay, but why—no." His eyes narrowed, becoming dark slits. "Oh, no fucking way," Mal bit out.

Damon nodded. "I contacted the council with what we found, and they went to the sleuth to look for evidence."

The sleuth? But only bears lived in.... Ivan and Teddy!

"It wasn't Ivan or Teddy," Alp insisted. "They love Cece and would never do anything to hurt her."

"It wasn't them," Damon confirmed. "It was their leader, Hiram, who reached out to Hyde. According to the emails we recovered, one of his people warned him about Hyde after finding the group on the web. Hiram sent a message to Hyde, saying that in exchange for money, he would give Hyde the proof he wanted that shifters were real." This time Damon roared, pouring all manner of rage into the sound. "He fucking offered up his family for money. According to the emails, he told them they needed to go with him. His wife apparently realized something was wrong and fought to protect the kids, and when he figured out he couldn't take them, he killed them instead, so they couldn't tell anyone what he'd done."

"That's why they couldn't scent an enemy. It was their leader all along."

"What's going to happen?" Alp asked.

"Hiram has already been executed" came the grim reply. "For his betrayal of the shifters, plus being complicit in all the deaths Hyde was responsible for. When things went south, Ivan and Teddy were convenient targets. Hiram, thinking he could get out from under this, if only he had someone to point at, found the perfect patsies. His email exchange with Hyde said that he could deliver Ivan and Teddy to Hyde if he was paid, but by now Hyde told him they'd found other means and wouldn't work with him."

Alp shook his head. Greed was something even shifters had to deal with.

"Why'd Cece go home?"

"She wanted to be with the boys. She ostensibly took Ivan and Teddy with her for protection, but also because they're not doing too well after finding out they were basically sacrificial lambs for their leader." Damon smiled. "When someone said they could go back to their sleuth if they wanted to, they said no, they had a home they were happy in. Cece was beside herself."

"But if this Hiram was willing to sacrifice his shifters and ulti-mately kill his mate and children, how did he stay in power?"

Damon rubbed the bridge of his nose. "He asked the council for money to help fund a school. They approved it. Hiram bounced that money around, using it to cover his crimes. The council has egg on its face for never checking on it or catching the lost funds."

"I weep for humanity," Alp grumbled. "Shifter and human alike."

"We're not all bad," Damon said. "But you're right. This paints everyone in a bad light. If the person in charge is corrupt, what does that tell us? What happens if the next one is successful in outing us to the world? And if that occurs, what will become of shifters? I think we'd be deluding ourselves to believe we'd be welcomed with open arms."

Mal had the same thoughts. There could well be humans worse than Hyde, and that scared him. "What did you do with the bodies of the humans?" Mal inquired, needing to get that thought out of his head.

"I think there are some things I can't share. It's better for everyone in the long run if the secrets are kept between as few people as possible."

"What are we going to do about the shifters who have no one to care for them?" Alp posed. "Especially the children."

This time Damon smiled. "I had a few thoughts I'd like to share with you both."

"Go on," Mal said, not altogether certain he liked the way Damon was grinning.

"First off, I'm in talks with the government to buy this property. The people I've spoken with seem only too happy to unload it, and I'm getting it for a fairly reasonable price."

"Why would you want it?"

Damon scrubbed a hand over his face. "This whole thing is a clusterfuck," he admitted. "Between Gwyneth and Lydia, we've barely scratched the surface of what's happened here and our response to it. I've put out a request to the packs looking for people to come here and help out."

That sounded good, but it also led to other questions. "Why here? Wouldn't it be easier to take them back to the packlands?"

"Before she left, Cece spoke with a psychiatrist who is a shifter. She wants to help out, but can't leave her practice to come here. She's offered to do Skype calls whenever she can, and she's also spoken with a few of her friends who are counselors. They've agreed to help out as well."

"That still doesn't explain why here. This place stole their lives from them."

"Yes, but you're forgetting one very important thing. To many of them, this is the only place they know. As awful as it was, there is a sense of familiarity here for them. Maybe as we help them out, the people will be able to heal and step out into the world again."

It was a twisted bit of logic, but Mal could see it making some sense. Better a place you know than to go somewhere totally new and have no idea how to deal with it.

"I was assured by the people who I've spoken with that we'll be able to get this property. When I asked for specs, they told me the complex goes down three stories, and each is connected by stairs, ramps, and elevators. If I had to guess, I'd say Alp made his way outside via one of the ramps. There are many exits for fire safety, but only two main ones for entrance and egress.

"There are hundreds of labs and research rooms. Hyde was only using about ten percent of the space available, so most of the building is untouched, which works in our favor. The whole complex sits beneath forty thousand acres of woods, a lake, and some of the most beautiful fields I've ever seen, full of lush foliage, flowers, and plants bursting with color."

It made Mal think of the day he and Alp had lain beside the lake and Alp had come to him, then shifted.

"I've also spoken with the Firsts and leaders of several packs. They're all horrified that this happened, and worse, that no one knew about it. Hyde made people disappear, and no one questioned it. The leaders have pledged money and people to help get this place fixed up. They're sending an advance team to see what needs to be done, but they're figuring if things are in good shape, it'll take a month or so to do it all. If they work section by section, at least people would have a place to live. There are three full kitchens, and several smaller ones throughout the building, so that'll help. The equipment needs a desperate upgrade, but that's easy to deal with."

Mal frowned. "And the government is just going to sell this to you?"

"Well, you see, old chap, I'm an eccentric millionaire who wants to have a bunker for the hard times I know are coming."

"That's all well and good, and I'm glad you're thinking about this, but how will you run the pack in Maryland and still oversee this one?"

"And now we come to the thrust of the story. I wouldn't. It would be physically impossible for me to take care of two packs on opposite ends of the country and still serve their needs properly."

"So you'd bring in someone? I mean, considering what happened, it would have to be someone you can trust not to abuse these people any more than they have been."

"Yes, that's my thoughts exactly. It would have to be someone strong enough to say no, but also flexible enough to understand that he doesn't know everything and is willing to listen to others."

The thought these people might get a real bastard made Mal's stomach churn. He couldn't imagine the hardships they'd have to deal with in the coming years.

"And he'd have to have a strong mate, someone who is kind, considerate, and won't let anyone walk over them. They'd also need to have the balls to stand up for these people, even if it's against their First."

"Good luck. I don't know where you're going to find anyone like that," Mal scoffed.

Damon shook his head. "Alp? Am I being too subtle?"

"No, I understood, and I think it's a fantastic idea."

Mal gazed from Alp to Damon and back again. "What are you two talking about?"

Damon waved a hand at Alp. "Go ahead and explain it to him."

Alp went back to the bed and lay next to Mal. He stroked a hand over his hip, then leaned in and kissed his chin. "What Damon is saying is he wants this to be your—*our*—pack."

Mal shook his head to clear the fuzz that settled in it, certain the toxins were responsible for him obviously being deaf. "He fucking wants what?"

CHAPTER 22

THEY'RE FUCKING INSANE. They have to be. That's the only answer. No way in hell could I run a pack.

Mal lay there, fuming. After Damon had dropped his bombshell, he left the room. Alp, the traitor, was grinning like a loon.

"Our pack," he said, clutching Mal's arm. "Maker, it gives me tingles to even think about it."

"Yeah, well stop thinking," Mal growled. "I am not running a pack. Hell, this isn't even a pack. It's a bunch of shifters whose only link is having been tortured by Hyde."

Alp sat up. "They're shifters who will understand why one of them is missing a hand, another is missing his eyes, or how about why some kids have wounds so bad, they actually scarred? Who else would understand like we do? Like they all do?"

Mal grabbed Alp's hand and pulled him back down onto the bed. "I can't be a First. I'm not cut out for it. Shit, Damon's people were all healthy, and they were in constant need of handholding. I couldn't stand that shit, so I left."

"See, I don't buy that." Alp moved closer, touching Mal lightly, his fingers stroking a gentle pattern over Mal's chest. "I mean, okay, maybe you did leave, but I know for a fact that it wasn't because you didn't want to be responsible for others. If that was the case, you should have stayed on your bike and ridden off, leaving me to be dragged back to the lab or to be killed."

The image of Alp—his fur covered in twigs and leaves and dirt, matted with blood, left to rot in a field somewhere, unclaimed, unloved, unmissed—sent a jolt through Mal.

"You killed four men to protect me. Does that sound like someone who didn't want to get involved?"

"It's different," Mal assured him.

"Okay, tell me how," Alp said, his gentle ministrations never stopping.

"I didn't want to get involved," Mal snapped.

"But you did. No one would have known if you had just kept on going."

I would have, and I would have regretted it my whole life. "You needed help."

"So do these people. Do you want me to tell you why I think you left Damon's pack?"

"Sure, dazzle me," Mal said, and even he could hear the sarcasm in his voice.

"Because Damon wasn't going to retire, and you knew it. It's been years since you left, and he's still there. I think that's why you went. You knew, deep down, you could never change anything because Damon wasn't going to be leaving as First. You wanted more, something you could call your own."

"That's bullshit."

"But it's not. What was it you said to me? Oh, I remember. 'No one wanted to keep me. I mean, don't get me wrong, I wouldn't have stayed, but it would have been nice to have someone at least ask.'"

"And?"

"I think you would have stayed, but only for someone who truly wanted you. You want to be needed, to make things right for people. You stood up for me against those men, then with Lydia when you were afraid she might tell people about me. Oh, and then for Lydia with Damon. Look at what you do, Mal. You're our knight. Our champion. Damon knows it, and that's why he trusts that you can handle this pack."

The fact that Alp believed in Mal made his chest tighten. When had he last had faith in himself? Was Alp right? Had Mal been needing this to complete him? When Alp pledged to him, something settled in Mal, because he'd known that he was needed.

"I don't know if I can do this," he whispered. "I'm not a good bet to lead anyone."

"You're the best bet. You have a few years of training under your belt already, and you pick up on things superfast. But that's not why Damon wants you. It's because you possess heart and passion and fire. You won't let anyone walk over your pack, and you will always— and I mean, *always*—stand between us and anything that would try to hurt us."

Did Alp really believe that about Mal? That he could be there for everyone in their pack, that they could guide them together? Did he truly trust Mal could do this?

And as the words hit Mal's brain, he realized he'd thought of this being *their* pack. Together. The two of them, First and First mate, leading and guiding them all. Being the buffer between them and the world that had already torn them apart.

And now it was time for them to be put back together.

"Do you really think we can do this?" Mal asked, his voice raspy.

"I think we're the only ones who can," Alp said, a dreamy expression on his face. Then he laughed. "Guess Mom was right. Our house is going to be bursting with children."

And for the first time, Mal wasn't as afraid as he thought he would be. In fact, he knew he should be panicked, but this adventure that lay before them was no longer scary. It thrilled him to know that the two of them would be standing together, making a life, a family.

THE FIRST THING Mal did as leader of the new pack was to take stock of his assets. There was Alp, of course. Lydia said she wasn't going to be walking away. He had Damon and Cece. The support of the council, which was important, plus the packs who'd already spoken to their groups and asked if anyone was willing to take up the challenge of starting a new pack.

When Damon told him there were people coming, Mal was stunned. He didn't think anyone would take them up on it.

Then there was the problem Mal would have to deal with right away. The kids.

Some of them, the older ones, shifted right after they were let out of the cages, groaning and stretching muscles that had gone unused for far too long. One of the boys, Kevon, had been there since his twelfth birthday, and he was nineteen now. Like Alp, Hyde had kept him locked in a pen unless he needed him for an... Maker, he loathed saying experiment. It was disrespectful to the people.

No, he amended. It was disrespectful to *his* people, and Mal couldn't have that. He'd taken to referring to it as the shameful incident. Kevon's muscles had atrophied and he could no longer stand straight. Lydia had said the bones of his legs had bowed, and she wasn't sure if it was possible to fix them.

Oh, how Mal wanted to kill Hyde all over again.

Then there were the kids who wouldn't shift back, either because they were too scared, traumatized, or they'd forgotten their humanity. Those were the ones who cowered in their cages, fearful of everyone, even Alp. One young fox kit yowled every time someone touched her, and she sprayed a noxious odor, which made Mal gag.

Despite the problems, the setbacks, and the uncertain futures of these children, Mal found himself energized. In the last week, he'd addressed the council to advocate for changes to how they dealt with missing persons. Any leader who found a packmate missing would be required to contact the council right away, so that word could be spread throughout the packs. Maybe if they'd been able to do that for the kids, an opportunity to find them would have been there. Maybe there wouldn't be nearly the level of trauma now.

He'd also butted heads with the council about money. He wasn't stupid enough to believe that any of the people under his care would be able to pay pack dues anytime soon. The kids, definitely not until they were at least eighteen, and that presumed the psychiatrists working with them would sign off on them getting a job. The ones that Hyde and his people had savaged? Mal knew how strong they were owing to the fact they survived, but their futures were in doubt until they could come to terms with their new reality.

Alp worried that keeping everyone sequestered underground wasn't going to help, and Mal agreed. He asked Alp to come up with a schedule so that everyone would have chaperoned time outside every day to get some vitamin D and have the chance to simply be kids.

And Mal was astounded with how everyone stepped up. Lydia would come for several hours after she closed the clinic for the day, then stay at the new packhouse for three to four hours a night, not getting back home until nearly eleven. Even Damon couldn't believe her level of dedication, but she told Mal in confidence that these kids needed someone, and she wanted to be part of it. Mal named her the official pack doctor, even if she could only deal with shifters in their animal forms. Damon arranged for the council to pay her, which left them with their mouths open at the fact a *human* knew about them. Damon railed at them, telling them this *human* had done more for the shifters in a few weeks than the council had done in years. That shut them up quick.

"Hey, you coming to bed anytime soon?" Alp asked from the door to Mal's new office.

"In a few minutes," he replied. "I'm going to try to squeeze a stone and get more money."

"The council?"

"Lydia needs some equipment, and it's not going to be cheap. The council and Damon are being extraordinary, but even their pockets aren't bottomless. We're funded for a minimum of twenty years, at which point everything will be reviewed, but Damon is certain we'll be getting money for as long as we live, due to the kids. More than a few are unlikely to be able to work. Marlon can't have anyone raise their voice to him before he shifts and scurries under the couch.

Obviously he will have problems working on the outside if he can't control his shift."

"And Teresa," Alp chimed in. "Anytime someone even gets close to her, she shifts and sprays. I had to burn my last set of clothes, because she was so damned scared." He grinned. "But there's good news too."

"Oh?" Mal leaned forward, elbows on the desk. "Hit me. I need some good news."

"Do you know Cody?"

"The little blond boy with the big green eyes? Yeah, I know him. What's up with him?"

Alp came into the office and took a seat. "He was crying earlier. And I mean big, sobbing tears. Teresa came into the room and found him. I was about to try to get her to move along when she did the most astonishing thing. She went to him and curled up in his lap. Cody cried a bit more, then looked down at the kit who was laying on him. He ran a hand over Teresa's fur and the tears stopped. Then he shifted into his cat form, and the two of them cuddled up and went to sleep."

"That is good news."

"I think Teresa is only afraid of adults, which makes sense, given that they're the ones who hurt her. She seems okay with the other kids. Maybe when she sees us interacting with them, she'll find out that we aren't the people who did her harm."

That was hopeful. Mal hated that anyone was afraid of him, especially a little girl with soulful brown eyes whose wary gaze went from person to person. Was she wondering when they'd do something awful to her?

"You know what?" Mal asked, straightening the papers he'd been working on. He stood and held a hand out to Alp, smiling when Alp took it. Mal pulled him to his feet, then slid an arm around Alp's shoulder. "I think that's enough for one night. Cece told me that I needed to make time for us to be together, because you were going to be the one who stood beside me when times got tough. I told her I wasn't sure they could get much worse, but she assured me it was possible this was the calm before the storm."

"And are you okay with that?" There was a touch of nervousness in Alp's voice, as though he was uncertain.

"Let me answer your question with one of my own. Will you be by my side the whole way?"

"Yes," Alp replied, without hesitation. "I'm one of these people. A survivor. And the wolf that saved me? He's the one who's going to save them too."

"Nah, the wolf is going to need help from his rabbit every step of the way. Tell you what. You help me through the rough spots, and I'll be there for you too."

"That sounds like a deal."

"Now, let's go make with the sex, yeah?"

Alp snorted. "You know it's almost one in the morning, right? And we have that meeting with Damon at seven."

The thought made Mal groan. "So no sex?"

"Tell me something. You've been burning the candle at both ends the last week. Which would you rather do: take me to bed and screw my brains out until I scream your name, or get five hours of sleep?"

Mal frowned. "Those are my only choices?"

When Alp stretched and yawned, Mal understood. His mate was exhausted too. He'd been running all day while Mal had sat behind the desk, poring over paperwork. That wouldn't do.

"How about I offer a third alternative?" He scooped Alp into his arms. "I'll take you home, make you a hot cocoa, then put you under the covers before I snuggle in with you and we both get some much-needed sleep?"

"You're turning down sex?"

"I'm not turning it down. I'm postponing it until we both are awake enough that we don't fall asleep midthrust. The idea of being buried in your ass all night has merits, but so does laying beside you and holding you as you sleep."

Another yawn, and Alp put his head against Mal's chest. "I think I might need to take your option," he whispered. "I'm sorry."

"Don't be. It's fine," Mal promised.

Before he could assure Alp more, Mal looked down and found his mate asleep in his arms. This moment couldn't be more perfect, at least as far as Mal was concerned. He carried Alp to their room, which wasn't anything more than a mattress on the floor right now. He knelt beside the bed, then lifted Alp's arms to take off his shirt. Once that was done, he manhandled him under the covers and pulled them up to his chin. He stood and stripped off his own clothes, never taking his eyes off Alp.

Mal smiled to himself. A few months ago, he would have taken someone at the bar to their place, fucked them, and left. Now? He stood here and watched his mate sleep, and nothing that had come before, no sexual encounter he'd ever had, could be better than this moment.

He went to the other side of the bed, peeled back the blankets, and crawled under them before slipping an arm around Alp's waist and gently pulling him close enough to nestle against Mal's body.

This, what Mal had right now, was all that was truly needed to make him happy.

"Good night, mate," he whispered into Alp's hair a moment before sleep claimed him.

CHAPTER 23

ALP COULD SCARCELY KEEP his eyes open. His head dipped, his chin touching his chest as he listened to Damon and Mal talk. The last four weeks had been exhausting, but ultimately satisfying. The workers Damon hired had found the base to be in remarkably good shape. There were a few walls that needed to be shored up where water had seeped into the masonry, but by and large, it was ready to be remodeled.

The crews that came in astounded Alp. There were shifters of every imaginable kind—lions, bears, tigers, lemmings, elephants, and so many others. The list was incredible, as was watching them strip off their shirts and get to work.

"Don't make me hurt them," Mal had said, his voice dark and dangerous.

"Huh?" Alp murmured, turning to face Mal.

"I don't like my mate staring at other men." He grinned and nudged Alp, tilting his head toward one of the workers. "Though that skunk shifter has a remarkable body, don't you think? Watch the way his muscles tighten as he lifts his arms. His back is smooth and sleek, and his ass flexes every time he bends."

Alp narrowed his gaze. "I will kill you in your sleep," he vowed.

Then he laughed when Mal reminded him that he only had eyes for his mate.

The crew worked almost seamlessly. The lion shifter—Alp couldn't recall all their names—had taken charge, and he kept everything on track. Spaces that had once been labs were remodeled into bedrooms. Cece had come with her boys—Ivan and Teddy included —and after Wiley conferred with Micah, they told the men what kind of rooms kids would like. Their suggestions were followed, and slowly the place took shape. Alp loved watching Wiley as he pointed out places things could be better. He was definitely his father's son.

Micah was the complete opposite. Where Wiley strode, Micah shuffled. Where Wiley stood proud and gave his opinion—he never ordered —Micah vanished into the background. What shocked Alp was when Wiley noticed, he stopped talking, went to his brother, and rubbed their cheeks together. He didn't miss Micah's sharp inhale, and he knew that Wiley was calming his brother through touch and pheromones.

"They're something, aren't they?" Cece asked, her breath ghosting over Alp's ear.

"Yeah, they're incredible."

"How he treats his brother is what tells us that Wiley will make a good First. He never pushes Micah, but he also won't allow him to hide away. Micah is an artist. He paints beautiful pictures that I love to frame and hang around the house. He glows with pride when he finishes a piece, and it's even more evident when Wiley praises it."

"Really? What does he like to paint?"

"He can do pretty much anything, but his favorites are the forests we run in." She fished out her phone and held it so Alp could see the screen. "This is the one he finished the night before we left."

The place looked so real. The trees were turning gold as fall settled in. There was a wolf standing there, and you could see the vapor from his breaths as they rose into the air and disappeared. Alp was amazed by the incredible detail. It was stunning that anyone could draw something like this, but even more that it was a fifteen-year-old boy.

"Oh, Maker. He's got talent."

That earned him a radiant smile from Cece. "Thank you. He loves doing it."

That gave Alp an idea. "Would you mind if I talked with him?"

"Why would I mind? Go for it."

Damn, he loved Cece. She'd told him all about taking his mother shopping. His mom thought they were going to the Wal-Mart, which was where she bought all the kid's clothes. She'd cried when Cece told her that they were going to New York, that there would be a private showing of fashions, and that Nura could pick out anything she wanted. Cece was shocked when Nura Dawkins turned her nose up at the "fashion" and said a good pair of overalls would do her just fine. What use did she have for an $1800 dress that would get spit up on by the new babies?

Just like she had with Mal, Nura wormed her way into Cece's heart. They ended up spending seventy-three dollars at Farm & Fleet to get her the overalls she wanted, plus some bulbs for her garden. Cece said she'd never realized people like Alp's parents existed and she was humbled to meet them.

"Alp? Are you with us?"

Shit. "Sorry, I was drifting."

Mal chuckled. "I kept trying too, but Damon would kick me every time I started to nod off."

"We were talking about the walls in the hallways leading to the kid's sleeping area. What do you think we should put on them?"

Alp sat up. "Oh, I have that covered."

Damon arched an eyebrow. "Really? Do tell."

"Well, see, Cece showed me the painting Micah had done before you all came here, and I loved it. I asked him if he'd like to do something for the kids in that wing, and he jumped at the chance." He swallowed. "I hope that's okay?"

That earned him a smile from Damon. "Thank you for making him feel included. Things like this are where Wiley shines, and Micah is always afraid he's invisible."

"Not to me," Alp promised. "His work was remarkable, and I think it would be a beautiful addition."

"I agree," Damon replied. "And look at you! Only First mate for a few weeks, and you're already stepping up." He sat back, folded his hands over his stomach, and smiled. "I knew you two were the only choice for this place." He sat up again and picked up his tablet. "Okay, back to work."

Mal groaned, but Alp knew it was teasing. He'd been intent on all the aspects Damon had discussed with him. How the council would be pumping funds into the newly minted Wald pack, helping them with the care of the affected shifters, and continuing to try and find out who the kids belonged to. Another problem facing them was identifying the bodies kept by Hyde. It was possible that the kids were the offspring of some of the people Hyde had killed, and they'd now be alone in the world.

The more Alp watched the interactions between Damon and Mal, the stronger Mal became in his eyes. He had started out tentative, but that had changed when Damon said they were going to make the rooms for the kids so they'd each have two people living there. Mal had nixed that, stating that the problems these kids may or may not have meant they needed their own safe space. He did offer an alternative. A group room, where mats could be laid out and the kids could all sleep together—in human or in shifted form—if they wanted.

"And you thought I'd made a mistake wanting you to be in charge here?" Damon said, his tone amused.

"Asshole," Mal had grumbled, but then he smiled.

"Where the hell are you, Alp?" Mal asked, tapping Alp on the head.

"Just thinking." He glanced down at their itinerary and realized he'd missed his cue. "Oh, is it my turn?"

"It is," Damon assured him, grinning like a loon.

"Okay, then." Alp stood, glanced over his notes, then turned to Mal and Damon. "The new kitchen equipment has been installed in all the kitchens. It's heavy-duty, restaurant quality and should last us for many years. From the people who have said they wanted to join our pack and work with the kids, eleven of them have asked about the cooking positions. We'll be able to feed everyone three meals a day, and have a few people who will help with cleanup. The doors are being changed to allow easier access to everyone. We want to ensure those missing limbs won't have issues going from room to room."

Alp took a deep breath, then continued.

"We're doing everything we can to make the place a home for everyone. Wiley had some amazing ideas, and even the workmen told him he was bloody brilliant, and if he was looking for a job, they'd all take him."

"Excellent," Mal and Damon echoed.

"And how many people will be part of the pack?"

Alp sighed. "We have seventy-two children and twenty-three adults, plus the incoming members of the other packs who will join ours."

"That's good," Damon said. "And the number will grow in the future, as more people hear about it. Though I have to say, I'm a bit concerned about the number of kids. There aren't enough people here to watch them properly."

"They'll be my responsibility," Alp said, crossing his arms. "I'll work with the incoming people, find out who likes kids, and go from there. I don't want to introduce too many new things all at once. I want to give them some stability first, so they know they're safe here."

"That sounds good," Damon agreed. "Let me ask, though. How bad is it?"

Now it was time to come clean. "Pretty bad. So many of them will bear the scars of what Hyde did to them. Because they're so young, their healing wasn't much better than a human, so it's probable they'll always carry the marks of the tortures they underwent. So, yes, the children are scared, but less so after getting food in their stomachs and receiving hugs every day."

"And who hugs them?"

Alp puffed up a bit. "I do. Every kid, every day. Eventually at some point, I'd like to have the rooms wired for sound so I can read to the kids every night."

"I am so proud of you," Mal said. "Thank you for showing them you care. And for thinking about story time."

"Don't thank me. They see my hand and know that I understand. Some of the older ones ask what happened, and I give them a variation of the truth. Maybe when they're older, but now? They don't need my trauma as part of their own." Alp bit back a sigh. "The electricians are wiring the complex, giving it a more natural lighting scheme instead of the harsh bulbs that Hyde and his people used. There will be dimmer switches to control each room, so if anyone has problems sleeping and would like the lights to stay on, we can do that. I've spoken with Cece's friend, and she has eight counselors who will be available to talk to the people who need help. I plan on insisting that everyone—myself included—speaks with them at least twelve times and we'll schedule other talks based on what the doctors say."

"Look at you," Mal marveled. "You've got this down cold."

The praise melted Alp's insides. "I'd like to take credit for it, but a lot of what I'm doing came from things my mom did for our family."

Nura Dawkins, Alp realized, had been the perfect mother who had a son that couldn't see it. She cooked delicious meals for the family every night and ensured everyone was at the table to eat together. She sat and helped the kids with homework, even though she couldn't get the hang of the weird math they were doing, and she always, without fail, was there to talk if you needed it. And while seventy-two kids was a lot more than fourteen, Alp wanted to be the kind of parent she had always been.

"Your mother is kind of amazing," Damon told Alp. "I met her when she went shopping with Cece. Even though she was with us only a few minutes before they left on their trip, Micah really blossomed under your mother's attention. He chatted animatedly with her, telling her about his latest work, then asked if she wanted to see it. He *never* does that. She told him she'd love to, and he took her hand and rushed back to his studio. That's what he calls his bedroom.

Your mom was moved to tears by the picture of a young wolf, laying under a tree, as rain poured down on him. She said she could feel his sadness, and that pleased Micah because someone got it without needing to explain."

"Yeah, she's kind of remarkable."

"I find I cannot disagree. And it appears as though her son shares the same qualities."

Alp stood. "Can you excuse me for a few minutes? I need to take care of something."

"Of course," Mal said, not looking up from his paperwork. "Tell her I said hi, and I look forward to seeing her soon."

"Alp?"

He turned to find Damon grinning. He tossed him a phone. "She's in my contacts as Nura."

Of course they'd know where Alp was going. It only made sense.

He stepped out of the makeshift conference room and pulled the door closed behind him. After a quick trip to the table that held the coffee and pastries for the workers, where Alp grabbed himself some juice, and he was ready. He held up Damon's phone, and his heartbeat sped up a bit. He found his mom's number and steeled his resolve with a deep breath, then pushed the button. It rang a moment later. When the call was connected, Alp could hear the chaos in the background as voices shouted over one another, asking for more cereal, to pass the soy milk, that the toast was almost gone. Alp remembered those days with a new fondness.

"Good morning, Damon. How's Cece?"

"Hey, Mom."

It was quiet a moment. "Alpin?" she gasped.

"Yeah, Damon loaned me his phone so I could call you."

"Oh, my dear. It's so lovely to hear your voice. How are you?"

"I'm... okay. Got a lot to catch you up on, though, if you have time."

"Absolutely. Give me a moment."

The voices in the background slowly vanished, and then with a firm click that Alp was certain had been a door, his mother came back.

"Are you okay? Is Mal?"

He sighed. She worried so, and that had Alp's eyes filling with tears.

"Mom, I'm sorry."

"For what, sweetheart?"

"Being a shitty son. I always thought I wanted to get away from everyone, but I guess what I really wanted was for someone to see me. Now I realize, you did. You always saw me."

"Of course I did. Why ever would you think I didn't?"

Alp sniffled and scrubbed at his eyes. "I was a stupid kid. I thought seeing me meant something else, and when that didn't happen, I figured I had to get away." He choked out a laugh. "But everyone in the family saw me, and I was too caught up in my head to understand that."

"You were a boy, love," she soothed. "Could I have been a better mother? Of course, I—"

"No!" Alp insisted, his voice pitching higher as his nerves kicked in. He had so much to say, and he didn't even know where to start. "You were an amazing mother. Don't think that you needed to be better, because you didn't. You made a home for all of us. It wasn't perfect, but family never is. That's why I'm calling you. Are you sitting down?"

"Yes. Are you sure you're all right? You're scaring me a little."

"I'm fine," he assured her. Then he told her everything that happened from the last time he'd seen her.

When he finished, she blew out a breath. "I'll have to thank Cece for killing that son of a bitch," she snarled. "Do wolves like chocolate?"

Alp barked out a laugh a moment before he dissolved into tears. "My mate was dead, Mom. I let him die."

"Hush, and listen to me, okay? Promise you'll hear what I'm telling you."

He scrubbed a hand over his face. "I'll try."

"Good. That's the best I can hope for. Shifters are more than animal, more than human. We're the best parts of both. The problem is, we also have the failings of both as well. Mal is a First wolf. He has to deal with increased aggression. You're a rabbit. For you, it's a fight or flight. It's not something you control—it's an inherent part of you. But you told me yourself, you pushed beyond it and went after Hyde. See, you went against your nature, and that's damned impressive."

"But I couldn't kill him!" Alp wailed.

She clucked her tongue. "Cece was right. You're not a killer. You're a nurturer. The people you're going to be working with? They need that Alp, not the one who slays giants. Work with your strengths, not ones you wish you had." She chuckled. "We're more alike than you know."

"I'm going to take that as a compliment," Alp replied, scrubbing a hand over his itchy eyes.

"That's how it's meant, sweetheart. I will give my life to protect my family, because that's how I am. You'll stand up for the people under your care, just like Mal, but yours comes with hugs and kissing skinned knees, telling the girls about periods, and—"

Alp froze and stared at the phone a moment, then brought it back to his ear. "Wait. What?"

"Oh, did you not know that? I'm so sorry," she said, but it was obvious she wasn't. "I know this isn't the perfect way to start a family, but it's one you and Mal are building with kids and adults who need you to guide them. And if you ever, and I mean *ever*, need me, I'll be on the next flight out. In fact, if you all need help now, we can get a caravan together and head there. We might be small, but we're scrappy."

Once again, tears pricked at Alp's eyes. "Mom, I love you so much."

"And I love you too," she whispered.

He cleared his throat. "So tell me what's going on in your life."

She chuckled softly. "Well, I hope you're sitting down, because this will take a while. Your Aunt Ruth and Uncle Tyler had another litter. They're up to twenty-seven kids. Oh, and...."

Alp smiled as he found a quiet spot and slid down the wall until he was sitting on the floor. He leaned back against the cool surface and listened to his mother as she caught him up on his family, which he swore he'd never take for granted again.

THE WORK WAS GOING SMOOTHLY. Well, as smoothly as it could with all the kids running around. Even when they put up barriers, somehow several of the rugrats bypassed them and were amusing themselves by looking at the machinery. Mal was grateful to see they hadn't lost their sense of wonder. In fact, he asked the workers to take a ten-minute break once a day, so he could show anyone who was interested what was going on.

Today he watched as Damon strode through with Wylie, pointing to various things they were adding. Wylie nodded, then seemed to be asking questions. Damon answered them with a smile. He was right about one thing: this wasn't the same Damon he'd known. He was always a good First, but now he was more... approachable.

"Mal?"

He turned and found Lydia behind him. "What's up?"

She winced. "I need to run and get some Pedialyte. A lot of the kids could use the boost, and I didn't get enough on my last trip to the store." She clenched her fingers tight. "I can see why so many shifters died," she snarled. "They didn't give a goddamn about their health. Oh, they died? We can just get another." She looked up at Mal, and he could see the hurt in her eyes. "I don't even know him, and he's dead and...." Her lip wobbled. "And I hate him so fucking much," she whispered. "That's not who I want to be."

He reached out and squeezed her shoulder. "That's not who any of us wanted to be," he told her. "Why don't I go? You can catch a nap or head out," he offered. "How much do you need?"

She frowned. "At least eight cases, and that'll probably only tide us over for a week. Some of the adults could use it too. They're almost all dehydrated. This will help them restore the electrolytes and keep them hydrated."

"That's no problem." Damon had given him a credit card for incidentals. True, it wasn't the black credit card that had fascinated Alp, but that was fine. He had one for Lydia too, after saying she shouldn't be spending her own money like that. He was going to be giving it to her tomorrow, which Mal was glad about.

"You'll need to take my truck."

"No, I should be...." Shit. Mal should have realized, after everything that happened with Alp, there was no way he could haul things they needed. Then he thought about the kids. What if they had to take them somewhere, like an emergency trip to Lydia's clinic? It's not like he could strap them to the back of his motorcycle. Still, Lydia looked shattered. Her eyes weren't bright, and her normally artfully messy hair was poking out in several areas.

"I appreciate that, but you need some rest. I'll figure something out."

She gave a wan smile. "I'll be okay for a couple hours. I still have a few kids to see before I close up for the night." She handed him the keys. "Go ahead. I'll need it for tomorrow."

"Yeah, okay. I'll do that. Thank you. Be back as soon as I can."

She nodded, then headed off toward her clinic. Thoughts were zipping through Mal's head. He knew what he needed to do—it was a matter of getting it done.

"Damon?"

Damon turned and tilted his head. "Malachi? Everything okay?"

"I have to make a store run. Wanna come?"

Damon said something to Wiley, who looked up and waved at Mal, then headed toward the kids' ward, probably to check in with Micah, who was hard at work sketching his designs on the walls. Once that was done, he'd paint them and give a glorious forest view for the shifters.

"What's up, pup?" Damon said, tossing an arm over Mal's shoulder. "Why so serious?"

"I had a realization." He swallowed hard. "I'm about to be a surrogate father."

"Yep, you are. Scared?"

Mal shook his head. "No, not in the least. I'm looking forward to the challenges, as well as the rewards."

"I knew you would, especially once you got out of your 'I'm not meant to be in a pack' attitude."

And that was the crux of Mal's thoughts. He'd lived as a lone wolf for years, catching the bus or thumbing for rides until he got his cycle.

"When you leave, how'd you like to take the cycle with you?"

Damon's jaw dropped. "Why would you give away something so beautiful?"

"I.... This isn't a pack like yours. My people will need hands-on care, probably for years. I won't have time to ride, and I need an actual vehicle to haul stuff and to have available for the kids. Yours are grown, and your pack runs like a well-oiled machine. I want someone I like to get use out of the bike instead of letting it sit in a garage and gather rust."

"I—I don't know what to say."

"You'd be doing me a favor," Mal told him. "Plus, I'm going to need you to help me pick out something solid and dependable to use for here."

"Sure, that would be amazing." He leaned in and hugged Mal, brushing their cheeks together. "Thank you."

Though Mal would be sad to lose his bike, he wasn't sad to be cutting the ties to his lone-wolf days.

Heh. Look at him now. All grown up and shit.

But he sure was gonna miss that bike.

CHAPTER 24

MAL SWUNG by the infirmary to check on everyone. Lydia nodded as he walked in, but then went back to examining Dobie, an eight-year-old beagle shifter who'd been blinded in one eye as a result of Hyde's experiments. Lydia said she'd been consulting with Gwyneth, and they hoped that together they could reverse the damage that had been done. Mal certainly hoped so, because there were too many people who would never heal.

Around him, workers bustled. Thankfully Lydia had some assistants now, because this job would be impossible for one person. Mal yawned and stretched as he headed out into the hall again. His meeting with Damon had gone on hours longer than expected, and Mal was worn out. Plus, it had been days since he'd been able to shift, and his body was feeling the stress. The aching back, the tired eyes, and the tight muscles that came with sitting and staring at numbers and charts until he was squinting at the screen, trying to get the numbers to stop dancing. He slipped into an empty room, leaving the door ajar, and stripped off his clothes, then shifted. Maker, it felt glorious as all the kinks worked out of his body.

He nudged the door open and stepped into the hall. He decided he could head to the ramp that led to the outside and take a quick run, maybe go down to the stream and lap up some of the ice-cold water.

He turned and headed for the exit, when one of the kids, a little girl whose name was listed as Alice on Hyde's notes, stepped forward. Mal had watched her hide whenever others were around, but now she came toward him, her palm outstretched.

"Puppy," she whispered, reaching out and touching Mal's snout. A few moments later, she leaned in close and threw her arms around Mal's neck. "Puppy," she said again. When she straightened, there was a look of sadness on her face that Mal couldn't stand. He needed to make her happy, right? That's what he was there for.

He nudged her hand, which made her giggle. She seemed to calm considerably when she stroked a hand over his fur, and that made Mal happy. He turned and trotted to the bags Lydia had brought on her last visit. This was going to be so embarrassing. It was a good thing Alp was helping out in the kid's area, because if he saw this, Mal knew he'd never live it down.

He reached into the bag and snatched a tennis ball. He took it back to the girl and placed it at her feet. She picked it up and turned it over a few times, then eyed him curiously.

Oh, shit. She has no idea what to do with it. He took it from her hand, then flipped his head and let the thing go flying. The bright yellow ball bounced along the hall, and Mal chased after it, grabbed it in his mouth, then hurried back to her and placed it at her pink tennis-shoe-clad feet.

She picked it up, looked at it quizzically, then at Mal. She seemed unsure. Just as Mal was about to try again, she tossed the ball. It skittered down the hallway, and Mal bounded after it. When he turned around, she was clapping and giggling, and so much warmth filled Mal. They played for a good twenty minutes, and this, Mal decided, was better than a run in the woods any day. Seeing Alice smile? Hearing her laugh? Yeah, way better.

"Alice?"

He spotted Lydia coming out of the clinic. He was so damned grateful for her. She'd already done so much, but there was more to go. Too many people had been maimed by Hyde, some of them far worse than Alp had been. He wished he'd been the one to kill that insane bastard, but at least he was dead. Damon's people ensured that everything on their closed computer network was still there. It seemed, from going through Hyde's files, he wasn't anywhere near his "miracle" and was zealously guarding his research, keeping the files under heavy encryption, even going so far as to not share with his counterparts.

When Alp asked how they could be certain, Damon told him they couldn't. The only thing they would be able to do was keep an eye on things and hope to hell their secrets died with the people in the labs.

When Lydia reached out to Alice, she smiled and took Lydia's hand. Alice turned and followed behind Lydia, glancing over her shoulder at Mal, who gave a chuff for her as she waved. As soon as Lydia had her in the examination room, Mal turned and came face to face with Alp.

Maker, please. Tell me he didn't see any of that.

Alp sauntered over and ran his fingers through Mal's thick coat.

"I missed you," he said brightly, scratching that spot Mal loved. His hind leg thumped, even as he tried to stop it. "Damon and Cece are taking the boys to the diner for dinner. She asked if we wanted to go, but I said no. I needed to come find you."

Mal inhaled, breathing Alp in, letting the scent fill his lungs. Alp was home for Mal, and he knew that to his heart.

Alp huffed out a breath as he turned in a circle. "I can't believe this place is home for us. And it's weird, you know? I walk through the halls, looking at the changes, and I don't see Hyde's face. I see the kids lighting up when we play a game, or Jerome Abernathy as one of the pack helps him learn to read braille. I spoke with him, and he said they took him while he was rooting for food. When we talked about what he wanted to do now, he said he had been homeless and now has nowhere else to go. He'd like to stay with us, if we'll allow it."

He'd been the man who'd had his eyes removed. Twenty-two years old, and they'd stolen his ability to see, to protect himself. For a cat shifter, it was hard to take, but he was doing his best to cope.

Damon said they'd spoken with an ocularist to have glass eyes made for him, but they'd also reached out to makers of visual prostheses about getting him on a list for the experimental bionic eyes. If he got them, he'd never be able to shift again, and it wouldn't restore his full vision, but maybe in the future....

"Mal?"

He snapped his gaze back to Alp, who was holding a soggy... aw, fuck.

"Wanna play fetch?" He danced around, waving the ball at Mal. "C'mon, be a good boy. Play fetch with your mate. Who wants the ball? Do you want it?" He pretended to throw it. "Where's the ball? Go get it!" Mal sat on his haunches and stared at Alp, whose eyes gleamed when he leaned in and whispered, "Or would you rather go home and play with some other balls?"

It took a moment for Alp's words to settle into his brain, but then Mal bounced up and took hold of Alp's hand. His mate's balls did sound way better.

"Mal?"

He stopped and looked up expectantly.

Alp leaned over and kissed him on the nose, then scowled. "Okay, won't be doing that again. I don't even wanna know why your nose is wet," he said, scrubbing a hand over his lips. "Just do not."

This man was way too adorable.

"I love you."

And all Mal's.

Even knowing there was a lot of hard work ahead of them, Mal wasn't worried. He and Alp would figure everything out together. For now, though? Mal dragged Alp down the hall toward their room, where they'd spend time decompressing, talking with each other about the problems, and, of course, having hot, sweaty sex.

There were still a lot of obstacles they'd need to deal with, but with the help of Damon and Cece, plus all the others who were joining them, it would be a good life for their pack.

Mal and Alp would make sure of it.

ABOUT THE AUTHOR

Parker Williams has always loved to write. Ever since he was a teen, one of his favorite things to do was put pen to paper and create worlds where men would find their everlasting love and be happy forever.

Now that he's older, he understands more about what it means to fall in love and the trials and tribulations that come with it, and he does his best to make sure his characters come across as real and alive.

Parker will always love to write, because every story starts when two men....

Parker's Website - Updates, free shorts, and more

ALSO BY PARKER WILLIAMS

Runner

Lincoln's Park - Links in the Chain #1

Galen's Redemption - Links in the Chain #2

Stained Hearts - Links in the Chain #3

The Collars & Cuffs Series with K.C. Wells

The Secrets Series with K.C. Wells

Haven's Creed

Haven's War

The Night Wolf

Reclaiming Quinn

The Spirit Key

Waiting On Life

Cultivating Caden

www.ingramcontent.com/pod-product-compliance
Lightning Source LLC
Chambersburg PA
CBHW030310200626
46816CB00002BA/842